WILEY'S LAMENT

WILEY'S LAMENT

LONO WAIWAIOLE

ST. MARTIN'S MINOTAUR

NEW YORK

www.minotaurbooks.com

ISBN 0-312-30383-1

First Edition: March 2003

10 9 8 7 6 5 4 3 2 1

TO VINCE KOHLER,
WHO LIVES ON IN HIS OWN BOOKS—
AND THIS ONE, TOO

ACKNOWLEDGMENTS

This book is not the shortest distance between any two points, and many hands helped guide it and me along our way. My thanks to: Dick Bailey, who turned me on to Richard Stark and Donald Westlake; Kaila, Poeko, and Kulia, who allowed me to find my way back home; the real Sam Adams, who convinced me Wiley's life was better told than lived; Vince Kohler, who showed me how to tell it; Michael Denneny, who put it on a printing press; and Ben Sevier, who took it off.

WILEY'S LAMENT

ONE

I picked Seattle because you don't piss in your own peonies, and because Seattle's tendency to look down on the rest of us had always rubbed me a little raw.

That's the problem with having the Space Needle for a nose— the thing sticks straight up in the air. But to me, Seattle was nothing but a safe-deposit box to which I had the matching keys. Every time I needed some money, I just drove three hours north and picked up a bag or two.

I got the idea from the evening news. You've probably seen the same story—a drug bust hits the airwaves, the first thing the cops do is flash the thousands of dollars they found. I could occasionally use thousands of dollars in those days, so I eventually decided to wage my own little war on drugs.

Ripping off a drug dealer sounds tougher than it actually is, mostly because I never met one who wanted his money more than his life. It makes perfect sense when you think about it, because money is easy to come by in the drug business and life isn't.

I liked midlevel targets, which is why I'd been on the skinny kid in the Seahawks jacket for almost five days without harming a hair on his cornrowed head. The kid was doing all right for himself that night, but he wasn't doing well enough for me— that's why I was waiting for his connection to arrive.

I'm better at waiting than most people, and waiting on the

skinny kid in the Seahawks jacket was a piece of cake because he looked right through me every time he glanced in my direction. You hear all the time that appearances can be deceiving, but I don't know many people who really believe it. It's amazing how invisible you can get when you mix two weeks without a shower or a shave with an overstuffed shopping cart and a bottle of Mad Dog in a brown paper bag. I was only half a block to the kid's right, but I could have been on the far side of the moon for all the attention he gave me.

The Lexus was late that night, so the kid and I were both ready to move well before it appeared. The car rolled to a stop, the window on the passenger side slid down and the kid leaned inside. I pushed my cart in his direction while he did it, using my right hand for the cart and my left to lift the Mad Dog bottle to my mouth. I don't drink alcohol, so the Mad Dog ran down my chin and collected in my grimy undershirt every time I tipped the bottle.

I could see the driver watching me idly as I approached, but my target was sitting next to him so I didn't give the driver much of a look. One of the odd things I had learned about this kind of gig is that you don't have to count the hired hands as long as you get your gun in the right guy's ear.

The kid was trading cash for product, and he and my target were absorbed by the transaction until I was only four or five strides away. They both looked my way at the same time, but the kid was the one who spoke.

"Get lost, muthafuckah," he said, but he was turning back to my target before the words were even out of his mouth. I staggered another step or two closer, hurled the bottle at the open window and then tried to beat it to the car. The bottle got there before I did, but not by much. My target saw it coming and ducked, but the kid was just beginning to turn back in my direction when it splattered against the door frame a few inches above his head.

The kid started to say something, but I hit him in the mouth with a forearm and knocked the words back down his throat.

He bounced off the door and fell to the pavement, but I kept my eyes on the prize.

"What the fuck?" someone shouted, but I'm not sure who. All I know for sure is that I grabbed the hand coming out of the window with a gun in it and cracked it against the door frame until the gun fell out. By that time, my .38 was in my left hand and I was jamming it into my target's closest ear.

"Everybody chill," I said quietly.

I looked at the driver and the kid on the pavement to my left, and they both showed me the palms of their hands. They didn't look afraid, exactly—the expression in their eyes more closely resembled curiosity than anything else—but they didn't look ominous, either.

"Get up," I said to the kid in the Seahawks jacket. "Bring the gym bag on top of the shopping cart over here." The kid got up and did as he was told.

"Get in the backseat," I said, and that's what the kid did next.

"Now put fifteen grand in that bag and throw it out on the sidewalk."

"What the fuck are you talking about?" said the guy wearing my gun in his ear. "Why fifteen grand?"

"Why not?" I asked, mostly because that answer was shorter than explaining the actual reason. I liked to give the victims something specific to do while I was setting up my departure from the scene.

"What makes you think we have fifteen grand in here, you fucking idiot?"

"I don't much care if you do or you don't," I said.

"What the fuck does that mean?"

"You live if you have it, you don't if you don't. It makes a lot more difference to you than to me."

"You think you can cap all three of us and walk away from it?"

"I think I can cap *you*, and I think I don't give a fuck what happens after that."

"You're fuckin' insane," he said.

"Possibly," I said, "but I don't see how that improves your situation."

"This is a fuckin' public street—you can't stand here and do this kind of shit!"

"Do you see anything stopping me so far?"

"How long do you think it's gonna be before someone calls the cops?"

"About sixty seconds," I said. "The cops are the reason you're gonna drive off and leave me standing here."

My target swiveled his head slightly to improve his view of me, and I swiveled my .38 right with him. His eyes were cold and lifeless, just like mine, but he smelled a lot better than I did.

"You are so fuckin' dead it's not even funny," he said finally.

"I know," I said. "The only question here is how dead *you* want to be."

"Give it to him," he said, his frigid eyes still locked on mine.

The kid reached down behind the driver's seat and picked up a dark brown satchel. The satchel was open, and I could see the cash inside it from my vantage point ouside the door.

"What am I supposed to do?" the kid asked. "Count this shit?"

"I don't know," I said. "Think you can tell by the weight?"

"What?"

"Start with the hundreds," I said. "Then you only have to count to ten fifteen times."

The kid looked at my target for directions, but my target was still looking at me. "Tell the kid to get started," I said.

"Do it," my target said, and the kid started shuffling through the satchel.

"Now pick up your phone," I said to my target, adding a little pressure to the gun in his ear for emphasis. "And make sure it's the phone—you don't wanna come this far and still not make it."

My target reached carefully between the front seats and produced a phone.

"Dial nine-one-one," I said.

"What?"

"Dial nine-one-one."

He punched the buttons and slowly extended the phone in my direction. I took it with my right hand and sent another little reminder into his ear with my left.

"I need to report a shooting across from that museum on First," I said into the phone. "Send an ambulance—it looks like there's at least one man down."

"I can't see the cross street," I said when the operator asked for that information. "How many museums do you have on this fuckin' street? It's the one with that piece of shit tin man out in front."

I cut the connection and tossed the phone into my shopping cart. "Do you think they'll find us?" I asked.

"What the fuck is wrong with you?" my target asked.

"Why? Does it make a difference somehow?"

"There ain't enough hundreds in here," the kid said from the backseat at about the same time as the sound of the first siren reached us.

"How many were there?" I asked.

"Seventy-six," he said.

"And a big parade," I said.

"What?"

" 'The Music Man,' " I said as the second siren horned in on the first. "We've got the seventy-six trombones, and here comes the big parade."

"What the fuck are you talkin' about?" the kid said.

"Never mind," I said. "You folks better be going. Just dump the rest of the cash into my bag and toss it out here."

The kid followed my instructions, so I tried my luck with his boss. "You can drive away from this gun in your ear whenever you're ready," I said. "If you don't get stupid on the way, you won't lose anything but money tonight."

"Let's go," he said to his driver, but his eyes were still fixed on mine. The driver did as he was told, even though he had to cut off a taxi to do it. My target finally turned away from me as the Lexus moved to the left lane, and after a block it turned uphill and out of sight.

I picked up my gym bag, dropped the .38 inside and closed the zipper. By the time the ambulance and the cops hit First, I was through the door of The Lusty Lady. I had paid Gladys in _rance, so she led me past all the naked girls in the fantasy booths and let me out on the fire escape.

It was five minutes from the back of the building to my old Subaru, and a shade over three hours from the Subaru to my front room in Portland. I was almost through with the count the skinny kid in the Seahawks jacket had begun when the phone rang and I found out I didn't need money anymore.

TWO

The *puta* knocked just as Fernando came out of the john. He padded over to the door, but he didn't open it.

She's a new one, he thought. *Let her fuckin' wait.*

He peered through the peephole in the door, and even through the fish-eye lens the girl standing on the other side began to change his mood. She was not blonde like Rebecca, and not tall and not stacked. *She's totally not my type,* he thought, but the longer he stared at her through the peephole, the less enamored of his type he became.

Fuck this waiting, he said silently. He opened the door, the girl slipped inside, and he locked and chained the door behind her. She looked him up and down for a moment, lingering around the halfway point long enough to make him glad that he was standing unclothed before her.

"You look ready to have some fun," she said, glancing from his nakedness to his eyes and smiling all the way.

"I am now," he said.

"I'm Lizzie," she said, extending her right hand in his direction. "I take it you're Fernando."

"And if I'm not?" he said, taking her hand in both of his.

"Then fuck Fernando," she said. "I know a good thing when I see it."

He liked the way that sounded, and the way she looked when she said it. He even liked the blue Nike sweats she was wearing and the white sneakers on her feet—they made her look like an athlete on her way back from the gym or the rink, and the sports bag slung over her shoulder did nothing to dispel that image.

Her grip was strong in his hands, and he found that he liked that, too. "Welcome," he said.

"Thank you," she said, stepping deftly around him and perching on the only chair in the room. "Please," she said, pointing toward the bed. "Make yourself comfortable."

He stepped to the bed and sat down, leaning back a little on his hands to make the muscles of his torso taut.

"So you called for Rebecca," she said, still smiling a little.

He nodded silently.

"And they told you she's out of town?"

He nodded again.

"Are you disappointed?"

"Not anymore," he said.

"Good," she said. "Why don't we take care of the service, and then I'll go get changed."

Fuckin' puta, he thought, his foul mood from before falling over him again. It always comes back to money.

"Take what you need," he said, nodding toward the roll of fifties next to the switchblade on the nightstand less than an arm's length from her chair.

She looked at the money and the knife, then back at him. "What's the knife for?" she asked soberly, the trace of a smile gone from her voice.

"It's a habit, mostly," he said. "I feel more comfortable with it than without it."

"I'm just the opposite," she said. "I'm much more comfortable without it."

"Take it with you when you change," he said. "You can leave it in the bathroom."

She thought that over for a minute. "Thanks," she said finally. "It's one-fifty for thirty minutes and two-fifty for an hour."

"How much is it for all night?"

"I'm sorry," she said. "I'm already booked for the rest of the night."

Booked my ass, he thought.

"One-fifty, then," he said.

She plucked three fifties from the roll and slipped them and the knife into the left pocket of her sweat jacket. "Just give me a minute to call the service," she said. "Then we can get this party started."

This party has already started, he said silently.

She rose from the chair, strode to the low bureau beneath the mirror, picked the receiver up, and began punching numbers. "This is Lizzie," she said after a moment or two. "I'm at the Evergreen, Room One-thirty-two. I'll call you back in thirty minutes. See ya."

You won't be done in thirty minutes, he said to himself.

She replaced the receiver and moved toward the bathroom. "Don't start without me," she said from the doorway. "I'll be right out."

Don't worry, you fuckin' puta, he thought. *I'm savin' it all for you.*

He leaned back on top of the bed, rested his arms on the pillow which covered the second knife, and then propped his head on his arms.

The Nike sweats were spilling out of the sports bag when she returned to the room, and the view of the girl provided by their new location almost changed his mood again. She was wearing something thin and red and slinky that pretended to cover her from the top of her shoulders to the middle of her thighs, but it was a sham all the way. He could see the hard nipples on her small breasts and the dark flash of her pubic hair when she moved.

"You like?" she asked.

"Sí," he said, almost in spite of himself.

"That's good," she said, dropping the bag next to the bed and herself next to him. "You're in for a real treat, Fernando."

I know I am, he said to himself.

"I am?" he asked.

"Yes," she said. "I can't do anything illegal here, so the rules are we can't touch each other. But I'm going to give you a show like you've never seen in your life. You won't be able to keep your hands off that beautiful cock of yours, I promise you. If you like it, you can tip me what you think it was worth when we're done. Fair enough?"

Unbelievable, he thought.

"Whatever you say, sweetheart," he said.

"Good," she said, almost humming it to him. "That's very good." Then she cupped her right breast in her left hand and began to caress the tip of it through the slinky red material.

"God, I feel hot," she said. "Just looking at you turns me on, Fernando."

Sure it does, he said to himself.

"Do you like what you do to my nipples?" she asked, moving one hand to each of them and touching them softly.

"Yes," he said, surprising himself a little.

"So do I," she said. Then she stood on the bed with her back to the wall and placed one foot on each side of his head. He looked up her legs and watched her bring one hand to her genitals.

"God, Fernando," she said. "You're making me so wet."

You're pretty good, he said to himself as he watched the ministrations of her hand. She continued what she was doing for several quiet moments, and he continued to watch her. Then she bent slowly at the waist and lowered her head until he could feel her breath on his penis.

"Stroke yourself, Fernando," she said. "I want to watch you do it."

Why the fuck not, he asked himself. He reached down with his right hand and began to do as she had requested, watching her stroke herself above him as he did it. Then she began to blow her warm breath up and down the length of his penis as he caressed it.

"Come for me, Fernando," she said. "Let me see you come."

Why the fuck not, he asked himself again. He watched the flicker of her fingers above him, savored her breath on his genitals, and stroked himself until he climaxed. She stepped down from the bed, reached into her bag, and handed him a towel.

"Nice, huh?" she said.

He nodded. "Very," he said, swabbing at himself with the towel. "Now you can blow me until I'm ready to fuck you."

She moved a step back from the bed and drew her bag up in front of her. "You know we can't do that," she said.

"Sure we can," he said. "People do it all the time."

"I explained that earlier, Fernando."

He reached beneath the pillow and extracted the knife with his left hand, releasing the blade as he did it. "And now I'm explaining something to you, you fuckin' *puta*."

She reached into the bag, then let it fall away. He saw the .22 before the bag hit the floor, and he watched in disbelief as she clasped both hands around the grip and raised her arms until the gun's unblinking eye was trained on his naked chest.

"No, Fernando," she said. "I do all the explaining here."

"This is supposed to scare me?" he asked, measuring the distance between the gun and the knife as he spoke. "You don't have the *cajones* to use that thing."

"It doesn't take *cajones*," she said. "All it takes is a finger."

"Really?" he said. "How many people have you shot so far?"

"Drop the knife, Fernando."

Sure, he said to himself as he rolled under the gun and slashed at her right arm.

The gun sounded like it went off in his left ear, but he felt the searing impact of the bullet high in his shoulder. Then his blade drew blood, the girl screamed, the gun fell to the floor, and Fernando began to grin.

"You shot me," he said slowly. "I can't believe you just shot me."

She made no reply, and neither of them moved until Morton started pounding on the door of the room. Then Fernando flipped the knife from his wounded side to the other and the girl darted to her right in an effort to get around the bed. She ran into a round kick that bounced her off the bureau, but when he closed in on her she came up with the phone in both hands and slammed it against the side of his head.

The blow staggered him enough for her to slip away and reach the door, but the chain did its job when she tried to pull the door open. He could see Morton through the gap allowed by the chain, and so could the girl.

"Help me!" the girl shouted.

"Fernando!" Morton said. "What the fuck's goin' on in there?"

"Shut the fuck up," Fernando said as he came up behind the girl. "And get the fuck away from my door."

The girl slammed the door in Morton's face and made a try at releasing the chain, but Fernando wrapped his left arm around her neck and pulled her close. The fire in his left shoulder almost made him scream as he held her, but he liked having his strong arm free for the knife so he tightened his grasp and let the shoulder burn.

"You should have just fucked me," he said into her ear. "Only one of us is gonna like this better than fucking."

The *puta* made no response except to hang all of her weight on his wounded arm until he couldn't bear it any longer. When he dropped her, she threw her right elbow into his crotch and twisted her way back to the door.

The blow doubled him over, but not for as long as the girl's escape required. She still had both hands on the chain when he came up behind her again, and this time he touched her with nothing but the knife. He made one swift incision, true and deep, and blood spurted from the artery in her neck.

Go ahead, he said to himself, *try to stop the bleeding with your hands.* She clutched her throat as if she could read his mind, then she stumbled and dropped heavily to the floor. Fernando stood over her and grinned quietly while her fingers turned crimson and her life slowly leaked out of her grasp.

THREE

"Jeezus fuckin' Christ," Morton said.

"Don't even start," Fernando said through a glare as he closed the door behind him. "Check my fuckin' back for an exit wound."

Morton stepped around the girl on the floor and gave Fernando's back a cursory examination. "Whatever went in the front is still in there," he said.

"Press on this," Fernando said, motioning toward the towel he was holding against the wound in his shoulder.

"Yeah, right," Morton said.

"It's either that or pull my pants on for me; asshole."

Morton chose the towel, and Fernando slipped into a pair of shiny brown slacks. "I'm gonna need a doctor," he said.

"A doctor of psychiatry," Morton said. "If you're not crazy, you're too stupid for words."

"Does that mean you'll shut the fuck up if it turns out to be stupidity?"

"It's not what *I* have to say you should be worried about. Avina's gonna go ballistic over this."

"Fuck Avina," Fernando said. "She doesn't have shit without me, and she knows it."

"Even she has a limit, wise guy. She's not gonna bury a homicide just to make a bust."

"This is the bust of her fuckin' lifetime. She'd trade her left tit for it, believe me. Besides, this ain't no homicide."

"Really? What is it?"

"Self defense," Fernando said. "I have a bullet in my shoulder to prove it. Now clean out the bathroom for me."

"Clean out the bathroom? Do you realize how deep the shit here is? Our chances of wiping every trace of you out of here before we get company are, uh, how do you say it—fuckin' *nada*, Einstein."

"Shut the fuck up and get my stuff out of the bathroom," Fernando said. "If something was going to happen behind the gunshot, it would have happened by now."

"If we wiped this room all night, we'd probably still leave a print behind."

"Prints are not a problem," Fernando said. "I ain't in nobody's computer. That's what you get for hookin' up with a solid citizen like me."

"That's what we get for hookin' up with a fuckin' psycho from a country that never heard of computers," Morton said on the way to the john.

We've heard of computers, Fernando said to himself. *We've heard of everything where I come from.* He walked slowly around the bed, fighting off a dizzy spell on the way. He picked up the .22 from the floor and threw it in the suitcase on the bed, then he fumbled through the *puta*'s bag for a moment and did the same with his three fifties and the knife.

"Where's Jimmie?" he asked when Morton came out of the john.

"What?"

"You know, Jimmie? The moron you rode out here with?"

"Yeah, I know Jimmie, but I'm not sure he's the fuckin' moron here."

"He's *not* here," Fernando said. "That's why I asked where the fuck he is."

"Her driver started for the door when the gun went off," Morton said. "Jimmie jumped him and ran him downtown."

"Call him," Fernando said. "We need the driver."

"He's not a problem. He never got a look at you."

"No wonder you're not the agent in charge, Morton. You think too fuckin' slow."

"Looking around the room here, I'd say I'm hearing this from someone who doesn't think at all."

"Call your fuckin' sidekick before he turns the driver loose," Fernando said. "We need him to get to the service that sent the *puta* here."

"What the fuck for?"

"Because they're gonna remember that I called for Rebecca, and Rebecca's gonna remember me."

Morton walked over to the bureau and picked the phone up off the floor. "There's blood on this fuckin' thing," he said.

Fernando touched the knot rising on the side of his head, but he didn't feel anything slimy. "Make the fuckin' call," he said.

"Do you still have the driver?" Morton said into the phone a moment or two later.

"Good," he said after a short pause. "Make him give you the location of the service before you turn him loose."

"You don't have to tell her a fuckin' thing," he said next. "I'll have our resident genius down there in a couple of minutes, and he can explain how he got shot by a fuckin' whore and thereafter committed self-defense on her sorry ass."

Fernando had finished flinging his clothes into the suitcase on the bed by the time Morton hung up the receiver. "He'll take care of it," Morton said, "but this is gonna cost you."

"You're already getting paid twice," Fernando said.

"It's not enough for this kind of shit," Morton said.

"Whatever. Throw me my fuckin' jacket."

Morton set the phone down on the bureau, but he was still wiping the surfaces he had touched when it started to ring.

"Who the fuck is that?" he asked.

"It's time to go," Fernando said. "Would you throw me my fuckin' jacket?"

Morton walked over to the mini-closet next to the john, plucked the jacket from a hanger, carried it to the bed, and draped it over Fernando's naked shoulders. Then he closed the suitcase, lifted it off the bed, walked back past the bureau and around the girl on the floor, and opened the door.

"Then let's go," he said. The phone fell silent as Fernando rose from the bed, slipped his bare feet into a pair of shiny brown loafers, and walked slowly to the door. He staggered slightly when he got there, and paused for a moment.

"Who was that on the phone?" Morton asked again.

"That was her people," Fernando said quietly. "She didn't call back when she said she would."

"Are you okay?" Morton asked.

Sure, Fernando said to himself, *I'm fuckin' feeling great.* He walked out the door, and Morton trailed after him without another word.

FOUR

"This is going to hurt," the doctor said.

No shit, Fernando said to himself. *It's been hurting since it happened.*

Then the doctor started digging for the bullet in his shoulder, and Fernando learned a little more about hurting than he had known before. He tried to ride on top of the wave as much as he could, but he began to regret refusing a painkiller before the probing ended.

"This man belongs in a hospital," the doctor said when he was done.

"I heard you the first time," Avina replied.

"No, I don't think you did," the doctor said. "I'm not signing off on this bullshit."

"Nobody's asking you to sign off on anything. I'll take it from here."

"You're still not listening. Do you realize how many ways this situation can turn to shit?"

"It already turned. What we're doing now is cleanup."

"You can't clean up this kind of shit. Don't you know that?"

"Please," Avina said. "It's too early for your moralizing."

"No," the doctor said. "It's too fuckin' late."

These guys used to be an item, Fernando said to himself, looking from Avina to the doctor and back again. He tried to imagine Avina's angular body intertwined with the doctor's, her hawk's eyes blurred with passion, her short black hair matted with sweat on her forehead, but he failed. *It would be like fuckin' a tarantula,* he thought, shaking his head slightly while he thought it.

"Are you okay?" the doctor asked.

"Yeah," Fernando said. "I'm just great."

"Keep this dressing fresh," the doctor said. "And keep up with these antibiotics. You're really at risk for infection here."

I'm from the sewers of Tijuana, Fernando said silently. *If infection could kill me, I'd be dead already.*

"And these are for the pain, in case you change your mind later," the doctor continued, handing him a pill bottle that rattled with the promise of relief.

Maybe later, Fernando thought. *First, I find that fuckin' Rebecca.*

"Thanks for coming," Avina said. "I owe you."

"You already owed me," the doctor said. He finished throwing his stuff together, slipped on a dark jacket, and strode to the door. "I hope it turns out to be worth all this shit."

"I hope so, too," Avina said. She opened the door, the doctor walked out, and she closed the door behind him. She stood there silently for a moment before she turned back in Morton's direction.

"Do you think we're covered at the motel?" she asked.

"The way we set it up will hold," Morton said. "Nobody'll get to us through the motel."

"How about the escort service?"

"That's not a problem, either," Morton lied. "The driver didn't see anything, and he's scared shitless anyway."

"How will you explain the hole in your shoulder when you get back?" she asked, turning her attention to Fernando.

"I'll just tell the truth," Fernando said as he slowly rose from the conference table in the middle of the room.

"And what's that?"

"Some fuckin' *puta* went crazy on me."

Morton came over from his perch in the corner and began to help him pull a shirt over the bandaged shoulder.

"That story's gonna work down there?"

"The truth sets you free, you know that."

"Take him to the Laurelhurst house," she said to Morton.

"Keep an eye on the wound, keep the dressing changed, what- ever—just make sure he doesn't die until after this thing comes down, all right?"

"I'm not a fuckin' nurse," Morton said.

"I know that. You're a special agent working on the biggest bust either of us will ever see, and I just asked you to make sure our inside man doesn't die from his own stupidity. All right?"

"Well, when you put it that way."

"Good," she said, turning back to Fernando. "Will staying up here a few days be a problem?"

Fernando shook his head. *No,* he said to himself. *I might need a day or two, anyway.*

"I'll just tell them the truth," he said again. He thought about saying more, but the look in Avina's cold eyes killed the impulse.

"Do you think you can fuck with me?" she asked.

Without a doubt, he said to himself. *Women are made to be fucked with.*

"Do you?" she asked.

"No," he said. "You're the one with the badge." *And you can stick that badge up your skinny ass,* he thought.

"You're fucking with me right now," she said. "And you don't even know why that bothers me."

Sure I do, he thought.

"I don't?" he asked.

"No, you don't. You can think whatever you want—it makes no difference to me what you get off on."

"So why are we having this conversation?"

"Because thinking you can fuck with me is stupid, Fernando, just like killing that girl tonight."

"Which means you're stupid to be working with me."

"Exactly."

"Don't worry about it. We're both smart enough to make this thing happen."

"I hope so, Fernando. And you should hope so, too."

Why is that? he said to himself, but her hawk's eyes were read- ing his mind somehow.

"Because if we don't," she said, "I will personally cut off your fucking balls and stuff them down your throat."

You're not woman enough to play with my balls, he thought. *And you're not man enough, either.*

"Don't worry about it," he said. "You're going to take Rodriguez down, I promise you."

"Just how good is your promise, Fernando?"

Read this, you fucking bitch, he said to himself. *My promise is as fucking good as gold.*

"Would you hand me my jacket?" he said to Morton. He leaned against the table until Morton walked across the room, retrieved the jacket from a chair along the wall, walked back, and draped it over his shoulders.

"Don't worry about how stupid we are," Fernando said. "We're smarter than Rodriguez, so we're cool."

"What makes you so sure?" Avina asked.

"Rodriguez trusts me," Fernando said. "How smart is that?"

The shadow of a smile flickered in Avina's hard eyes, but it didn't stick. *Fuck you,* Fernando said without a sound, and he shuffled in the direction of the door. Morton walked with him and opened the door when they reached it, and Morton pulled it closed behind them when they crossed to the other side.

"She's probably staring at us right through the door," Morton said as they moved toward the elevator bank at the end of the hall.

"Let her fuckin' stare," Fernando said softly. "Where's Jimmie now?"

"He'll meet us at the Laurelhurst house. He should be done at the escort service by now."

Good, Fernando thought. *Maybe I can pop a couple of these pills after all.* He was leaning slightly against Morton's shoulder and dreaming of uninterrupted sleep when the elevator arrived in front of him. The door whispered open, and after a moment they had another wall between themselves and Avina's cold hawk's eyes.

FIVE

"Yeah," I said softly. "That's Lizzie."

Sam pulled the sheet back over my daughter's lifeless face, placed his big black hand on my shoulder, and guided me gently out of the room. We walked for some unrecognizable length of time until we entered a brightly lit room filled with metal chairs and shabby wooden desks. He led me to one of the desks, ushered me into one of the chairs, and draped his 250 pounds of muscle on another.

I looked at him sitting there, looking back at me through those big glasses with the ugly black frames, and the only thing I could think of was the time Leon knocked those glasses off that thick head in a scuffle for a rebound back in the days when I didn't have a daughter and my daughter wasn't dead.

"Do you still play?" I asked.

Sam chewed on the question and eyed me intently for a while, but he eventually answered. "Not as much as I'd like," he said. "But, yeah, I still get out there now and then."

"Do you still get all the fuckin' rebounds?"

"Pretty much," he said.

"Where do you play? I can't remember the last time I saw you."

"I play with some guys from work here. The Bureau has its own gym."

"I guess that's a good thing," I said. "I can't think of who else would want to play with you guys."

"The feeling is pretty much mutual," Sam said.

"I guess it would be."

"Even if it wasn't, I wouldn't be lookin' for you two. You guys beat me enough in high school to last a lifetime."

"We're not in high school anymore, Sam. We could all be on the same team now."

"Yeah," Sam said, still looking at me as though his eyes were focused on a different conversation than his mouth. "Wouldn't that be something?"

"I've never been able to figure out what that means. Isn't everything something?"

"Yeah," he said. "I guess everything is. Maybe it's just an expression."

"An expression of what?"

"Of awkward nervousness in this case. You know, something to say until we're ready to deal with this situation."

"I don't think I'll ever be ready to deal with this situation, Sam."

"I'm sorry about that, Wiley. I truly am. But I have a job to do here, and I think we both want me to do it."

"I know," I said softly, and then I drifted off inside myself for a while. Sam let me go, but he continued to watch me relentlessly. I began to shrink under the weight of his gaze, and then I began to think I might disappear entirely if I could only hang onto the nervous silence between us long enough.

I don't know how long we sat there waiting for me to evaporate, but I finally gave up when I noticed that I was diminished but not gone.

"What happened, Sam?" I asked.

"I don't really know too much," he replied. "I don't have the M.E.'s report yet, but there are two knife wounds on her body—one on her right arm and another across the front of her throat. It looks like she bled to death."

"What's the story?"

"I don't know. I was hoping you could help me a little there."

I laughed at that, but it was one of those laughs that won't come out of your mouth until you rip it away from your ribcage.

It sounded more like a scream than a laugh by the time it finally hit the atmosphere.

Sam looked like he wanted an explanation, but I didn't have a thing to say. "I'm talkin' about some general information," he continued. "Why she might have been at the scene of the crime, who she knew, just basic stuff like that."

"You need to talk to Leon, not me."

"Why's that?"

"This is the first time I've seen her in more than a year."

"What's Leon got to do with it?"

"I haven't seen him in more than a year, either."

"But they saw each other during that time, I take it."

"Yeah," I said. "They saw a lot of each other during that time."

"Jeezus," Sam said quietly. "That's fucked up."

"Tell me about it," I said.

"So you can't help me at all?"

"I don't know shit, Sam."

"How 'bout where she was working, or what line of work she was in?"

"Why?" I asked. "Is there some occupation that'll make her a little less dead?"

Sam's eyes narrowed a little in response to that, but neither of us said anything else for a while. He finally saw what he was waiting for or got tired of waiting for it.

"I'm trying to figure out what your daughter was doing at the scene of the crime," he said, and by then his gaze was hot enough to burn holes in my forehead.

"Where was that?" I asked.

"A motel out by the airport," he said, his eyes fixed intently on mine as he said it.

"Where?" I asked, but I barely had enough breath in me to get the word out of my mouth. I tried to inhale, but either my technique no longer worked or the air was gone from the room.

Sam did not reply. He sat there behind those ugly black frames and watched me try to catch my breath, and when I finally did he sat there and watched me some more.

"What motel?" I asked.

"The Evergreen," he said quietly.

"Never heard of it."

"Neither had I," he said, and then he disappeared. One moment I was staring at him staring back at me, and the next moment he was gone and all I could see was Leon.

I had been carrying a cold fury over Leon for more than a year, and at that moment in Sam's squad room my anger achieved critical mass—some internal switch flipped from cold to hot. I could feel the heat radiating through my veins, and I reveled in the warmth for a moment.

I didn't know how Lizzie had ended up in a room at the Evergreen Motel, but I did know that the path had run directly through my oldest friend in the world. My cheeks began to burn as I contemplated what needed to happen next, but that's when I learned that Sam was still in the room.

"Doesn't Leon own an escort service?" he asked, just letting it hang out there like he was checking on tomorrow's weather forecast.

"Leon has a lot of businesses," I said, but by then I had already made the same connection. I couldn't think of many ways to explain Lizzie's presence at the Evergreen late Thursday night, and being there to work was by far the most likely of them.

"I think you're right," Sam said. "I do need to talk to Leon. If you really have been avoiding him for a year, I suggest you avoid him for a while longer."

"He's all yours," I lied, and then I told the truth: "He's the last person on earth that I want to see." *After one more look at Leon,* I thought, *I won't want to see anyone else.*

Sam watched me soberly, mulling over what he saw as I rose from my chair. "I'm glad it's you," I said, telling the truth again. "Thanks for leading me through it."

"We're not through it yet," he said softly. "But we will be."

"Yeah," I lied. "That's what I meant." Then I turned my back on Sam, walked out of the room, and down the hall to the front stairs. I could still feel Sam's eyes on my back by the time I reached the street, but he asked no more questions so I kept the rest of the answers to myself.

SIX

"You shouldn't have let me drift off," Fernando said. "We've wasted the whole fuckin' day."

"It wasn't like I could stop you," Morton said. "Your system crashed, and that was that."

I could keep you awake, Fernando thought, *no matter how many times your fuckin' system crashed.* "What'd you get from the guy at the escort service?" he asked, looking past Morton to where Jimmie was stretched out on the sofa across the room from the wet bar.

"Fuckah wasn't theah," Jimmie said. He was sprawled on his back with his head spilling off one end of the sofa and his feet spilling off the other end, and he was flipping through a notebook which was propped against his chest.

You look ridiculous like that. Fernando thought, *but then you always look ridiculous.*

"That's it?" Fernando said. "You got nothin'?"

"Ah didn't say that," Jimmie replied, brandishing the notebook. "Ah got the fuckah's log book."

"And?"

"And that gives us who went wheah when."

"We already know the who and where we're interested in. What we need is the where from."

"Plus it gives us the numbah they'all was at befoah they went."

I really hate the way you talk, Fernando thought. *People from my side of the border might have an accent, but at least they started with another fuckin' language.*

"Can you guys get an address to go with a number?" Fernando asked.

"Yeah," Morton said. "But there's no guarantee it'll be current. We aren't talkin' about the most stable element in the population."

I'll stabilize her right up if I find her, Fernando thought.

"I feel lucky," Fernando said. "Give it a try."

SEVEN

I couldn't find Leon by the time I made up my mind to kill him. He was like piss on a hot rock—his smell was still in the air, but he seemed to leave no other traces.

I started looking for him the same way a kid looks for the prize in a Cracker Jack box, and it should have taken about the same length of time. But when I turned the town over and shook, Leon didn't spill out in the palm of my hand.

When I finally admitted my decision to myself, it was four on Friday afternoon. My system had crashed after my session with Sam, but I was not refreshed by the down time. My dreams had been filled with Leon's blood flowing on the wrong side of his skin, and I rose from that empty respite determined to make my dreams come true.

I called Leon's office, but a voice I didn't recognize told me he was out for the rest of the day. I called his house in Lake Oswego, but I didn't leave a message when his machine clicked on for the same reason that I didn't call his cell phone—I didn't want to talk to Leon, I wanted to blow his brains out the back of his head.

When he didn't show up on the surface of his life, I began to scratch a little deeper. I started with Ronetta—not because Leon favored her over all his women, but because I did.

Ronetta lived in a well-kept, two-story house on Ainsworth, which was a street of well-kept houses even though it ran through what Leon's neighbors in Lake Oswego thought of as the wrong part of town. I took advantage of some rare winter sun and walked the fifteen blocks between her house and mine, a distance I frequently thought of as the shortest span from one unreachable point to another on the face of the earth.

She wasn't home when I got there, so I waited on the steps of her porch. I thought about Leon and I thought about Ronetta, and after a while of doing that she showed up with JJ and Scooter. The twins rolled over me like a pair of cocker spaniels, and I horsed around with them both while Ronetta stood in front of her gate and watched without a word.

Ronetta had a way of looking at you that could melt the shoes right off your feet, but that wasn't the look she was giving me. I ducked under her silent glare and concentrated on the kids. They chattered, they wriggled, and they burst occasionally into sudden squeals of laughter, and I rode along on the wave of their innocent energy while I waited.

I didn't have to look at Ronetta to see her. I had frames of her image frozen in my memory going back at least a quarter of a century. And I added to that private catalog of images as frequently as possible. That day, for example, I had already registered what she looked like standing at her gate: the turbulence growing in the green of her angry eyes, the irritation in the tilt of her head, the glimmer of brown skin where her white silk blouse did not reach, the provocative curve of her body against the soft fold of her skirt, the long angles of a face that time had yet to touch. So I ducked under her hard glare and watched her with my mind's eye while I fooled around with the children she had made with Leon rather than me.

I thought Ronetta would eventually break down and say something, but what she eventually did was walk around us and slam into the house. After a while, the kids clambered after her and I was alone again.

I went right back to thinking about Leon and thinking about Ronetta. I thought about the old days, when we were young and crazy and full of life, but I got no joy from doing it. I felt old and numb and full of death, and I had made up my mind to breathe as much of that death into Leon as I could spare.

Finally, the door behind me opened and I heard Ronetta on the porch.

"Have you talked to Julie yet?" she asked.

I didn't say anything, but I rose and turned two blank eyes in her direction.

"Why not?" she asked, taking my silence as an answer rather than a hint.

"Julie doesn't want to talk to me."

"She doesn't want to talk to you, or you don't want to hear what she's going to say?"

"How the fuck would I know what she's going to say?"

"Just call her, Wiley. She's going through the same thing you are."

That almost made me laugh out loud. "Believe me," I said, "it's not the same thing."

"Oh," she said, drawing it out a little. "I see. Poor little Wiley is all alone in this."

"I have always been alone, Ronetta. You should know that better than anyone."

I saw the flash in her eyes right before she slapped me, but I wasn't ready for it. It was quick, but there was still plenty of sting to it. Her eyes were raking mine, and when she saw that the slap had registered fully, she slapped me again. This one snapped my head around a little, but otherwise I didn't move a muscle. We stood there glaring at each other. I could see her contemplating another swing, but eventually that drained out of her eyes and a somber resignation took its place.

After what seemed like an hour or two, Ronetta raised her hand and touched me where my face was burning. The pressure of her fingertips was so light that it almost wasn't there, and I began to feel it somewhere else entirely. Then she stepped in to me, drawing my head down just by subtly increasing the pressure of her touch on my cheek. Her lips brushed my other cheek softly on the way to my ear, and I closed my eyes and drank her in through the pores in my skin.

Her right foot was planted between my feet, and her leg was brushing lightly against the front of me. When I began to harden there, she pressed in even closer. When she spoke into my ear, I was listening to her leg more than her words.

"It's time for you to grow up," she said softly. "Call Julie."

I didn't react for a moment, but her words eventually got through. I opened my eyes and moved my head back so I could see her. She tried to say something to me through her eyes, but I was reading too slowly so she kissed me. Her lips were both soft and insistent on mine, and I opened up to them. We stood on the porch of her house like that for another hour or two, her hand on my hot cheek, her right leg unflinching between my legs, her lips trying to talk directly into my mouth. And when she had said everything she could think of to say, she bit down hard on my lower lip.

I jumped back with the taste of my own blood in my mouth, and then she slapped me again. This one had her shoulder in it— I could feel it in my toes. I looked at her blankly again, still trying to track what was happening.

"One more thing, Wiley," she said, her voice low but with an edge to it. "If you're all alone out here, how'd you just get the shit slapped out of you?"

EIGHT

The address that came up with the *puta*'s phone number turned out to be in a new apartment complex about fifteen minutes south of the Laurelhurst house. Fernando watched the scenery change from the backseat while Morton drove their government-issue Ford and Jimmie rode, as ridiculous as ever, in the front passenger seat.

"I thought we were supposed to be in the good part of town," Fernando said. "This here looks like shit."

"It comes and goes," Morton said. "It gets pretty good again a little farther, down around the college."

Sure, Fernando thought, *but we probably aren't going that far.*

Rebecca's complex was one of many in a scruffy area Fernando guessed had formerly been dominated by the small, plain houses which still survived here and there. Her complex was divided into a series of quads, and the apartment they were looking for was in the farthest quad from the asphalt parking lot. Fernando took his time getting there, and his companions did the same.

"If the bitch is out of town," Jimmie said, "why the fuck are we comin' heah?"

"That's why you're not the agent in charge, Jimmie," Fernando said. "You think too fuckin' slow."

"And y'all is fuckin' Einstein, raht?"

"More like fuckin' Sherlock Holmes," Morton said. "We're gonna look around for clues as to her current location."

"Unless we really get lucky and come up with a roommate of some kind," Fernando said. "Then we can forget the fuckin' clues and just ask."

When they got to the right quad, they had to climb some stairs to get to the right door. Morton knocked on it briskly as soon as he could.

"Who is it?" someone said from the other side.

Morton drew his ID from his jacket and held it close to the peephole in the door. "Drug enforcement, ma'am," he said. "Open up, please."

Fernando listened to the sounds of the door locks coming undone and watched the door swing open. A tall coffee-colored girl dressed in baggy gray sweatpants and a University of Oregon tank top looked back at him from the doorway.

"What is it?" she asked.

What it is, Fernando said to himself, *is my lucky day.* He stepped around Morton and drove his right fist deep into the girl's flat gut. She folded over his arm and sagged to the floor, and he knelt right with her.

"As soon as you can breathe," he said into her ear, "tell me your name."

Fernando saw more panic than understanding in the girl's eyes, but he waited on one knee until the balance shifted. "Caramelle," the girl said finally.

"Caramelle," Fernando said softly, "you are a very beautiful girl."

Caramelle blinked slowly, as if she wasn't sure how she was supposed to answer that. Then Fernando slipped a knife into his right hand and filled the empty spots in her eyes with fear.

"Do you see this blade?" Fernando asked as he flicked it into position. "Nod if you see it."

Caramelle nodded.

"Here's what's going to happen," he said. "I'm going to ask you a question, and then I'm going to start cutting you until you answer it. Nod if you understand me."

Caramelle nodded emphatically.

"I hope I don't have to change the way you look," he said.

"You really are a beautiful girl. Nod if you're ready to start."

She nodded again.

"Where is Rebecca?"

"Vegas," Caramelle said quickly.

Fernando nicked her right ear lobe, drawing a shudder from Caramelle and a thin line of blood from her ear. "Where in Vegas?" Fernando said.

"Circus Circus—Room Fifteen-thirty-four."

"That's good, girl," Fernando said. "You done real good." Then he made one short, quick movement with his right hand that Caramelle never saw coming and drew a deep incision across the front of her throat. Blood spurted when the blade hit the right spot, but Fernando knew where the blood was going and he wasn't there.

Caramelle's last move was to clasp her neck with her hands, and Fernando quietly watched her do it. *It's funny how they all try to stop the bleeding with their hands,* he said to himself.

"Man," Jimmie said from the doorway, "y'all is good with that thang."

No shit, Fernando thought. He rose from the floor, stepped around Caramelle and the blood pooling faster than the plush carpet could absorb it, and crossed to a phone resting on an end table next to a low divan.

"It's me," he said after he punched some numbers for a while, "I need you to do someone in Vegas tonight. Room Fifteen-thirty-four at Circus Circus—a tall blonde. Make it look like an OD if it's not too much trouble."

"Shee-it!" Jimmie said as Fernando hung up the receiver. "Just like that and it's done?"

Just like that, Fernando said to himself. *And you could be done the same way.*

"Are you finished?" Morton asked. "Or do you have to work your way through the whole fuckin' logbook?"

"I'm done," Fernando said quietly. "The others have no reason to remember me." He recrossed the room, skirted around Caramelle again, and walked out the door. He was almost back to the Ford before he remembered the Asian bitch with the natural blonde hair.

NINE

Ronetta turned and walked back into the house, and for the second time that day I felt most of the oxygen in the air disappear. When she was gone, I slumped against the door frame and tried my best to string a few breaths together.

I don't know how long I stood like that, because the next thing I remember I was approaching the Jefferson gym. I said a small prayer of thanks for my automatic pilot, because I couldn't have picked a better destination if I'd tried. Friday nights meant high-school hoops in that part of town—and no matter how many houses Leon bought in the upscale burbs, he was still from that part of town on Friday nights.

The usual crowd was already starting to spill out onto Commercial Street, and the usual authorities were there to keep an eye on it. I saw four or five guys from the Gang Enforcement Team, three squad cars, and two policemen on horseback, and I didn't give them a thought as I looked for Leon in the throng.

He wasn't there, so I didn't have to shoot him in front of several cops. I drifted into a ragged line near the ticket window so I could get inside to shoot him in front of fifteen hundred basketball fans instead.

Three gang-bangers dressed in khaki pants and navy blue sweatshirts with the hoods pulled up were playing grab-ass on the sidewalk behind me, until the smallest of the three cut away from his homies and slammed into me. There were a lot of ways to play that scene, but I only felt like one of them. So I drained every drop of expression from my eyes and turned and looked straight at the kid who had bumped me.

The kid was laughing and carrying on until he looked over his shoulder and into my eyes. Then he downshifted in a hurry.

"What the fuck you lookin' at, bitch?" he said, squaring up so that we were standing almost face to face. Actually, I was looking down on him—he was three or four inches shy of my 5'10". He didn't like that angle, so he stepped back a stride as his partners fanned out on each side of him.

The kid hadn't turned the volume up much when he spoke, but the heat in his voice activated the radar possessed by most crowds in that part of town. The people closest to us started moving out of our way and the people farthest from us started pushing in to get a better view. That meant the various authorities would soon be in the picture, so I didn't change a thing—I just stood there with my cold eyes locked on the kid's.

The kid didn't like that much, but he didn't know what to do about it. We stood like that for another second or two, until our freeze-frame started leaking cops from both sides.

"Do we have a problem here, fellas?" asked the first one on the scene. We didn't acknowledge the cop's presence in any way, but one of the kid's homies answered the question.

"No problem," he said. "We're cool—we're cool." He seemed to be talking to the kid more than the cop, and the kid started to listen. He let his partners shoulder their way into the space between us, but his eyes didn't waver for an instant.

"All right, break this up," said another cop.

"Who is this punk-ass bitch?" the kid asked, but he let himself be guided backward by his homeboys while he waited for the answer.

"Whoever," one of them said. "Who the fuck gives a shit?"

They were halfway across Commercial Street by this time, but the kid was still trying to burn holes into my eyes and I was still showing him my cold stare. When they reached the sidewalk on the far side of the street, the kid pointed at me and said, "Later, muthafuckah!" Then the three of them walked up to the corner, turned right, and strode out of sight.

The kid didn't know that later had already come and gone, but I wasn't blessed with the same degree of ignorance. Which is probably why I had ruffled the kid's feathers in the first place—that night I had flaunted the freedom that comes with not giving a fuck about what happens next because it was the only freedom I had left.

The crowd had completely lost interest in the situation by that time, and so had the cops. I turned back toward the gym and drifted along with the line to the ticket window, hoping as I went that Rea was not at her customary perch. When I finally got to the window, the seller was someone I didn't know. I took this to be a good sign; Rea would have demanded an explanation of the scene with the gang-banger, and I didn't have one.

My reprieve was short-lived, however, because Art was at the door. I saw him watching me over and around the fans filing past him while I rode the line in his direction.

"Hey, man!" I said as I got to him. "Seen Leon yet?"

"Don't try to change the subject," he said. "What was that all about?" Art had the subtlety of a sledgehammer, so I can't say his directness came as a surprise. I tried to shrug his question off, but he wouldn't let it slide.

"Are you all right?"

Art was about my height and roughly twice as wide, and he had the kind of face that shows up in the nightmares of kids who don't scare easily. His voice was deep enough to originate somewhere below the ground he stood on, and it came out with a rumbling Southern rasp to it. He laughed easily and joked around with most of the people he admitted to the game, but there was something serious just behind his humor that kept the baddest gang-bangers from messing with him no matter what they thought of his Gang Enforcement T-shirt.

He was talking directly into my ear, and people were crawling all around us on their way into the gym. Somehow, the situation wasn't conducive to generating a good lie—the only thing that came to mind was the truth.

"I guess I've been better," I said.

He wrapped his big hand around my shoulder and looked me

in the eye. "I'm sorry for your loss," he said gravely. "But you hang in there, you hear me?"

I couldn't think of anything to say to that, so I just nodded.

"No," he said then. "I haven't seen Leon yet. I'll tell him you're lookin' for him when he gets here."

"Don't bother," I said. "I'll try to catch him before that."

"All right," he said as I turned to leave. "Just remember what I said, Wiley. Everybody loved that girl."

"Apparently not everybody," I could have said, but I didn't want to stop long enough to say it. So I cut the voice away from the words and let them drop without a sound while I picked my way back to the sidewalk against the flow of the crowd.

TEN

"You're way outside the lines now, *amigo*," Morton said.

What lines, Fernando said to himself. He was back in his spot in the Ford, this time watching the neighborhoods improve as they drove north.

"How many people do we have to watch you waste before you're done?"

"Close your fuckin' eyes," Fernando said, "and you won't have to watch any."

"I'm not jokin' around here," Morton said.

Sure you are, Fernando thought. *You have no idea how funny you are.*

"We have a thing going here," Morton said. "I don't have a problem with that. But you seem to forget that we're still federal agents."

Fernando leaned back against the seat and closed his eyes. The wound in his shoulder was throbbing, and Morton's incessant whining was making his head hurt, too.

"Are you going to talk about this or not?" Morton said.

Fernando did not reply, except to lay a naked blade against Morton's throat so swiftly that he could have sliced the question mark off the last word out of Morton's mouth.

"What's to talk about?" Fernando said as Morton slammed the car to a halt. "Your asses are mine, Morton. I can fuck you any time and any way I want. That's all you need to remember about our relationship."

"Shee-it!" Jimmie said. "Did y'all see the way he moved?"

"And you keep your fuckin' mouth shut," Fernando said as he returned to his former position against the backseat of the car. "I'm sick of the way you fuckin' talk."

ELEVEN

I walked down Commercial Street, past the main school building and the baseball field. Alberta Street was busy, so I turned west and walked to the light at Albina before I tried to cross. Drunk Oscar was waiting in front of the store on the other side of the street, but he took one look at me as I walked up and swallowed his request for a handout. We ignored each other while I waited for the light to cross Albina, and as soon as the light changed I started ignoring him a lot more.

Most of the garbage cans were at the curb on the next two blocks, and I remember making a mental note to myself to do the same with my can when I got home. This was not thinking of a particularly high order, but I took some encouragement in it. Taking care of my garbage seemed a legitimate achievement at that point in that day, although I was conveniently ignoring the fact that only a small fraction of the garbage in my life was ready for curbside pickup.

Except for the din of travel rising from the freeway a block to the west, Michigan was silent. I found a kind of solace in that imperfect silence, and I tried to cloak myself in it as I turned south and walked the remaining block to my door. My house resembled the others on my street—dark and uninhabited—and it still looked dark and uninhabited after I walked in and closed the door behind me.

I didn't disturb the darkness until I reached my bathroom, where I turned on a light so I could see myself in the mirror.

The face staring back at me from the glass was familiar, but oddly so—the individual elements all seemed the same, but the sum of the parts no longer matched the answer given in the back of the book.

My lip was getting puffy where Ronetta had made her mark, but otherwise my face was as lean as usual. My close-cropped black hair was still blended liberally with gray, my eyes and my skin were still brown, and my broad shoulders still seemed to link me to a long line of people who had dipped wooden oars all over the Pacific Ocean. Yet the more I studied myself, the less connected to that mirror image I felt.

I splashed cold water on my face and walked back into what once had been the dining room. I didn't do much eating there, so I had it set up like an office—a desk, a lamp, a chair, a Mac, a printer, a filing cabinet, and a phone. The living room was to my left, the kitchen to my right, and the single bedroom next to the bathroom behind me. It was probably Leon's smallest house, but that was cool with me because I didn't take up much space at the time.

I went to the phone, turned on the lamp, and let my fingers do the walking for a while. I called Leon's card room in LaCenter, his porno shop on Sandy, and his topless bar on the far east side, but he didn't turn up at any of them. Then I called Ginger, Lisa, Michelle, and Linda, but only Linda picked up the phone.

"This is Wiley," I said.

"So?" she said.

"Is Leon there?"

Linda's response to that was a short snarl that might have been born as a laugh had there been any humor in its family tree. I waited for a moment for a more formal answer, but it turned out that a moment was not long enough.

"Linda," I said, "is Leon there or not?"

"Jesus Christ," she said. "Are you ever out of the fuckin' loop." Then she hung up the phone.

I followed her example, but the phone began to ring almost as soon as it left my hand. I sat back and waited for my machine to switch on.

"You know what to do," I heard my voice say. That was followed by a beep, and then my wife's voice leaked into the room.

"This is Julie," she said, and then she paused for a moment. When I didn't pick up the phone, she continued. "Call me. We have to talk about this."

After Julie cut the connection, I played the message through again.

It sounded exactly the same as it had the first time. I got up, went to the closet in the bedroom, picked up the athletic bag, and set it on the bed. Some of the light from the lamp in the next room drifted through the bedroom doorway, but I didn't need it.

The bag was about half-filled with money, and I extracted a handful of it. I counted it out in the half-dark, and it turned out to be $1,100. I straightened the bills out, folded them once, put them in my front-left pants pocket, rezipped the athletic bag, and threw it back on the floor of the closet. Then I went back out to my desk, picked up the keys to the old Subaru parked next to the house, turned off the lamp, and walked through the dark of the kitchen to the back door and out to the driveway.

After I dragged my garbage can to the curb, I climbed behind the wheel of the car, started it up on the first try, pointed it at the night lights of Portland, and set off to find out where Leon was spending the last night of his life.

TWELVE

Avina's eyes were colder than the ice in the drink she was nursing at the wet bar when they came in the front door.

"Where've you been?" she asked sharply.

"Romeo here had to see another girl," Morton said.

"You're unbelievable," Avina said, shifting her frosty glare to Fernando.

"That's what the girl said," Fernando replied.

"You move from the living room to the kitchen," Avina said, "I want to know about it."

"I have to take a dump, you wanna come over and watch that, too?"

Avina hit the drink in her hand and said nothing for a moment. Morton moved off to the kitchen on the right, Jimmie headed for his sofa to the left, and Fernando continued to stand in front of the door.

"How's the shoulder?" Avina asked.

Maybe you should kiss it, Fernando thought. *The ice might numb the pain.* "It hurts," he said.

"Good," she said, and then she hit the drink again.

THIRTEEN

I drove north on Michigan to Alberta, east past Jeff to MLK, and south all the way to the Morrison Bridge. I drove under the bridge, wrapped around the eastbound span, and popped out on Belmont Street so I could check the Monte Carlo.

The Monte Carlo was hot among the hip that winter, which meant it had become a fixture on Leon's Friday-night itinerary—with the exception of that particular Friday night, I discovered.

I abandoned Belmont at Twelfth and headed north for Sandy Boulevard, where I made another wasted stop at the porno shop at Fifteenth with "Live Dancers" splashed in neon across the front. I never quite understood that sign—does it mean that someone else has dead dancers?—but when I tried to rib Leon about it he just looked at me in sympathy. Maybe that was the main difference between us—more things made sense to Leon. Maybe that was why he owned half of Portland while I lived in the smallest of his houses.

Leon was not on the premises—dead or alive—so I drifted along Sandy for several blocks, scanning both sides of the street for a glimpse of Suzie. I finally spotted her near the Wendy's at Twenty-ninth. The tire shop next door was closed for the night, so I pulled into its parking lot and waited. A moment later, Suzie opened the passenger door of the Subaru and slipped in beside me.

"When are you going to get a car, Wiley?" she asked, tilting the rearview mirror down with her short, stubby arms so she could get a look at her face.

"This is a car," I said.

"This is a piece of shit," she replied. She fussed a little with her lipstick, ran her fingers through her hair, tilted the mirror back up, and leaned back in her seat.

"What's up?" she said after a moment.

I slipped another bill from my pocket like the one I had left with the counterman at the porno shop and handed it to her. "Can you do me a favor?" I asked.

"What do you want?"

"Have you seen Leon go by tonight?"

"Nope."

"Will you give me a call if you do?"

"That's it?"

"That's it."

"Give me your number before you totally lose your mind."

I recited the number to her and she said it back to me. "Do you need to write it down?" I asked.

"I don't collect that many numbers in the course of my day," she said. "I've got it."

"If you see him, just leave the time and the direction on my machine."

She opened the door and scooted out, but she peered in at me from the pavement. "You must want to see him pretty bad," she said.

"Yeah," I said.

"Does he want to see you?"

"No."

"Can I get into trouble here?"

"Maybe," I said.

"Fuck it," she said. "I'll call you if I see him."

"Thanks," I said, but she slammed the door on top of it. I rolled down my window as she walked back toward the Wendy's.

"Suzie!" I said.

She looked back at me but didn't stop.

"Take care of yourself."

"You mean I don't have you to do that?" she said with a smile. Then she blew me a kiss and turned her full attention to the cars streaming by her on the street. She was still there, fishing for eye contact with solitary drivers, when I caught a break in the traffic and pulled away.

FOURTEEN

"Give me the logbook," Fernando said as soon as Avina went out the door.

"If you don't know the bitch's name," Morton asked, "how the fuck are you gonna look her up?"

That's why you're not the agent in charge, Fernando said to himself. *You think too fuckin' slow.*

"Just give me the fuckin' logbook," Fernando said.

Jimmie tossed it to him from the sofa, and Fernando caught it against his chest with his good right hand. He sat in the armchair that matched Jimmie's sofa, propped the book on his lap, and began to flip through the pages to the date when he had met the unusual Asian chick with the natural blonde hair.

It's a shame she didn't work out, Fernando thought. *I never saw hair that light with eyes that dark before.*

"What are the odds this bitch would remember you?" Morton asked, still stuck in slow. "How many different guys you figure she's seen since last summer?"

"She'll remember me," Fernando said, but a shadow crossed his face while he said it that gave Morton pause.

"What?" Morton said.

"What was the date I was here last July?"

"Beats me."

"The twenty-second," Jimmie said from the sofa.

"How do you know that?" Morton asked.

"Just a mental giant, ah guess."

"Seriously," Morton said.

"It was Tammy Jo's buthday," Jimmie said. "She still ain't fu-given me foah missin' it."

"That date isn't in this book," Fernando said, flipping through the pages some more. "The twenty-first and the twenty-third are here, but not the twenty-second."

"You sure it was the same service?" Morton asked.

What, Fernando said to himself, *this one just shut down that day?* "I've only used one service," he said.

"Any othah dates missin'?" Jimmie asked.

"Yeah," Fernando said, flipping through the book. "It happens every now and then."

"Prob'ly ain't the only logbook," Jimmie said.

Fuck, Fernando thought.

"Why would they have another one?" Morton asked.

"Guy prob'ly has the calls fuhwuhded somewheah else now and then. Bet y'all a dollah we got anothah book wheahevah that is."

"Fuck it," Morton said. "No way the whore would remember you, anyway."

"I had to cut her a little," Fernando said. "She'll remember me."

"Yup," Jimmie said. "That'd do it."

"Jeezus Christ," Morton said.

"Call the service," Fernando said. "See if they answer."

Jimmie picked up the receiver of a phone tucked away on a low table at the end of the sofa. "What's that wuhd?" he asked. "The one that stands foah the numbah?"

"Fantasy," Fernando said.

"Raht," Jimmie said as he punched out the letters. "Ain't that a hoot?"

"Jeezus Christ," Morton said again.

"Hey!" Jimmie said into the phone. "Y'all open? Awraht! Now y'all hang on jus' a minute—ah'll be raht back."

Jimmie cradled the receiver against his chest and grinned in Fernando's direction. "She wants ta know what she can do foah me," he said.

"You're talkin' to a woman?" Fernando asked.

"Yup."

"Get a girl over here," Fernando said.

"You're shittin' me," Morton said. "Please say you're shittin' me."

"Ask for the Asian with the blonde hair," Fernando said. "Maybe it's still my lucky day."

Jimmie poured Fernando's request into the phone, then cradled the receiver against his chest again.

"She says Alix ain't on call tonight. That name sound familuh?"

"Yeah," Fernando said.

"Well, she ain't available."

"Get someone else."

"Can we talk about this?" Morton asked, but no one answered while Jimmie went back to his conversation on the phone.

"What's the numbah heah?" Jimmie said after a moment or two. Morton gave it to him and Jimmie relayed it into the phone.

"She's gonna have a sweet lil' dahlin' call raht back," he said with a grin. "This is on y'all, raht, boss?"

"Hold it," Morton said, his voice rising a little as he said it. "We can't have one of your fuckin' slasher scenarios here. The agency is tied to this place."

"Wait until she leaves, then," Fernando said.

"That's not all. If it's just a phone switch, the girl won't necessarily know where the relief location is."

"The service is gonna get its cut at some point. All we have to do is follow the money."

"Then what—you slash another throat?"

"You don't like that scenario, you guys follow the girl and come up with the logbook. Flash your badges, throw some of that federal fear into her. I'll stay here and play Jimmie's part."

"Hey," Jimmie said. "I'll play my own damn part."

"Think how Tammy what-the-fuck's-her-name would feel," Fernando said. "I wouldn't want that on my conscience."

"You don't have a fuckin' conscience," Jimmie said.

True, Fernando thought, *but I do have a need for a good fuck. Might take my mind off this fuckin' shoulder.*

"Ain't this a bitch," Jimmie said, but he didn't reach for the phone when it started to ring a moment later.

FIFTEEN

My next stop was Leon's topless club on the far east side, so I slipped off Sandy at Thirty-ninth in favor of the freeways. After a couple of minutes east on Interstate 84 and a couple more south on Interstate 205, I was rolling into Leon's crowded parking lot.

Nothing was parked in his private parking space, so I climbed out of the car and walked to the phone booth on the corner, called my own number, and found out I had no messages.

By the time I got back to the club, a pimp named Sylvester was following his hired muscle through the door. Sylvester was sporting the classic ghetto-cowboy look—his skinny feet were ensconced in a pair of snakeskin cowboy boots and he was wearing a wide-brimmed cowboy hat with a feather stuck in a snakeskin hatband. We made eye contact as I walked up, but neither of us spoke. He made a show of flashing his roll when he paid the cover charge for his partner and himself, but the guy working the door did not seem visibly impressed.

"Hey, Henry," I said when it was my turn to pass by.

"Hey, Wiley," Henry replied.

"Has Leon been in since I talked to you?"

"Nope. Hasn't called, either."

"How's your night?"

"It was great until Sylvester showed up. We'll have to wait and see now."

"Won't that be a thrill," I said.

Henry grimaced and turned his attention to someone coming in behind me, so I walked on down the short hallway into the club. The bar was on the left as you came in and the two stages were down a few stairs to the right. There was some room at the long counter overlooking the stages, but the tables were almost full and the rails around each stage were jammed. I didn't know the dancer on the second stage, but Ginger was doing her thing on the main stage.

After admiring her for a moment or two, I turned to the bar and found a stool next to the wall farthest from the door. Abby came over with a diet Pepsi as I sat down.

"Thanks," I said, but the music was so loud she probably didn't hear me. She smiled and nodded at me anyway, then went back about her business behind the bar while I settled down to wait.

Abby returned at the end of a song about fifteen minutes later to find out if I wanted anything to eat. I didn't realize that I was hungry until she asked, but I passed in favor of holding onto that lean, edgy feeling in the pit of my stomach. She gave me a fresh drink, and I sipped it slowly while I went back to waiting for Leon to walk in the door.

Every thirty minutes or so, I walked back to the office to check my messages, but either Leon was flying low that night or my early-warning system wasn't up to the job of tracing him. I was pondering what my next move should be about an hour before closing time when Sylvester gave me something else to think about.

The crowd that night was lively but nice, mostly a lot of young guys having some fun on a Friday night. Sylvester and his bodyguard had been quietly drinking all night, and by the time all hell broke loose I had almost forgotten about them.

It started when the bodyguard bought a table dance from the dancer I didn't know. Or maybe it started somewhere deep in the murky history between Leon and Sylvester, and it came to the surface during the table dance. The dancer was a little short for my taste, but cute in a perky kind of way. And she was giving the bodyguard his money's worth, shedding her outfit with some style, and stirring some heat into the routine.

Sylvester's table was near the same wall that I was up against, only down a level, so I had a good view of the proceedings. I was taking full advantage of that view when everything turned sour. The dancer had her back to the bodyguard and was bending low, giving him one of the standard poses in the business. But he reached out and put his meaty paw on her butt.

The dancer tried to play it off, and it was a good try. She slapped his hand away but kept on dancing, not even turning to look at him. I was admiring her poise when the bodyguard made another move, this time grabbing her right between her legs. She shrieked and jumped away, then came back at him with a glass from the next table.

"Motherfucker!" she shouted as she flung the glass at his face.

He turned his head slightly, but the glass hit him on the cheek right below his left eye. Time seemed to stand still for an instant while the big guy blinked and shook his head, then he stood up. I was up by this time, too, and I could see Henry coming from the corner of my eye. But before we were close enough to do anything, Sylvester hit the dancer hard in the face and she went down in a heap on the floor. Then the bodyguard timed Henry right and floored him with a left just below his ribcage.

The bodyguard sensed me coming and turned, but I ignored him completely and focused on Sylvester instead. He felt me coming, too, but when he turned to look I slammed my fist into his mouth. The cowboy hat with the feather in it flew one way and he bounced off the wall the other way, and I followed right after him. By the time the bodyguard started coming at me, I had the .38 stuck in Sylvester's face.

I fired one shot into the wall next to Sylvester's head, and the big guy paused. Then the DJ cut off the music and gave me some talking room.

"Back off," I said, talking to the bodyguard but looking straight at Sylvester. He looked back at me without a word, and the big guy stood above me like an avalanche waiting to happen.

I turned my gun hand slightly and rammed the side of Sylvester's face with the butt of the .38. That got a howl out of him, but the big guy still didn't cut me any slack.

"Back off," I said again.

"Jesus Christ!" Sylvester interjected. "Do what the fucker says!"

The big guy backed off a step or two, but I still didn't like the feel of his hulking presence.

"Farther," I said, and he moved back a little more.

I looked up for a moment, and noticed for the first time that almost everyone in the room was frozen in a ring around us. I saw a flash of movement from the periphery, but it turned out to be Ginger working her way through the throng.

She was coming up behind the big guy, so I returned my attention to him. "Bend over," I said.

"What?"

"Bend over," I repeated.

"Fuck you!" he said, so I turned in his direction and shot him through his left foot. He hollered even louder than Sylvester had and crumpled like a house of cards when the door slams.

"What the fuck's wrong with you?" he screamed.

"Shut the fuck up," I said quietly.

He started to argue with me, but he shut the fuck up when I pointed the .38 at his other foot.

"Stand up," I said.

"You just shot me in the fuckin' foot!" he said. I just looked at him blankly and waited, and when he didn't do anything I said it again.

"Stand up."

This time he did it, although it took him a while.

"Now bend over," I said.

"What?"

"You know, like a table dancer."

He hesitated again, so I let my .38 give Sylvester a foot just like the one it had given the bodyguard.

"God damn, Tee!" Sylvester howled. "Do what he says!"

Tee slowly bent over, but his eyes were locked on mine all the way down and the message in them was something less than friendly. Then I told him to spread his legs apart a little more, and our friendship flickered more dimly still as he did it.

His gaze didn't waver until Ginger kicked him hard between his legs. He fell to the floor with a scream and grabbed his crotch with both hands, but he didn't get much sympathy from Ginger.

"That's right," she said. "Keep your fucking hands where they belong, you fucking asshole."

By that time, Henry was getting his breath back and the new dancer was back on her feet. "Go get some ice from Abby," I said to the dancer, motioning with my head to the bar. She followed my instructions without a word, moving off with her face in both hands.

"Are you okay?" I asked Henry.

"Yeah," he said.

"Can you take care of the rest of this?"

"Yeah."

"I don't think Sylvester here is gonna want the cops. Do you have to call 'em?"

"Probably," he said. "Someone might have done it already."

I got up, put the .38 away, and started to walk out of the room.

"You're a dead man," Sylvester shouted after me. "Do you hear me, motherfucker? You're a dead man!"

No shit, I said silently to myself as I walked back out to the Subaru and drove deeper into Leon's last night.

SIXTEEN

The *puta* was busy between Fernando's legs, but his penis seemed oblivious to her ministrations.

What the fuck is going on, he thought.

"Slow down," he said.

The girl followed his instructions, but his response did not change. He watched her blonde head bobbing gently over his genitals and felt nothing but the throbbing in his shoulder.

"Forget it," he said. "Get the fuck out of here."

"Don't ask for your money back," she said as she rose from the sofa and moved to the matching armchair. "I kept my end of the bargain."

If I want my money back, Fernando said to himself, *I won't have to ask for it.* He watched her dress without a word, marveling at how quickly she made the switch from Frederick's of Hollywood to Levi Strauss.

"I'm sorry it didn't work out this time," she said when she was done. "How 'bout I give you a discount the next time you call?"

Sure, Fernando thought, *that'll be just fuckin' great.*

"Let yourself out," he said. He watched from the sofa as she picked up her bag and walked herself across the room and out the front door.

After the door closed behind her, he rose slowly and moved to the picture window overlooking the street. He made a space in the blinds and watched the girl walk past the garage, out the driveway, and up to a Miata convertible parked at the curb. She climbed into the front passenger seat, and a moment later the car coughed to life and pulled into the eastbound lane. By the time it reached the park at the end of the block, Morton had his Ford moving in the same direction.

Fuckin' idiots better get the job done, he thought. *If they don't, I'm the idiot.*

He looked down at himself as he turned away from the window. He was nude except for the condom clinging to his limp dick. *The safest fuckin' sex I never had,* he thought as he slipped the sheath free and dropped it on the hardwood floor. Then he returned to the sofa, stretched himself along the length of it, settled into the incessant throbbing in his shoulder, and began to wait for the waiting to end.

SEVENTEEN

Without a conscious thought from me, the Subaru pointed its nose back to the freeway. I rode wherever it went, using the time to review the night's events.

I could feel Leon in the atmosphere around me no matter where I turned that night. But he seemed somehow just behind my field of vision, lurking safely in my blind spot as he watched me lurch from one end of Portland to the other.

I came out of these ruminations as the car rumbled over the Markham bridge and spilled me out on Highway 26—the freeway that ran through my life like a blacktop timeline. It was built in the late forties to connect Portland with the resort town of Seaside on the northern Oregon coast, but what it did for me was hook the life I was living to the life I had lived before.

I generally drove west on 26 about as often as I called the Devil collect. I had tried to escape where it led me several years before, but I guess turning your back on the past doesn't make it dry up and blow away—every time you turn around, it still stretches out behind you as far as the eye can see.

The Subaru labored going up the Sylvan hill, but I just sat back and waited. I knew we would eventually crawl over the crest, and that's what we eventually did. Once we were on the flat heading past Beaverton, we were home free—or would have been, that is, if home were ever accessible at that price.

The first thing I noticed after we got up to speed was a storm front swallowing stars as it scurried toward me. Before long, I was driving into the rain. Visibility shrank on both sides of the Subaru, but I didn't need to see where I was going. After forty minutes of beating against the rain, I parked across the street from the house I had shared with Liz and her mother.

I turned off the Subaru and sat there silently, watching the house through the rain. The windows of the car began to steam up, but otherwise nothing happened for ten or fifteen minutes. I used the time to try to remember what I was doing there, but nothing had been clearly identified by the time the porch light came on, the front door opened, and Julie appeared in the doorway.

I saw her clearly for a moment in the porchlight, but then the light was behind her as she came striding off the porch and into the rain. Not that it mattered—just like Ronetta, I could see Julie with my eyes closed.

I watched her knife through the rain toward the car, walking unflinchingly and without haste. When she passed in front of me, I reached over and unlocked the passenger door. She opened the door when she got to it, slid into the seat beside me, and closed it again.

She didn't say anything at first, so I said the same. We just sat there in the silent darkness and looked at each other. I don't know what she was seeing, but the view for me was nearly unbearable. I would have looked away, but somehow it seemed important not to be the first to do it.

"How long were you going to sit out here?" she asked at last.

I didn't know the answer to that question, so I made no reply. She took my silence as my response, nodded almost imperceptibly to herself, and then looked away.

I did the same, but I could see her just as clearly as before. Her short brown hair was damp from the rain, and the pale skin of her face seemed to pick up every available trace of light. I thought there might be a slight residue from the rain on her forehead, and I felt a sudden urge to kiss her lightly along the line of her bangs just in case. I did nothing, of course, until the urge withered in the edgy silence and faded back where it belonged.

Then Julie began to weep. Her body started to tremble, and tears were streaming down her face when I turned to look at her again. I wrapped my right arm around her slowly, as though a sudden move might spook her, but she leaned away slightly and continued to sob without a sound.

"Come here," I said softly. I increased the pressure of my hand on her far shoulder until she folded into me. She pressed her face against the leather of my coat where it covered my heart and wept without reservation, and I wrapped my other arm around her and held on as hard as I could until she finished.

"What did we do?" she asked finally, her voice muffled oddly by the leather of my coat.

"It wasn't you," I said. "It was never you."

She pushed away from me in response to that and sat up straight in her own space. "We've had this conversation before," she said. "I don't have the energy to do it again right now."

She began to dab at her face with the sleeve of her sweatshirt, so I offered her a handkerchief from my coat pocket.

"I'm fine," she said, but she shifted to the other sleeve and worked a while more. When she was finished, she leaned back with a ragged sigh and closed her eyes.

"Do you know what happened?" she asked.

"Not really," I said.

"What was she doing there?"

"I don't know."

"I want to know what you know, Wiley," she said, sitting up straight again and locking her eyes on mine. "You owe me at least that much."

"I'm working on it," I said, "but I really don't know anything yet."

"Well, what do you think happened? How does our daughter get murdered in the middle of the night in a motel out by the airport?"

She was starting to shake a little again, but this time more from rage than grief. I waited for the tremors to subside, and after a couple of minutes of silence they did.

"Try not to beat yourself up with questions we can't answer

yet," I said. "Believe me, Julie, I'm going to find out exactly what happened." I left off the part about "if it's the last thing I do," even though I was certain that it would be.

She looked at me sharply for a while more, then she leaned back against the seat and closed her eyes again.

"Sam came out to question me," she said. "Is he any good?"

"I don't know, really. But it wouldn't surprise me if he is."

"He wouldn't tell me anything, either."

I thought I had already fully explained that phenomenon, so I let that comment slide. She saw what I was doing immediately, so she let it slide as well.

"We're going to have to make some arrangements," she said.

"I know."

"Can I count on you to help me with that?"

She was looking at me sharply again, trying to see my answer more than hear it. I tried to match her intensity as I looked back while I lied with all my heart.

"Yes," I said simply.

"Thanks," she said. "I really appreciate it."

Neither of us spoke for a while after that, and when she finally did I missed the silence keenly. "I know this is hurting you just as much as it is me," she said. "Why aren't you feeling it?"

"This is another conversation we've had before," I said. "I don't have the energy to do it again right now."

"Don't you dare mock me," she said. "You don't have that right."

"And you don't know a damned thing about what I'm feeling, so don't start acting like you do."

"Oh, that's right. Nobody understands Wiley."

Since I was hearing that line for the second time in the last twelve hours, it knocked me back a step. When I failed to respond, Julie looked close enough to see the shadow of bemusement on my face.

"That's funny to you?" she asked.

"Not really. It's just that Ronetta said the same thing earlier tonight."

"And this surprises you?"

"I don't know."

"Those are the truest words you've ever spoken, Wiley—you don't know, you never have known, and you never will know."

"I don't know what?"

She shook her head, opened the car door, and climbed back out into the rain. After she slammed the door and started out into the street, I climbed out my side to intercept her.

"I don't know what?" I asked again.

"You don't know shit," she said as she walked around me. I turned and cut her off again on the sidewalk in front of our house.

"That's not an answer," I said.

"I don't owe you any answers—you owe me, Wiley." She whipped around me again and strode up the walkway to the porch. I stood motionless in the rain and watched her go, and then I watched her turn and stride right back.

When she got within arm's reach of me, she put one hand on each side of my face and drew my mouth to hers. She walked into the kiss that followed, which might explain how deep she got. She brought everything she had in the vicinity into play, and I tried my best to match it. By the time she broke it off, I was deep into my second erection of the night.

She reached down and brushed the hardness between my legs with the back of her hand, then she stepped away.

"Do you get it yet?" she asked.

"Do I get what?"

"I'm the same as Ronetta—I always have been. That's why you were attracted to me in the first place. My only problem is you met her first."

"There's more to it than that, Julie."

"Really? Name something—name one thing that isn't just a rationalization for why you never gave me an honest chance."

We stood there speechless in the rain while she waited for an answer, and when it didn't look like one was coming she nodded emphatically. She wheeled toward the house and then paused and turned back.

"Actually, you're right," she said, "but you don't get that either, do you?"

"What?" I said.

"There was one difference between us, not that it ever mattered to you."

"What?" I said again.

"She wanted Leon, and I wanted you."

She waited to see if that sank in or rolled off me like the rain, and I don't know which one she saw because she turned away, strode up to the porch, and slammed through the door until she was out of my sight—or until I was out of hers.

EIGHTEEN

I stood on the sidewalk where Julie had left me like a fish on a stick, but it was far from the first time she had bagged and tagged me. That's what I hated most about her—every time she took a shot at me, she pulverized the neon bull's-eye only she could see in the center of my chest.

When I finally realized the rain would never wash me clean, I recrossed the street and climbed back into the Subaru. I wiped the water off my face and the back of my neck with the handerchief I had offered to Julie, then I ran it over the steamy windows until I could see well enough to drive.

I cranked up the car and wandered slowly through the old neighborhood, passing familiar houses looming in the darkness like ghosts from my former lifetime. I stopped when I rolled up at Lizzie's old elementary school, one of those mistakes you have to make once in a while to prove you're still alive.

The building still looked the same, chunky and longer than it was wide. I drove down Main Street across the front of it, turned left on Eighteenth, and drove headfirst into a parking slot facing the large yard behind the school.

I kept the motor running and the lights on so I could watch the rain leak through the twin beams stretching out from the car, but before long all I could see was a snippet of a girl with an intellect bigger than the building to my left and a heart deeper than the whole outdoors to my right. She was dancing effortlessly across the yard, flowing first one way and then the other, until she suddenly stopped and peered in my direction. She cupped her little hands around her eyes in an effort to shield them from the glare of the headlights, and she walked slowly like that until she reached the cyclone fence at the edge of the yard. She pressed up against the barrier, staring intently, and then she moved her right hand tentatively until it became a cautious wave.

I don't know how long I saw her standing like that, waving from a timeless tableau where the rain couldn't touch her, but it was long enough for me to read the haunting question in her eyes. *Is it you,* she seemed to be asking. *Are you there?*

When my tears finally did begin to come, they came hard. I sobbed uncontrollably until dehydration cut the water off, and somewhere along the way the girl dissolved into the night and I was sitting alone in the car with the rain pouring down.

After I got what was left of my bearings back, I pointed the Subaru back toward Main, drove north to Nineteenth and then east to the Plaid Pantry on Elm. I used the pay phone outside to discover that I still had no messages and the clerk inside to hook me up with some ice-cold caffeine, and then I went back to work.

I couldn't explain how the little girl in the schoolyard with all the tools she would ever need to conquer the world became the young woman who couldn't get off the floor of an airport motel Friday morning. But I did know that her life had taken a wrong turn when she hit Leon, and he was going to pay for it.

As I had learned several years before, the trip from my old life to the life which followed it was downhill all the way, and in less than thirty minutes I was back where I had started the previous afternoon simply because I couldn't think of anywhere else to go.

I pulled into my driveway, parked, cut the engine off, and dragged myself out of the car. I threw the cup from the Plaid Pantry into the garbage can next to the stairs, climbed to the side door, and opened it with my key.

That was all reasonably routine, although something about the garbage can struck me as strange. But I didn't worry about it for long, because the kitchen floor jumped up and slapped me square in the face as soon as I walked through the door.

NINETEEN

It had begun to rain in earnest shortly after the girl's departure, but four hours later the storm was beginning to ease. Fernando thought he could see the first hint of light in the sky, but he wasn't sure.

Can't tell the difference between day and night in this fuckin' town, he thought. *All these clouds, you don't know if it's the sun or the moon that ain't shinin' through.*

He peered from his vantage point behind the blinds down the street all the way to the park and saw nothing but wet, empty pavement.

Fuckin' idiots, he thought. *How long can this job take?*

TWENTY

I was on the wrong end of my .38 when I woke up. The first thing I saw from where I was sprawled on the floor was my own gun pointed right between my eyes.

Leon was straddling my kitchen chair so he could rest his arms on the back of it while he looked at me over the top of my gun. He was the second thing I saw, and I lost my appetite for looking around after that and closed my eyes. The right side of my head felt like two or three of Portland's many fine drummers were keeping time on it, and when I reached up to touch it my fingers came away slimy.

"There's not that much blood," Leon said, "but you're going to want some ice on that lump." I heard something metallic sliding along the floor, and when I looked in the direction of the sound I saw Leon edging a bowl of ice toward me with his foot.

I grabbed a handful of cubes and clasped them to my head until my fingers began to get numb and water started running down my wrist. I knew there was something wrong with my technique, but I didn't stop to try to figure it out because the cold seemed to encourage the drummers to skip a beat now and then.

I heard Leon rise from the chair and walk to the sink, but my eyelids had fallen again and I didn't give a fuck what he was doing anyway. I heard the water in the sink come on for a moment, then he was back and fumbling around with the ice in the bowl. He moved my hand away from my head and placed a damp cloth wrapped around some more cubes where my hand had been.

"Hold that," he said.

I did what he told me to do while I watched him reclaim his perch on the chair. He was still dressed for Friday night—silk suit, silk shirt, silk tie, Italian shoes, those thin socks you get when you rent a tux, and every bit of it exactly the same shade of gray, just like the guy in the John R. Tunis books I used to read when I was a kid. I can still remember the look of approval on Leon's face when I first told him about the dude who only dressed in one color at a time, and Leon started doing the same as soon as the money started flowing his way.

The gray flattered him. He had the same shade here and there in his close-cropped hair, but I couldn't think of a color that didn't work for him some way or another. His complexion was a dark chocolate, which probably had a lot to do with it, and his 6'2" frame was a natural to hang clothes on, which was probably the rest of it.

I don't know how long I was lost in this fashion reverie, but I finally focused on the fact that his eyes were focused on me. He didn't say a word—he just leaned on the back of the chair and watched me. I tried to read his expression, but his lids were drooping over most of his eyes and what was left offered no clues. I had seen that heavy-lidded look before, and my guts suddenly felt colder than the ice in my hand.

"You ready to talk?" he asked finally.

"Fuck you," I replied, closing my eyes again so I wouldn't have to watch him watching me through those slits.

Closing my eyes didn't work, of course. I could still see him sitting there like it was painted on the back of my eyelids—his slitted eyes watching me patiently, his muscular body at ease in his fine gray threads, his arms propped languidly on the top of the chair, my .38 dangling in his right hand. I eventually opened my eyes again just to change the picture.

"What did you hit me with?" I asked.

"I didn't hit you, homeboy," he said with a trace of a grin. "Why would I hit my oldest friend in the world?"

"Fuck you, Leon."

"You keep saying that. I'm starting to think that's why you've been looking for me all night."

I didn't respond to that, so he watched me through those hooded eyes for a moment before he continued.

"Is this what you were going to fuck me with?" he asked, brandishing the gun in his hand.

When I didn't respond to that, either, he seemed to switch his attention from me to the gun.

"You know, I really hate these things. I miss the way it was when we were kids, when people used to settle their differences and live to tell about it—back when we used our fists instead of these fuckin' things. Now nobody comes from the shoulder anymore—it's all from the pocket. I miss the old way."

"Sure you do," I said. "You used to kick everyone's ass the old way."

"I still kick everyone's ass, Wiley. I just don't like doing it as much."

I slipped back into silence, and Leon went with me. He had probably been waiting for me most of the night, and he didn't seem to mind waiting some more.

"If you didn't hit me," I said after a while, "who did?"

"Elmer," he answered. "He's a bit more deft than I am. I was afraid I might hit you too hard."

"Thanks for the concern."

"You're welcome."

"Where's Elmer now?"

"He went home. We're quite alone now, if you're still feeling romantic."

I started to respond to that, but I suddenly felt overwhelmed by our conversation, like I didn't have enough energy to read my next line. I think I started to drift off somewhere, but Leon nudged my shoulder with his foot.

"None of that," he said. "We're still on concussion alert here. How's the head?"

I dropped the ice and probed my head cautiously. The lump was still there, but the drummers seemed to be on a set break.

I raised my head off the floor for a moment, and when nothing significant happened I raised up enough to lean against the door under the sink.

"It's fine," I said. "Tell Elmer I really appreciate his deft touch."

"I'm guessing you're going to want to tell him yourself, but if I see him first I'll be sure to give him the message."

"When have I ever wanted to see that idiot?"

"I think you're going to want to see him now."

"What makes you think that?"

"It's just a hunch—kind of a feeling, you know?"

"What the fuck are you talking about?"

"You're right. Here we are talking about Elmer when we should be talking about you and me and this nasty thirty-eight."

"There isn't anything that needs to be said on that subject, Leon. Just give me the gun back and I'll clarify the situation for you completely."

"Fine," he said, and he tossed the .38 into my lap. "Enlighten me."

I picked the gun up and stared at it dumbly. Then I stared at Leon the same way. Then I pointed the .38 at his face. His hooded eyes stared back at me, intent but still patient, waiting for whatever was going to happen next.

What happened next was my arm got tired and I lowered the gun back down to my lap. I felt like I was sitting in a cloud; I shook my head to clear my vision, but that only woke the drummers up. After a moment or two, the throbbing in my temple subsided again, but the cloud remained.

I don't know how long I sat there in a befuddled daze, slumped on the floor of my kitchen with my best friend waiting patiently for the fog to lift. Somehow the denseness of the atmosphere seemed oddly familiar, even comforting, while the concept of clarity and penetrating light seemed unbearably hostile and exhausting. But after a while, even my hazy silence began to tire me; and when that happened, Leon's patience was rewarded.

"I think I hate your fuckin' guts," I said quietly, just to get things started.

"No shit," Leon replied.

"No shit?"

"No shit, Sherlock."

"How long have you known this?"

"Where the fuck have you been all your life? You've hated my guts since day one."

"Then why have we been tight all this time?"

Leon didn't answer that immediately; he sat there behind those hooded eyes and began to shake his head. "You figure it out," he said finally. "I don't have the time to explain your whole fuckin' life to you."

Actually, I wasn't quite as dense as I sounded. I don't know if love and hate are just mirror images of each other, as some people say, but I do know they are not mutually exclusive. In the case of Leon and me, one was every bit as old as the other.

"I guess you think the love is stronger than the hate," I said, looking down momentarily at the gun in my hand.

"Something like that," he said. "Or maybe I thought it was time to find out."

"Kind of a risky method of discovery, isn't it?"

"Not really."

"No?"

"No," he said, still studying me from a place where I couldn't really see him. "I already know the answer, Wiley. You're the one in the dark."

I chewed on that for a while, and when I had my fill I tried to bounce the conversation from my back to his.

"I think you're responsible for what happened to Lizzie, Leon," I said.

"I figured as much," he said quietly.

"Do you deny it?"

"Absolutely."

"I'm not saying you were the guy with the knife, Leon, I'm saying you are the reason she was there with the guy with the knife. I'm saying that if not for you, she'd still be alive, and I don't think I can forgive you for that."

"I can see you didn't know shit about Liz."

"What are you talking about?"

"The question is what are *you* talking about?" Still slow and deliberate, stretching everything out for me like I couldn't grasp anything thick. "What are you saying—Liz was this fragile little thing who started turning psycho knifer tricks as soon as I got my evil hands on her?"

"I'm not saying that's what you intended; I'm saying she bounced off you in that direction, and I'm saying if you had stayed the hell out of the way it wouldn't have happened."

"You might be right, bro'. But we're all bouncin' around out here, aren't we?"

"What's that supposed to mean?" I asked.

"If you had gone to LaCenter tonight instead of the club, Sylvester would still be able to walk on both of his feet. Some things happen, some things don't."

"You couldn't keep your fuckin' hands off her, could you?"

I could feel the heat rising in my cheeks, and so could Leon. He shifted down to an even slower gear and proceeded to wait for me to match him, watching me intently from deep inside his skin somewhere.

"What?" I said without thinking. I guess I saw a question behind his face, and it turned out I was right.

"I'm wondering just what it was about Liz and me that sticks in your throat so bad," he said, after eyeing me carefully for another moment or two.

"Isn't it obvious?"

"No."

"It should be, Leon."

"Then straighten me out, old friend. Lay it out for me."

I looked up at him and he looked down at me, patiently, like he had all the time in the world. I kept trying to peer through those slits in his eyes, and he just sat there and watched me try.

I wanted to explain it to him—I wanted him to see exactly what he had done. But time ticked by minute after minute without a word passing between us, him waiting for me to start and me waiting to figure out where.

"What it is," he said softly, when he finally got tired of waiting for me, "Liz and me happened. She wanted me and I wanted her back, then she didn't want me anymore and that's the end of another story in my sorry life. I'm not about to apologize for it—she was the best thing that happened to me since Ronetta, and if it was up to me I'd be with her right now.

"You see what I'm sayin'? Whatever your problem is and why it's a problem don't mean shit. Your next move remains the same, bro'—you only have one move that makes a fuckin' difference."

"What is it?" I said. I don't think I've ever spoken with less volume in my life, but Leon heard me loud and clear.

"You know what it is," he said, and he was talking way down low with me.

"What happened to Liz, Leon?" I said finally.

"I don't know, homeboy," he replied, and then he waited some more.

"What?" I said, tired of the pregnant silence and the entire night which had come before it.

"Are you ready to quit jackin' off all over town and find out?" he asked.

This time I was the one who nodded, and after a moment he got up, walked around the chair, and stood over me.

"All right," he said. He leaned over, slipped a hand under each of my arms, and lifted me effortlessly off the floor. Once I was standing, he drew me close and held me there, I think waiting to see how my head was taking it but maybe saying something else at the same time. When I seemed to be okay, he stepped away and looked into my eyes, the hoods over his gone, two old friends peering into matching brown pools.

"Then let's do it," he said.

And that's exactly what we did.

TWENTY-ONE

Fernando was just below the surface of awake when the phone began to ring. When he reached over his head to pick up the receiver, hot spikes richoteted through his shoulder. He was cursing under his breath by the time he got the receiver to his ear.

"What?" he said.

"It's me," Morton said.

"What?" Fernando said again.

"The bitch hasn't moved for two hours," Morton said.

"So?"

"So we've been out here all fuckin' night!"

"So?"

"So we started thinkin'."

I've heard everything now, Fernando thought. *These fuckin' idiots started thinking.*

"So?" he said again.

"Maybe we don't need this bitch after all. Maybe we should have just looked Alix up in the logbook we already have, seen if she's in there. You know, once Jimmie found out her name."

Fuck me in the motherfuckin' ass, Fernando thought. He reached over to the coffee table in front of the sofa—nice and easy, nothing too quick, the whole move thought out well in advance—and picked up the logbook. He flipped through the pages until he saw the name, and he flipped through the pages some more until he saw the name hooked up to a number.

"Hey!" Morton said into his ear. "Are you there?"

Yeah, Fernando said to himself. *I'm motherfuckin' here. Idiot fuckin' Fernando is motherfuckin' here.*

"Come on back," he said. He returned the logbook to the coffee table, hung up the receiver, yanked until the phone came free from the jack, fired it across the room, and watched it bounce off the wall slightly to the left of the wet bar.

Come on back, he said to himself, *so all us idiots can be here together.*

TWENTY-TWO

"Where do you want to start?" I asked.

"You know what they say about the shortest distance between two points," Leon said.

"Yeah," I said, "I know what they say, but I think that shit only works when you know the location of both points."

"We'll always know two—this one and the next one."

"So where's the next one?"

"For you, it's the shower—you're a fuckin' mess. From there, it's Ronetta's in an hour for breakfast. Think you can handle all that?"

"Fuck you," I said.

"See you there, then," he said with a smile, and then he went out the door and down the steps.

"You brought the fuckin' garbage can in from the curb, didn't you?" I said from the landing by the door.

"Might have tipped you off that I was here, huh?" he asked. "In an hour or two, maybe."

We both laughed at that, and the laughing felt good.

"Leon!" I said. He paused at the end of the driveway and turned to look at me.

"I'm glad you were here," I said.

"Likewise," he said. "See you in sixty." Then he walked down the street toward where I guess his car was stashed and I went back in the house. The .38 was still in my hand, so I cleaned and reloaded it before I did anything else—just to prove that Leon didn't know shit. Then I stripped, showered, threw on some fresh clothes, and learned why I would be seeing Elmer sometime soon.

Leon picked Ronetta's phone up on the first ring. "Talk to me," he said.

"I might be a minute or two late," I said. "I have to make a stop on the way."

"We'll be here," he said.

"Why did you let him walk out with it?"

"I told him not to, but he didn't wanna listen."

"You could have tried a little harder."

"True," he said. "But I wasn't feeling all that generous toward you at the time."

"Tell those twins not to eat everything before I get there."

"I make no promises in that area," he said. "Sometimes they don't wanna listen, either."

"Later," I said, and I smiled in spite of myself as I hung up the phone. A minute later I was in the Subaru and headed for Elmer's place on Hancock. The morning was cloud-gray but dry, and the town was starting to stir. The traffic was still light, so I pulled into the lot in front of his apartment complex without undue delay.

I had thought about how to handle the situation during the short ride over, but nothing brilliant had come to mind so I just walked up the stairs and knocked on his door. Nothing happened, so I knocked some more. Finally, a woman's voice filtered out to where I was standing.

"Who is it?" she said.

"Tell Elmer Wiley wants to see him."

"Elmer's not here."

"If you're not going to tell him, stand away from the door."

"What are you talking about?"

"If he's not coming out, I'm coming in."

"You ain't comin' in—the door's bolted."

I stepped back from the door and fired a kick right at the center of it. The wood splintered around my foot, revealing the empty space between the outside panel and the inside panel.

"What the fuck are you doin'?" the woman shouted.

I thought what I was doing required no further explanation, so I ignored her question and kicked the door again. The outside panel crumbled some more, so I kept up my assault, using one foot and then the other. After a couple of minutes, I heard some scuffling on the other side of the door and then it opened.

Elmer stood in the doorway wearing nothing but boxer shorts and a .45. He was shorter than me but significantly larger, and his skimpy attire revealed more muscles than I like to see at one time. The only thing small about him were his eyes, which were set kind of close together and always gave me the impression that he couldn't quite comprehend whatever he was looking at.

"Have you lost your fuckin' mind?" he asked, and the way he said it was vintage Elmer. He didn't yell it out or express displeasure in any way—it sounded more like he was sincerely curious.

"My question exactly," I said.

"What?"

"That's what I came here to ask you."

"What you talkin' about?"

"I'm talking about my money, Elmer, and what the hell you were thinking when you took it."

"Shit, that didn't take no thinkin'. I took it 'cause it was there and you cain't take it back."

"See," I said, stepping in closer to him and slipping the .38 into my hand, "that's the part I wanted to ask you about. Let me show you something—look into my eyes."

"What?"

"Look into my eyes, Elmer."

I was crowding him pretty good by then, and he had to rear his head back a bit to focus those beady eyes on mine. His brow furrowed while he did it, like what he saw there didn't quite add up.

"Do you see it?" I asked.

"Do I see what?"

"Do you see the truth?"

"What fuckin' truth?"

"That one or both of us is going to die in your fuckin' doorway unless I get my money back."

"Shit, Wiley, you ain't no fuckin' killer, and you sho ain't gonna die for no money."

"You better look a little closer, Elmer. You're missing something."

That was the thing about Elmer—when I said that, he actually did try to look a little closer. His beady eyes squinted up at me while he did it, but I could see that he was still having trouble coming to the right conclusions.

"You're right about one thing, Elmer," I said.

"What's that?" he asked.

"I wouldn't be dying for the money," I conceded. "I have my own reasons for dying—I just don't want to be ripped off by you before I do it."

He blinked a couple of times after that, like he heard me but couldn't quite decipher it all. I waited a moment or two, but he didn't say or do anything so I tried the direct approach.

"Elmer," I said quietly, "bring my money out here." He blinked again, but except for that neither of us moved.

"Do it now, Elmer."

Finally, he turned slightly in the doorway and jerked his head at the woman standing in the room behind him. She moved out of my sight for a minute and then returned with my gym bag. She handed it to Elmer without a word, and he handed it to me.

"I spent some," he said, but I could tell by the weight of the bag that it hadn't been enough to notice.

"That's the only thing it's good for, Elmer," I said. "Don't worry about it." Then I returned the .38 to its customary place beneath my coat and started to walk back the way I had come.

"Hey, Wiley!" Elmer said. I stopped and turned toward him, half expecting to see him lifting that .45 in my direction after all.

"How's your head?" he asked, his gun still dangling at his side.

"Damn fine," I said. "You have a real deft touch, Elmer."

"Thanks," he said with a grin, and then he went back into his apartment and closed the splintered door behind him.

TWENTY-THREE

Fernando watched a long line of car lots and fast-food shops drift by his window. The morning was cloud-gray but dry and the town was beginning to stir, but the traffic was still light and Morton had them moving easily.

"That's it theah," Jimmie said, "raht in front of the chink-food place."

Morton turned right when he got to the Chinese restaurant, and two blocks later he pulled onto a shoulder where the curb would have been on a street with a greater degree of development than this one.

"That's it right there," Morton said, nodding at a small ranch-style house across the street from the car.

"Ain't nobody home," Jimmie said.

"How do you know that?" Morton said.

"No cah in the driveway."

"How do you know it's not in the fuckin' garage?"

"Ain't a garage in this paht of town with a cah in it."

"What the fuck are you talkin' about?"

"Bet y'all a dollah it's full of junk. Garage is just anothah wud foah dump in this paht of town."

"What part is that?" Fernando asked.

"Mah paht," Jimmie replied. "Same kind of fo'ks we got back home."

"Check it out," Fernando said. "If she's there, get her out here."

"Y'all got mah dollah?" Jimmie said as Morton climbed out of the car.

"Fuck your dollar," Morton said, slamming the door on top of the words. He walked across the street, up the driveway, down a path which skirted the garage, and knocked on the front door. After a moment, he knocked again. Then he retraced his steps and eased himself back behind the wheel of the Ford.

"Now what?" he asked.

"Now you owe Jimmie a dollar," Fernando said. He leaned back in his seat, shifted his shoulder around in a fruitless effort to find a comfortable angle, closed his eyes, and began to wait.

TWENTY-FOUR

My Subaru didn't have wings, so I didn't take a straight line from Elmer's to Ronetta's—even if it was the shortest distance between the two points. Instead, I dropped two blocks in the wrong direction to pick up Broadway, went with the Saturday-morning flow all the way to Grand, took a turn to the north and through the jog to MLK, and then all the way up to Ainsworth. From there, I did have a straight line to Ronetta's, and I rode it for a minute or two until I slid the Subaru into a spot behind Leon's Mercedes.

Ronetta was sitting on her front steps when I got there, bundled up in sweats and a parka and sipping something hot from a mug. She watched me come in the gate and move up the walk toward the stairs, and I watched her watch me. As usual, she was laughing at me quietly somewhere deep behind those sly green eyes. A trace of that laughter was dancing where I could see it, but I was long past being offended by it. Anytime I can make the world a happier place, I'm all for it.

"So you found him, huh?" she said.

"It was more like he found me," I replied as I slouched into the space beside her.

"And now you're here for breakfast," she said, smiling over the top of her mug at me.

"Yup. And now I'm here for breakfast."

She took another sip from her mug, then she reached over

and brushed the back of her right hand across my cheek. "How did it go with Julie?" she asked.

"What makes you think I saw her?" I said.

"How did it go, Wiley?"

"About the same as it always does."

She didn't respond to that, so I just sat back and watched her sip from the mug until I couldn't stand it anymore.

"How'd you know I saw her last night?"

"Wiley," she said, laughing quietly around the edges of the words, "the fact that you don't know what you're going to do does not mean the rest of us are equally in the dark."

"Funny," I said.

"Kind of," she said. "But it's kind of sad, too, don't you think?"

I knew the answer to that question, but I didn't feel like sharing it so I kept my mouth shut for a while. Ronetta did the same, and eventually I was the one who broke the silence.

"How long has this breakfast thing been going on?" I asked.

"Every Saturday for quite a while now," she said. "Sometimes I can't stand to watch what the three of them do to my kitchen, but the damage never seems to be permanent."

"It sounds kind of nice," I said.

"It is," she agreed. "It's very nice."

"Ready to see what they're up to?"

"I already know what they're up to, but I guess I'm ready anyway."

We got up and I followed her across the porch and through the front door. As soon as the door was opened, we ran into the joyful noise spilling out of the kitchen. We could hear Leon and each of the twins, but somehow the total effect was greater than the sum of the parts.

The kitchen was at the opposite end of the house, and we walked down a hallway to reach it. We passed a stairway, the door to the basement, and a bathroom on our left; to the right were the living and dining rooms. There was a swinging door at the end of the hallway, and we used it to walk in on three galloping gourmets.

Scooter was up to her elbows in a bowl of pancake batter at

a table in the corner of the room, JJ was turning bacon on an electric griddle on the counter next to the stove, and Leon was fussing over a pan full of eggs and at least half of the vegetables known in the western world.

"Uncle Wiley's here!" Scooter shouted when she saw us. "You're just in time!" She hopped away from her chair at the table and grabbed the batter bowl with both hands. Leon dragged the chair to the counter, and before you could say "Maple syrup!" Scooter was throwing batter at the griddle and making it stick.

JJ brought his bacon to the table and Leon did the same with the scrambled mess he had made, and by the time the two of them finished setting the table, Scooter had six perfectly golden tops staring at her from the griddle.

"Come on, Scooter," JJ said. "Everything else is ready!"

"You can't rush a good pancake," she said, studying each of them elaborately. "Tell him, Daddy!"

"You can't rush a good pancake, JJ," Leon confirmed.

"They don't have to be perfect," JJ argued. "They're gonna look like a mess when I get through with 'em, anyway."

"That's all the more reason to get 'em right in the first place," she said, and she continued to nurse them along for another moment or two before she unleashed her spatula and cleared the griddle.

"How high, guy?" she asked.

I looked at everyone seated around the table, each in his or her own turn, and then I looked at Scooter standing next to me with six golden flapjacks on a plate between her small, strong hands.

"One will do," I said, "and I love you."

"I love you, too, Uncle Wiley," she said, and she filled my request before she flipped one to each of her folks and two to JJ. She took her seat, we all joined hands and bowed our heads, and no one made a sound for a moment. Then we ate that breakfast right down to the tabletop.

TWENTY-FIVE

"Ready to hoop it up, bro'?"

"You've got to be kidding," I said.

"Trust me," he said. "You'll sleep better after a little exercise."

"Leon," I said, "I don't have any trouble sleeping after staying up all night."

"Let's go—the timing's just about right." He rose up from the porch steps and headed down the walk toward his car. He was wearing black sweats and black sneakers, and I would have bet a lot of money on the color of the shorts and shirt lurking beneath the surface.

"Leon," I said, "I'm not even dressed for it."

"Don't try to tell me you don't have everything you need in the back of that piece of shit you call a car," he said, pausing at the gate to look back at me. "I know you, homeboy. Let's go."

"I should have gone to a Denny's for breakfast," I said as I got off my ass and followed his example. "They might not always serve everyone, but they don't chase you out to a gym when you're done."

"Should've, could've, would've," he said. "The story of life in these times."

When I joined him at the gate, I noticed him staring over my shoulder and turned to see what he was looking at. The house loomed silently behind us, its inhabitants already out the door for swimming lessons and a stop at the downtown library.

"That's kind of a special scene you've got going there," I said.

"Yeah," he said. "It is."

"But?" I said, after a moment or two.

"But it ain't the scene it should've, could've, would've been, my man. Let's go."

After moving my gear and my money from the back of the Subaru to Leon's trunk, we went. Two or three minutes later, we pulled into the lot in front of the Moore Street Salvation Army complex. The Sal had hoops for the thirty-and-over crowd on Saturday mornings, and a lot of hoopers from our generation congregated there regularly. The games were four-on-four going crosscourt rather than full, a concession to age which Leon and I didn't actually need. Consequently, we rarely played at the Sal on Saturdays—the only hard part about kicking everyone's ass there was getting up early enough to do it.

The first game of the morning was just getting underway when we walked in the door. Leon went over to sign our names on the waiting list and I went into the shower room to change. When I came back out, Leon and Sam were stretching together on the open court.

Sam appeared to be wearing the same ugly black glasses and the same set of muscles I had seen the night before, except now he had an elastic strap fastened to the glasses to keep them from falling off his big head. He looked up at me from a straddle stretch when I came up on them.

"Hey, Wiley," he said.

"Hey, Sam," I said, looking straight at Leon while I said it.

"He called right before you showed up for breakfast," Leon said. "Hell, we can all use a good run, so I told him we'd meet him here."

"If I wanted a social secretary, Leon, I sure as shit wouldn't choose you."

"Why not?" Leon asked. "I think I have a lot of potential in that area."

"What do you want, Sam?" I said.

"I want to do this thing here for a while," he said, "and then I want to talk. Is that okay with you?"

"And if it isn't?" I asked.

"Why worry about that?" Sam said. "I'm sure it's okay with you."

"I must have missed something over the last couple of decades, Sam. Just when was it that you got to know me so well?"

"It's been a relatively recent phenomenon," he replied. "Now shut up and stretch—I don't want to have to carry your ass all morning." Then he got up off the floor, picked up a ball, and walked off toward one of the open hoops.

"Way to go, Leon," I said.

"Had to be done, son," he said. "We need to know what he knows, right?"

I didn't bother to respond to that question. We both knew he was right, so what was there that needed to be said?

The first play of our first game made it look like Sam *was* going to have to carry me. Pooh was on the team that had already won a game, and he came right at me as soon as the ball was in play.

Pooh normally played like he had a red-hot pogo stick up his butt, and I had a hard time keeping up with him at my best. On that first play, he turned me into a statue—he went by me before I could even turn my head to get his license number. But it didn't matter, because Sam rose up in front of the rim and slapped Pooh's shot all the way to the top of the key. I chased the ball down and whipped it crosscourt to Leon flying down the sideline. He saw Sam busting up the middle, so he lobbed the ball toward the front of the rim and Sam jammed it emphatically.

I got into the proceedings pretty good after that first play, and we conducted an informal clinic on the court for the next hour or so. When we had all the exercise we could stand for one morning, we gave up the court and drifted outside to listen to Sam talk.

We followed him to his car, an old Dodge Dart that turned out to be parked right next to Leon's Mercedes. He threw his gym bag on the trunk lid, drew a towel out of it, removed his glasses, and attacked the sweat streaming down his face.

"I need to do this more often," he said after a moment. He removed the elastic strap from his glasses and threw it in the bag, then began to apply a corner of the towel to cleaning his lenses. After what seemed to me like forty or fifty minutes, he put the glasses on and looked at us through them.

"I can use your help on this thing," he said, "but you guys scare me."

"You seem to be handling it pretty well," I said.

"Seriously," he said. "When you're not in the gym, I think you guys are a couple of clowns—and that's scary out here in the real world."

"This is what you wanted to talk to us about?" Leon asked. "Ringling Brothers or fuckin' Barnum and Bailey?"

Sam looked at Leon through those black-rimmed glasses, then he looked at me, and then he mopped his brow with the towel. "I just love this repartee," he said finally. "It's so fuckin' amusing."

"What do you want, Sam?" I asked.

"I want to know if we can work together."

"On what?"

"On finding out what happened to your daughter."

"I thought you told me to stay out of it."

"How 'bout we cut the shit, okay? You're both going to jump all over this, and we all know it. And there's a chance you'll even find out some things along the way, because there are probably some people in this thing who will talk to you before they'll talk to me. So my question is, can we work together on this?"

"Let's say you're right," Leon interjected. "What do we need you for?"

"I can think of a couple of things. For one, I know what the doc found out."

"Such as?" I asked.

"Like I said," he repeated, "can we work together on this?"

"What was the second thing?" Leon asked.

"If we don't work together on this, I'll harass your ass every step of the way. Believe me, you don't want that."

"Now guess who's scared," I said, but I was looking at Leon as I said it and he was looking at me.

"What do you want from us?" Leon asked.

"I tell you what I know, you tell me what you find out."

"That's it?"

"That's it."

"You're on," Leon said. Sam scoured Leon with his gaze for a moment, then he turned to me and did the same. I nodded my acquiescence, and he began to tell us what we didn't know.

"Your girl didn't go out easy," he said. "Not all of the blood on the scene was hers, and she had powder residue on her hands."

"She shot the motherfucker?" Leon asked.

"Looks like it."

"If what you're saying is true," Leon said, "what's the scenario? How do you think it came down?"

Sam seemed to chew on that question for a moment while he stared at me from behind those ugly black frames. And when he finally did answer, he kept his eyes on me.

"The order in which she incurred her wounds suggests he came at her with the knife, she popped him, but he didn't go down and she eventually did. It looks like they tussled a bit before it was over."

"Why?" I asked.

"Motive is one of the questions on the table," Sam said carefully. "And there are a couple more."

"Such as?" I asked.

"Just the obvious ones," he said. "Who she was with, why she was there, stuff like that."

"Why do you think she was there, Sam?" I asked, drawing it out a little, lacing it with ice.

He continued to look at me, his eyes unblinking behind his glasses. "I don't know, Wiley. Why do you think she was there?"

"Fuck you, Sam."

"I'm not here to pass judgment on your daughter," he said quietly, his eyes still gouging mine with that unblinking glare. "I'm not even here to pass judgment on your sorry ass. I just want the bad guy. Understood?"

"Yeah," I said. "I understand you perfectly."

"Good," he said. He mopped his brow with the towel again, threw it in his bag, opened the trunk, and dropped the bag in-

side. Then he moved around the side of the car and folded himself into the driver's seat. He closed the door, rolled down the
window, cranked up the engine, and backed out of his parking
space. When he drew up even with where we were standing, he
stopped and looked us over again.

"Call me from time to time," he said.

"You'll hear from us," Leon said.

"Thanks for the game," Sam said. "You know, it's a lot more
fun playing with you than it was playing against you."

I thought about returning the compliment, because the same
was true going the other direction. But I let the comment drown
on the back of my tongue, and after a moment he pointed the
Dart out of the parking lot and left me standing next to Leon
like a stone.

TWENTY-SIX

Ten minutes later, I was dialing Alix on the phone in my office. Leon and I had gone our separate ways to crash for a few hours, and I was looking for a soft place to land. After two rings, her voice mail kicked in.

"If you want me," it purred, "leave a message after the beep."

I did as I was told, then stripped off my workout gear and hit the shower. I stood with my forehead almost touching the spout for I don't know how long, but the water stung my face until it ran cold. I leaned into the icy needles long enough to determine that the cold water would scour me no cleaner than the hot water had, then I abandoned the shower and slowly went to work with a towel.

There was no time limit for the toweling process in my house, but when I began to fall asleep with the towel in my hands I gave up my delay game and padded into the bedroom with my bare ass following close behind. I remember throwing back the blankets on my bed and the cool caress of the sheet as I sprawled across it, but whatever happened next got by me.

I slept without dreaming—or maybe just without remembering my dreams, if the experts on such things are correct. Not that the difference matters—you wake up just as clueless either way.

Or maybe dreams do come true whether you remember them or not, because on this particular occasion I awoke with Alix spooned enticingly behind me. She was still sleeping, so I remained motionless while I savored the press of her naked flesh against mine.

Eventually, she reached across my hip and cupped my penis in her hand. "You rang?" she said.

"You came," I answered.

"Not yet," she said, her hand beginning to move almost imperceptibly where she was holding me. "But I remain hopeful."

"How long have you been here?" I asked.

"That depends on what time it is now."

"The clock is behind you."

"That's okay," she said softly. "I'm not curious enough about what time it is to give up this position."

"I give you my solemn oath that you shall lose nothing in the transition."

"I don't know. What other oaths do you have?"

"Shut the fuck up and roll over so I can see what time it is."

She responded to that by shifting her hand from my penis to my testicles, digging her nails in a little, and squeezing just enough to indicate how bleak she could make my immediate future.

"Wiley," she said, "is that any way to speak to a lady?"

"Pardon me," I said. "I didn't realize I was in the presence of one."

"But?" she asked, squeezing harder.

"But I most certainly realize it now."

"You say the sweetest things," she said, unhanding me and turning toward the opposite side of the bed. I followed her example, molding my body to the slender curve of hers. Alix was almost exactly my height, so when my feet slipped under hers everything else tended to line up just right. After all the appropriate adjustments were made, I reached around her and placed my hand over her heart.

Alix covered my hand with one of hers and wiggled back against me where a wiggle would do the most good. I could see the clock radio over her shoulder, but I didn't like what it was saying so I rubbed my nose against the soft blonde hairs barely visible on her upper arm and banished the time from my mind for what turned out to be a fraction of a second.

"Wow," Alix said lazily. "I've been here almost four hours."

"And it took almost all of that just to get my attention," I said.

"As sweet as your attention is," she said, "I think I needed the sleep even more."

"Sounds like a rough night."

"A rough week. I've been out of town since Monday, and it was already starting to go bad Tuesday morning."

"But now the worst is over," I said, kissing her softly where my nose had been nuzzling.

"Yes," she said, moving my hand from her heart to her right breast and molding it exactly the way she wanted it. "The worst is over now."

There was something about the way her breast fit into the palm of my hand that I could feel a long way south of my fingertips, and I didn't change a thing for quite a while so I could savor that feeling.

Alix finally slid away from me a little until she was flat on her back. She tilted her head in my direction and locked her dark Asian eyes on mine. Like me, Alix's family tree had roots on more than one continent; but, unlike me, her disparate elements had combined in a way that could stop traffic on the freeway flowing just a stone's throw from my bed.

I tried to peer through her black eyes, but she seemed to see farther with them than I could. After more time slipped between us without a word, she began to lightly stroke the fingers cupping her breast. Then she brought her left hand to her uncovered breast and began to stroke it as well, letting her fingers linger at her nipple until it rose to her touch. And while this was happening, she continued to use those blank black eyes to watch me watch her.

"I'm starting to run out of time," I said finally.

"You won't need much time," she replied, continuing the ministrations of both hands. When I still hesitated, she reached up and guided my head to her lips. She kissed my forehead tenderly and then drew my left ear close enough to whisper into it.

"Wiley," she said, "just do what you want to do."

So that's what I did. I started by kissing her forehead right in the gap between her eyebrows and the sweep of her curly blonde hair, and when she closed her eyes I lingered at both eyelids for a moment.

Alix sighed audibly and seemed to settle deeper into the bed. Her left hand returned to her breast, although languidly, and I eventually followed its example. After I tongued the scar which ran along the edge of her right breast, I rolled up on my knees so I could lean over her body and bring my mouth to either of her nipples. Then I spoke to her as sweetly as I could through one and then the other until she moved her left hand to my shoulder and pressed gently.

"Wiley, please," she whispered.

I sat up for a moment and threw the bedding still draped over us off the end of the bed. Thus liberated, Alix flexed her dancer's legs slightly at the knees and let them drift apart. There is no degree of abandon quite so exquisite as a beautiful woman's legs drifting apart before you, and I moved between them determined to give as good as I was going to get.

I tried to tease Alix by kissing the inside of each knee, but we both knew where I wanted to go and that it would not be long before I went there. After a moment or two of this diversion, she cradled my head gently in her hands and drew me to her genitals.

After a rather enjoyable period of trial and error, I think I found her clitoris. Alix said something to that effect, but I have found that you can't listen to what women like Alix say while they are working. I think I found that particular spot because of something her body said to me when I got there, and the message got louder as I focused my attention in that vicinity.

Don't get me wrong—I don't believe the clitoris is the center of a woman. What I do believe is that it can occasionally be made to feel like the center of a woman, and I was hoping for such an occasion with Alix that day. When she began to shudder silently and press more vigorously on the back of my head, I allowed myself to believe that my hopes had been realized.

"God," she said finally, urging me to move alongside her. "I can't tell you how much I needed that."

"Sure you can," I said.

"I'm serious," she said. "Sometimes I think you should be charging me for this instead of the other way around."

"Fine with me," I said, "except you need the money and I don't."

"Yeah, there's always that."

We stopped talking after that. She went back behind her black eyes, and I began to slip ahead to where my last Saturday night was likely to take me. After a moment or two, I got up, found the gym bag, and brought it to the bed. I fished a fistful of bills out of it and laid them on top of the radio on the nightstand.

"Would you do me a favor?" I said.

"What is it?" she asked.

"I'd like to pay in advance for our next several sessions."

She reached over, took the bag away from me, and peered inside it.

"There might be enough money in this bag for a lifetime pass, Wiley," she said.

"Sounds good to me."

"What's going on?"

"Nothing for you to worry about, really."

"Wiley, you don't know me well enough to be doing this."

"Sure I do. The problem here is you don't know *me* well enough."

"Why do I suddenly feel like I'm never going to see you again?"

"Oh, you'll see me again," I lied. "Like you said, there might be enough money in that bag for a lifetime pass."

She looked at me sharply for a moment, and then the sharpness evaporated. "Can I do anything for you?" she asked, reaching down with her left hand to cup me softly.

"What you just did was for me," I said.

"Can I do anything else?"

I drew her up from the bed, kissed her on the side of her neck, and pulled her close inside my arms. I thought of death falling on my daughter without warning while I had been granted the chance to prepare for it, and the thought made me shudder in Alix's embrace.

"You've already done more for me than I deserve," I said, and I tightened my grip until the silent shudder began to subside.

TWENTY-SEVEN

Fernando was deep inside a black dream of Tijuana when Morton's phone began to ring. *Why is the phone ringing,* he thought from inside the dream. *We had no phone in Tijuana.*

In his dream, he was huddled against the wall opposite his mother's narrow bed. Rodriguez was stretched across the bed on his back, his head turned toward Fernando and his cold eyes burrowing into Fernando's brain. Those cold eyes made Fernando's innards freeze, but he gave himself up to them, buried himself in them, wrapped himself in their icy grasp.

In the dream, he could not see his mother at all. Then the phone began to ring, Rodriguez closed his eyes with a groan, and his mother's low gurgle drifted under the phone's insistent trill.

Freed from the cold eyes, Fernando turned his gaze to his mother. She wiped her mouth with her arm and shielded her slick breasts from his view, and when he did not turn away she spoke to him.

Answer the phone, Fernando, she said, which was bullshit because his mother did not speak English. And because they didn't have a fuckin' phone in Tijuana.

"This is Morton," Morton said into the phone.

"Relax," Morton said a moment later. "We just went out to get some Chinese. We'll be back directly."

Motherfuckin' Rodriguez, Fernando thought. *He's about to get a fuck he'll never forget.*

"We have to go," Morton said. "Avina's having a cow again."

"Why'd y'all say we went out foah Chinese?" Jimmie asked. "Ah hate that fuckin' shit."

"Jeezus Christ," Morton said. "We don't have to fuckin' do it just because I said it. What percent of what we've actually done in the last two days have we told that bitch?"

"Ah raht!" Jimmie said. "Ah'll get a Whoppah on the way back."

Fernando opened his door and slowly disengaged himself from the backseat of the car.

"What the fuck are you doing?" Morton said.

"I'm goin' inside. You guys do whatever you want."

"What are we supposed to tell Avina?"

"What the fuck do I care?"

"We can't go back without you. Period."

"Like I said, do whatever the fuck you want." He slammed the door of the Ford and began to walk across the street.

"Fuck!" he heard Morton say.

Then Jimmie: "What about mah fuckin' Whoppah?"

Then he was on the driveway in front of the garage and he couldn't hear them anymore. He went to the right, away from the path that led to the front door of the house. He walked along the edge of the garage until he reached a patio and a muddy yard. He stepped across the patio to a sliding glass door shielded on the inside by a full-length drape. He tugged on the door, and it slid open.

Nice security system, Fernando thought. He pushed his way through the drape, closed the door, and stood without further movement for a moment in a small dining area. A tiny kitchen to his right. Both rooms neat as a pin—not a stray cornflake or a dirty dish in sight. He moved around the table and chairs. A hallway ran off to his right, the living room and the front door to his left.

He went to the right. The first door he came to opened into a bathroom, also cleaned up neat, and the next revealed another neat room with an undersized bed and a large box which overflowed slightly with toys.

Fuckin' bitch, Fernando thought. *Why does every fuckin'* puta *in the world try to raise a kid?*

He stepped across the hallway and peered through an open door into what turned out to be the *puta*'s room. Big bed covered in some frilly shit, but nothing out of place.

He walked back down the hall to the front room. He had a choice between a sofa stretched under the picture window facing the street and two armchairs slanted toward an entertainment center in one corner. He picked the sofa. He put his head at the end further from the front door, stretched his feet the opposite way, closed his eyes, and settled down to wait.

TWENTY-EIGHT

My phone rang as Alix and my gym bag were descending the steps to my driveway. I said good-bye for a final time and moved back to my office to let Leon talk into my ear.

"Are you ready to do this thing?" he said.

"Yeah," I replied.

"Let's go, then," he said. "I'm across the street."

I hung up the phone, double-checked my .38, slipped it into its spot on the back of my hip, covered it with my leather jacket, and went out the door to wring some answers from the rest of the day.

"How long have you been out here?" I asked as I slipped in the passenger side of the Mercedes.

Leon pulled away from the curb, drove to the end of the block, turned left, turned left again at the next corner, and then rolled up the street to the stop sign at Alberta.

"Not that long," he said while he waited for a break in the traffic.

"How long is not that long?" I asked.

"Long enough."

I could hear the grin in his voice, but he was looking to his left so I didn't have to see it in his face. I tried to leave it alone, but I failed by the time he pushed the Mercedes into the east-bound lane.

"Long enough for what?" I asked.

"Long enough to see your money bag walk out of the house again."

"Don't even go there," I said. "You wouldn't understand it in a million years."

"Well, let's see," he said. "I don't understand you and money, or you and women, and here we've got you and money *and* women, no doubt combined obscenely. I guess you're right—I'm not likely to understand it."

"Fuck you," I said.

"That makes it even more confusing," he said.

I cut my losses after that by keeping my mouth shut as we slipped through a yellow light at MLK and continued east on Alberta. When we turned south on Fifteenth, however, the silence seemed less appropriate. Portland didn't get much bleaker in those days than the corner of Fifteenth and Alberta.

"Where are we going?" I asked.

"We need to see George," Leon said.

"Fat George?"

"The very one."

"Why him?"

Leon turned right on Prescott and pulled over to the curb as soon as we recrossed Eleventh. He looked over at me without a word, and I looked back at him the same way.

"I'm thinkin' there's only one way to proceed on this thing," he said finally.

"Same here," I said.

"Squeeze all the questions until the answers pop out?"

"Exactly."

"What's the first question?"

"Don't get delicate with me, Leon. I'm way past being afraid of anything we might find out."

"What's the first question?" he asked again, still looking at me unblinkingly.

"Why was Lizzie in a motel room with a guy who needed to be shot."

"That's why we have to see Fat George," he said. He climbed out of the car, and I followed his example. A light drizzle was slowly draining a dark, ominous sky, but I could barely feel it on my face as we walked toward Tenth.

"I thought Fat George lived over by the Lloyd Center somewhere," I said.

Leon paused on the corner after we finished crossing Tenth, and I paused with him. "George is like most of us," he said. "He lives wherever he happens to be. And right now, he happens to be in that white house across the street."

"If you knew where he was, why didn't you just call him?"

Leon started across Prescott, so I did the same. "George isn't returning my calls today," he said as we walked. "That's why I know he's the one we have to talk to."

"How do you know he's here?"

"Let's just say George and I have a mutual acquaintance at this address."

We walked up a short flight of stairs to a covered porch, and a caramel-colored woman dressed for the kind of work women undress for opened the door when we knocked. Whether you looked in her eyes or through her transparent wrap, you could see at a glance that she had been a beautiful woman.

She stepped aside without a word and we entered a living room in which the living was not particularly good.

"What did you tell him?" Leon asked.

"Nothing," she said flatly, and then she closed the door behind us.

"Tell him to get his sorry ass out here," Leon said.

"He's sleeping," she said.

"Say it loud."

She walked across the room without another word and disappeared down a narrow hallway. I looked at Leon after she was gone, and he shrugged slightly and grabbed a seat on a sofa covered with a worn bedspread.

"It was a long time ago," he said, and then he didn't say any more.

I considered the various alternatives for sitting available in the room—an already reclined recliner, a boxy armchair with cotton showing through the arms, and a seat next to Leon—and decided to slouch against the wall by the door instead.

We waited quietly for a moment or two before the muffled sounds of a scuffle emerged from the hallway. I could hear George's whine but not the words he was saying, and then the sharp crack of a slap.

George entered the room shortly after that. The white boxer shorts he was wearing didn't cover much of his bulging flab, which meant he was flashing more flesh than I really liked to see in one place. His beady eyes were scrunched up in his fat face and his cheeks were flushed, but the steam he had generated out of our sight quickly dissipated when he focused on Leon.

"Sit down, George," Leon said.

George moved to the boxy armchair and did as he was told. He started to say something, but he swallowed it when Leon held up his hand.

"I'll tell you when to talk, George," Leon said. Then no one said a word for a while. George didn't like the silence much, but I just gave him a blank stare when he turned to me for relief.

"What's wrong with your phone, George?" Leon said finally.

"Whaddaya mean?" George said nervously, turning back toward Leon.

"I mean what's wrong with your phone, George."

"Ain't nothin' wrong with it."

"Oh," Leon said, drawing it out a little. "That's too bad."

Sweat started leaking from George's forehead. He swabbed at it with the back of one arm, but I couldn't see that it did any good.

"The fuck's he talkin' about?" George asked, looking in my direction. I still had my blank face on, and I threw a noncommittal shrug in with it. He turned back to Leon.

"Whaddaya mean?" he said again.

"Why is it that you can't understand me, George? Do I stutter? Am I speaking some foreign fucking language?"

"No, no—it's just that I don't know what you're talking about, man."

Leon rose from the couch, pulled a 9mm Glock from behind

his back somewhere, and jammed it in George's face. When George's mouth dropped open, Leon buried the gun in the gap.

"Nod your head if you understand me now," Leon said.

George nodded vehemently. The sweat was pouring down his face, but he made no more attempts to swab it away.

"When I call you, George, I expect you to call me back. Understood?"

George nodded sharply.

"Good," Leon said. "Now it's almost your turn to talk, George. But if I don't like what I hear, I'm going to terminate the conversation. Understood?"

George nodded again, and Leon removed the Glock. He stepped back to his spot on the couch, sat down easily, and rested the gun on his right knee.

George squirmed in his chair, and the longer Leon sat there without a word the more George squirmed. He tried to wipe the sweat out of his eyes with his arm again, but his arm was sweating, too, so the maneuver met with the same result as it had the first time. Then his head began to swivel, first swinging toward me and then swinging back toward Leon, but neither direction seemed to soothe him.

"Jeezus, Leon," he said finally, "whaddaya want?"

"You know why we're here, George. Cut the fuckin' whining and tell me what I want to know."

George chewed on that for another anxious moment, and then his eyes caved in on themselves and he started to talk.

"Look, man, I don't know what happened. It was just like any other call, I swear to God."

I watched the coil behind Leon's eyes tighten a turn or two, and he glanced at me and probably saw the same thing. Leon may have been shooting in the dark, but he sure as hell knew when the ball went through the hoop.

"George," Leon said, "either you're stone stupid or you're lyin' to me."

"I swear to God, Leon, I'm tellin' you the truth. The dude called for a girl, I gave his number to Lizzie, she took it from there. I don't know what happened after that. It was just like any other call, Leon, on my mama it was."

"You're mama's dead, George."

"God damn, Leon—on my mama's memory, then! You know what the fuck I mean!"

"Where'd he call from, George?"

"What?"

"Where'd he call from?"

"From the fuckin' motel, I guess. Whaddaya mean, where'd he call from?"

"I don't think so, George."

"What?"

"You think he rented a room and then sat down and gave us a call, is that it?"

"Why the fuck not?"

"Because if he had done that, George, the police would have his name, address, and license number, and we wouldn't be having this conversation."

"Fuck me," George said finally.

"You see what I mean, George?"

"Yeah," George said. "I see what you mean."

"How often do the girls get their own room, George?"

"I don't know, man. I don't think it's very damn often, but who knows? They don't always tell me the truth, you know what I mean?"

"I need the number he called from, George."

"I don't have that with me, Leon. I'd have to look that shit up at home."

"Who's working the phones right now?"

"Rosey's got 'em, but they're on call forward to her place."

"Give me your keys before I leave. You don't want to go home for a while."

"Why the fuck not? You already found me."

"Sam'll be coming by one of these days. You don't want to be home when that day comes, George."

"How's he gonna get to me in all this?"

"Same way we did, George, only not as fast."

"Fuck me," George said again.

"Now tell me the rest of the story, George."

"Fuck, Leon! What rest of the story?"

"What name did he give?"

"The name don't mean shit, Leon! These fuckers give all kinds of names."

"George, how many times do you think I want to ask you the same fuckin' question?"

"Fernando, man. He said his name was Fernando."

"What did Fernando say when you asked him if he had used our service before?"

"He said yeah."

"But you don't remember a Fernando."

"No."

"Did he ask for a particular girl?"

"He asked for Rebecca, but she's in Vegas this week."

"Why Lizzie?"

George swallowed hard and glanced at me while he mopped his soggy brow with his arm again.

"Why Lizzie, George," Leon said.

"She was up—she was on-call that day and it was her turn. What can I say—it was just another fuckin' call, man."

"And she said what?"

"I don't know—she took the number."

"I want to know what she said, George. Exactly."

"The fuck difference does it make what she said, Leon? She took the number, all right?"

Leon locked his eyes on George, and what I could see in them from across the room almost made *me* shiver.

"Wait, wait—she asked did I know him."

"And you said no."

"No. I mean yeah—I said I didn't know him."

"And then?"

"That's it. We hung up."

"Did she call when she got to the room?"

"Yeah."

"What'd she say?"

"You know, nothing. She said everything was cool and she'd be done in half an hour."

"Tell me what she said exactly, George."

"She said she was in One-thirty-two at the Evergreen, and she said he wanted thirty minutes."

"Then what happened?"

"Then she didn't call me back in thirty minutes."

"What'd you do?"

"I tried to call the room, but no one answered. Then I called back and asked the office to check the room, but they put me on hold so I hung up."

"What happened when you called her driver?"

"Fuckin' Albert didn't answer, and I haven't seen or heard from him since."

"Anything else, George?"

"No. No, that's it, I swear to God."

"Now let me see if I've got this straight, George," Leon said. "A Fernando calls you Thursday night. He says he's used our service before, but you don't recognize his name. He asks for Rebecca, but she's not available so you hook him up with Lizzie instead. Lizzie goes to the Evergreen and gets a room for Fernando, then she calls in and says everything is cool. But thirty minutes later her driver has disappeared and she has been on the wrong end of a knife a couple of times. Is that the basic story, George? Does that about sum it up?"

"Yeah," George said quietly.

"You still think it was just like any other call, George?"

George closed his eyes and bowed his head. I watched the sweat stream down his face. Some of it ran off his nose like raindrops until he cradled his head in his hands.

"Do you, George?" Leon said again.

"No," George said. "I don't."

Leon got up and put the Glock away. "Miriam," he said, talking toward the narrow hallway, "bring me George's keys."

The caramel-colored woman came into the room a moment later. She was dressed in jeans and a Lakers shirt, and her face was made up so well you could barely notice the welt high on her left cheek. She handed Leon a cluster of keys on a Nike key ring.

"How long have you been bookin' Lizzie, George?"

"It's been about a month."

"And you didn't think either of us would want to know?"

"Fuck, Leon. She said if I told either of you I'd just get my ass kicked and the gravy train would stop."

"George, you're too stupid to work for me. What, you thought we'd never find out?"

George raised his head slowly, but he didn't speak until he saw the key ring. "Hey, you've got the keys to my ride, too."

"You're not goin' anywhere, George. You're stayin' right here until I get back to you. Understood?"

"Yeah," he said, sinking down again. "I'll wait right here."

"And George," Leon said, his voice so cold George looked up in spite of himself, "if you ever hit this woman again, I'll make you eat your fuckin' wisdom teeth. Do you understand me, George?"

"Yeah, I understand you, man."

Leon turned toward the woman. Their eyes met briefly, but neither of them said anything. After a silent moment, we both went out the door, down the steps, and back into the ragged remnants of that drizzling day.

TWENTY-NINE

Fernando woke with a start, wrenching his shoulder sharply. He started ignoring the pain as soon as he noticed it, focusing instead on the sound of the car in the driveway. When he heard the doors slam, he rose from the sofa, slipped a knife into his right hand, and moved silently to the door.

He listened intently to the footfalls approaching the house. Two people, one bigger than the other.

She has the fuckin' kid, he thought. He leaned forward slightly on the balls of his feet, his head craned toward the door, his ears tuned to receive every ripple of sound. He heard the screen door open, then a key in the lock.

He moved a step to the left so the door shielded him as it opened. A boy maybe four or five years old carrying a Star Trek pillow popped into the room, but Fernando waited for the kid's companion to clear the entrance before he slammed the door shut. That got a jump out of the companion, who turned sharply in Fernando's direction and showed him the black eyes he had seen on the Asian girl with the natural blonde hair.

But these eyes belonged to a Vietnamese woman, a middle-aged woman who was frozen in front of Fernando with a scream stuck in her throat.

She got your fuckin' eyes, Fernando said to himself. He held the knife in front of the woman's face and released the blade. The woman flinched soundlessly and stepped back toward the boy with the pillow.

"Sit down," Fernando said, motioning with the knife toward the sofa. The boy said something softly in a language Fernando did not understand. The woman shook her head, gathered the boy in her arms, and sat them both down on the sofa.

"Where is your daughter?" Fernando said quietly.

"She is out of town," the woman said.

"Out of town where?"

"The beach."

"Where at the beach?"

"I don't know."

"You don't know?"

"I don't know."

"She takes off, leaves no way to contact her?"

"She said she'd call when she stopped somewhere."

"When was this?"

"Maybe an hour ago."

"When she calls, you tell her it's time to come back. Understood?"

"What happens until then?" the woman said, her eyes focused on the blade in Fernando's hand.

"Nothing," Fernando said. "Nothing at all."

THIRTY

Neither of us spoke as we walked back to the Mercedes. Leon was punching a number into his phone and I was making certain that my left foot alternated with my right.

"I'm lookin' for you, Albert," Leon said into the phone. "Call me before I find you." Then he broke the connection, waited a moment, and began pushing buttons again. He looked at me briefly as we approached the car, but neither of us spoke.

"It's me," he said, returning his focus to the phone. "Switch the phones back to George for me, would you? Thanks. I'll get back to you later."

Leon broke that connection as he let me into the car, and a moment later we were winging west on Prescott. We had turned south on Seventh and were waiting for the light to change at Fremont before I figured out what was bothering me about his last call.

"Who's going to answer the phones at George's place?" I asked.

"Let the motherfuckers ring," he said soberly, looking away from me while he watched the westbound traffic.

I could only see one kid on the covered basketball courts in the park across the street. He was a white kid about JJ's size, dressed in baggy black shorts and a Blazers sweatshirt which was too long for his arms. I watched him pull up both sleeves and then launch a red-white-and-blue outdoor ball from the top of the key. The colors revealed a nice rotation on the shot, and it feathered through the chain-link net without touching the rim.

"What's wrong with that picture?" I asked, nodding at the kid jogging after his ball. Leon glanced in the direction of my gaze and then turned back to me.

"I know what you mean," he said. "Kids are all home playin' hoops on fuckin' Game Boys and shit. You could dynamite these courts most of the time and never hurt a soul."

I watched the kid retrieve his ball, return to the same spot at the top of the key, and repeat the same routine. The ball arced cleanly through the chains and slapped the pavement again. Then we got the light, and Leon drove us past the courts and the kid and my reflections on the days when basketball was all we had to worry about.

We turned east on Knott, then south on Fifteenth, and a few moments later we pulled up in front of some condos just east of the Lloyd Center. The curbs on both sides of the street were already crammed with cars, so Leon pulled into the parking lot of an apartment complex half a block from the condos and planted the Mercedes in front of a sign that read TENANTS ONLY. Some time dripped by then, until I finally realized that Leon was sitting there studying me.

"Ready?" he asked.

I couldn't think of what to say to that, so I just climbed out of the car instead of answering. Leon did the same, and we both headed through the rain to a door George's keys could open.

The phone was ringing when we entered the apartment. Leon went to the table with the phone on it, but he ignored the ringing while he rummaged through the assorted papers on the table. When the ringing stopped, he picked up the receiver and punched in a number.

Our eyes met while he waited for an answer, and I felt my back stiffen and my weight shift to the balls of my feet. "Put George on," he said.

"Where's the logbook, George?" he said a moment later.

"That's funny, George. I'm standing in front of the table right now, and there is no fuckin' logbook in sight."

"God help you if you're lyin' to me, George," he said finally, and then he put the receiver down.

"What?" I asked.

"The logbook is missing, and George swears it was here when he left."

I turned and walked back to the door, opened it, and bent down to examine the locking apparatus and the door frame.

"I can't really see anything," I said. "If someone forced it, they were slicker than shit about it."

"That's one question," Leon said. "How someone got in the door. Another question is how that someone found the door."

"What?"

"You call our number, you don't know where we are."

"If you followed your money long enough, you might get here."

"True, but this time the money didn't get back here, did it?"

"They must have got it from Albert, then."

Leon nodded silently, the lids drooping over his eyes again, the remaining slits revealing nothing as his mind continued to whirl. "Albert," he said after a moment, "but why?"

"To keep us from getting this fucker's number?" I offered.

"Maybe," Leon said. Then he looked at me like I was a quadratic equation he needed to factor, and when he was done he nodded slowly.

"So what's next?" he asked.

"It's either Albert or the Evergreen," I said.

"Yeah," he agreed, nodding again. "And we know where the Evergreen is."

I turned and started out the door, but I hesitated when the phone started ringing again. Leon pressed me gently on the shoulder and ushered me out.

"Just let the motherfucker ring," he said.

THIRTY-ONE

We used the overpass on Twenty-first to get across Interstate 84, then bent west along Irving past the Nationwide building to the freeway entrance at Sixteenth. A moment later, we were flowing in a stream of light traffic sluicing east.

Leon had his wipers on an intermittent cycle, and they swept the windshield in front of me seventeen times before he switched to Interstate 205. I lost track after that, but it only took a few swipes to get from there to the parking lot of the Evergreen on Airport Way.

The Evergreen was a long, two-story complex with all of the units opening out on the parking lot. Leon turned in near the office but kept on going until he got to Sam's Dart. He drove up on the left side of it and stopped, then he pushed a button on his door that made the window on my side start dropping.

Sam was eyeing me from the driver's seat of his car. His window was already down, so there was nothing to hinder a conversation between us but the absence of words. And after a moment or two, Sam took care of that.

"Got anything for me yet?" he asked.

"Sam," I said, starting out several shades lighter than I felt, "you gotta get a life. Don't you know it's almost Saturday night?"

"Yeah," he said, "That's why I'm already out on the town. Just like you boys."

"Havin' any fun yet?"

"It's been kinda slow, but I figured it would pick up when you guys showed."

"How long were you going to wait for that?"

"It's hard to say. You know how it is—once you're out here, you just go with the flow."

"Yeah, that's you, Sam—real spontaneous."

"Got anything for me yet?" he said again, his eyes behind the black-rimmed glasses staring at me blankly.

"Fuck 'anything for you yet,' Sam."

"I guess that's a no," he said, after watching me without expression a while more.

"You like guessing games, Sam?"

"Not particularly."

"Neither do we."

Sam looked away from me for a moment, then opened his door and unfolded from the car. By the time he hit the pavement, Leon was doing the same to my left. I followed suit after a heartbeat or two, and the three of us strode through the drizzle to the only door in sight set apart by crime-scene tape.

The room we were heading for was at the end of the bottom floor. When we got there, Sam pulled the tape away and opened the door. He stood aside while Leon entered the room, and when I walked by him he fixed me with the same blank expression that he had been using in the car. I turned it back at him without a word and followed in Leon's footsteps.

The room would have been close to the standard of its species except for the rumpled queen-sized bedspread splattered with blood and the dark stain on the carpet between the bed and the door.

"We're almost done here," Sam said from behind me, "but it might be best if you didn't wander around too much."

I started to respond to that, but my remark died in my diaphragm when I saw Leon stagger slightly and catch himself against the wall. He stood like that for a long moment or two, his back to us, his head canted downward, his right hand touching the wall.

"You okay?" I asked finally.

"Yeah," he said. "I'm fine." He stood up straight and looked around as if he'd just come through the door.

"What'd you find in the bathroom?" Leon asked.

"Nothin' out of the ordinary," Sam said.

"What was the story out here?"

"We found her body on the floor there, but it looks like the tussle started on the bed and traveled around the room a bit."

"What do you know about the guy?"

"Right-handed, probably under six feet tall, type A-positive blood."

"That's it?"

"So far, I don't even know it was a guy."

"I take it you didn't find either weapon."

"Nope."

"Witnesses?"

"Not really. Somebody a few rooms down probably heard a gunshot, but he thought it was a car backfire at the time."

"Did you find the bullet?"

Sam shook his head, but he was looking at me rather than Leon.

"How long after it happened did they find her?" Leon asked.

"I think just a few minutes. Someone called the office and said they couldn't reach their friend in that room. That's when they found her."

"Do you know who made that call?" Leon asked.

"Nope," Sam said, still watching me closely. "He hung up sometime after they put him on hold. Do you?"

"I'm workin' on that," Leon said. "I'll keep you posted."

"About how far back?"

"About how far back what?"

"How far back are you gonna keep me posted?"

"About as far back as you're keeping us, Sam."

"What makes you think you're not right up to the minute?" Sam asked, turning his attention from me to Leon.

"When were you plannin' on tellin' us this room was regis-tered to Lizzie?" Leon asked.

"Oh," Sam said, "*that's* the stick up your butt."

"What's the story, Sam?"

"I'm workin' on it."

"What's to work on? All you have to do is read the name off the fuckin' registration card."

"There is no registration card for this room," Sam said. "It apparently was not available for general use."

"What the fuck does that mean?" I interjected.

"Like I said, I'm workin' on that."

Sam didn't exactly get out of my way when I turned and shouldered past him, but he didn't stop me, either. I strode out of the room without another word and didn't slow down until I reached the office.

I spilled through a glass door, and I remember hearing a bell clanging behind me as I vaulted over the registration counter. The dark teenager seated at a desk behind the counter didn't say a word, but she sucked in her breath sharply and her eyes expanded as I flashed by.

The only thing still between me and what looked like a small apartment was one of those beaded curtains like hippies used to hang across everything back in the sixties, so I slipped through it and followed the sound of a television set. It led me through a cramped kitchen and into a tidy living room where no one was parked on the stuffed sofa in front of the set. I turned toward a short hallway on my right, but I paused when a woman dressed in a blood-colored sari entered the room from that direction.

She might have been surprised to see me standing there, but it didn't cause her to miss more than a beat or two. "Please get out," she said, pointing off behind me somewhere. "You do not belong here."

"I know that," I said. "Forgive me."

She continued to stand with her arm pointing over my shoulder while she processed what was happening, and then she slowly lowered her arm. "What do you want?" she asked.

"I need to know about Room One-thirty-two," I said.

"I have already told the police everything I know," she said, still eyeing me carefully.

"I'm not the police," I replied quietly.

"I am fine," she said then, raising her voice slightly. It took me a moment to realize that she was speaking to the girl I had left behind the beads, and by the time I got that straightened out she was motioning toward an old chair across from the sofa. "Please sit," she said.

I followed her instructions while she settled into the sofa. For a silent moment or two, we stared at each other while the television droned on unattended.

"If you are not the police," she said finally, "then who are you?"

"I'm the father of the girl who died in that room last night."

"Ah," she said slowly. "I am so sorry for your loss."

"Thank you," I said.

"Still, it might be more appropriate for you to speak with the police."

"Tell me about Room One-thirty-two," I said again.

The woman raised her eyebrows slightly while she thought over her answer. "You are quite to the point, are you not?" she asked next.

"Yes," I said.

"That room has been retained by a company called Pacific Industries," she said after another slight hesitation. "We were told it would be used for employees in town for meetings and that kind of thing."

"How long has this been going on?"

"Seven or eight months."

"How often does the company actually use the room?"

"Infrequently, I believe."

"You believe?"

"It is possible that we do not observe every occurrence, but it does not appear to be in use very often."

"Then why rent it by the month?"

"Perhaps that question could better be answered by the company."

"Then why rent it by the month?" I said again.

"There might be some advantages," she said, raising her dark eyebrows again as she said it. "Guaranteed availability, increased convenience. And confidentiality, of course."

"Yes," I said, more to myself than to the woman. "But why would employees in town for meetings require this degree of confidentiality?"

"Again, that question might better be answered by the company."

"Please," I said.

"I can only say that the question you are asking has occurred to me as well."

"Who made this arrangement for the company?"

"We were contacted by telephone, followed by a company check which was sent by mail to pay for a year in advance. The check was good, so we sent the key to the company's post office box."

The woman's voiced trailed off for a moment while she closed her eyes and gently massaged her temples. "Actually," she added as if from a distance, "we have had very little contact with this company."

"How about with the guests?" I asked.

The woman opened her eyes slowly and regarded me intently for a moment, as if waiting for the answer to a question she had asked herself. She removed her hands from the sides of her head and folded them demurely in her lap, gazing at me some more.

"How about with the guests?" I said again.

"I believe there has been only one guest," she answered.

"What?" I asked blankly.

"I believe there has been only one guest," she said.

"Why do you think this?"

"I do not think it, exactly. It is more of a feeling. When we clean the room, the aura is always the same. It feels like we are always cleaning up after the same person."

I said nothing in response to this, but my body stiffened and I felt myself rising to the edge of the chair.

"Does this sound silly to you?" she asked finally.

"No," I answered.

"I did not think it would," she said.

"Have you seen this man?"

"No," she said, but it came out a little tentative around the edges.

"But what?" I asked.

"But I have seen what he has done. There is always a woman, and usually the residue of their conjunction is evident. Everything is left for us, of course—magazines, lotion bottles, used condoms, soiled towels. Everything is left for us."

"But what?" I asked again.

"But I believe your daughter was not the first woman hurt in that room by this man."

"Why do you believe this?"

"As I said, everything is left for us."

"When did this happen?"

"Late in the second month," she said with an audible sigh. "I am unable to recall the exact day."

"And you told all of this to the police?"

"No," she said.

"Thank you," I said, rising to my feet and turning to leave. "You've been extremely helpful."

"Please forgive me," she said quietly.

"For what?"

"For turning away late in the second month," she answered.

"Forget about it," I said. "I turned away a long time before that."

THIRTY-TWO

Sam and Leon were standing between their cars in front of the office when I came out. Neither of them was speaking when I joined them, so I did the same. We stood there silently and watched each other breathe until I finally opened my mouth.

"Pacific Industries?" I asked.

"Don't get your hopes up," Sam replied. "It's a dead end so far, and it's probably going to stay that way."

"The post office box?"

"Canceled and reassigned already."

"The checking account?"

"No longer open."

"What about the bank's records? Somebody's name was on that account somewhere."

"That's the part I'm workin' on. I should have the subpoena Monday."

"But what?" I asked, even though I was starting to get the picture by the time the question came out of my mouth.

Sam gave me a little shrug instead of an answer, and we went back to standing there without a word for a while. "If there's a name we can use at the bank," he said finally, "why bother with this setup in the first place?"

"Who would bother with it?" I interjected. "What's the point?"

"That seems to be the question of the day," Sam said. "I'll let you know when I come up with an answer."

I was already settling into my seat in the Mercedes by the time he finished the sentence. Leon followed my lead, but Sam continued to stand there with his eyes locked on mine.

"Thanks, Sam," I said. "We'll do the same."

"Yeah," he said. "You do that."

I shut the door while Leon brought the car to life, backed away from the office, and pointed us at Airport Way again. I watched Sam in the rearview mirror until we slipped into the traffic headed back toward the interstate, and I saw him turn and head for the office door just before the mirror lost him.

"What's up?" Leon asked.

"What's in that logbook we couldn't find at Fat George's besides the names and numbers of the callers?"

"The names of the girls who took the calls, the addresses they went to—that's about it."

"The manager thinks only one guy has been using that room since this fuckin' dummy company booked it."

"No shit?"

"No shit."

"I see where you're goin' with this," he said, looking sideways at me for a moment. "But even if we find someone through the log who's seen the motherfucker, it might not do us any good."

"Why not?"

"Most of these girls see a lot of guys. You ask her to describe the guy she met in Room One-thirty-two at the Evergreen once upon a time, she's not gonna be able to do it."

"He made one of them bleed while she was there," I said. "I think she'll remember him."

Leon's eyebrows jumped a notch at that, but he didn't say anything.

"What?" I said.

"That should help, I agree with you there."

"But what?"

"But we don't know where the fuckin' logbook is."

"Just shut up and drive," I said, and that's what he did. I guess the rain had stopped somewhere along the way, because I noticed when we veered off I-84 at the Lloyd Center exit that Leon's wipers weren't on and we could still see through the windshield. Then we pulled up to George's place and I was right back to seeing through a glass darkly.

"What are we here for?" I asked.

"When did this girl get cut?"

"Late in June or July."

"Maybe we'll get lucky. If the missing book doesn't go back that far, George might still have the book we need."

We parked in the same spot as before, but I could feel something was different before we even got to the door. The apartment didn't seem tossed, exactly, although the first thing I saw when Leon let us in was the empty drawers of George's bureau all hanging at various stages of open.

Leon crossed the room to a filing cabinet next to the table, opened the top drawer, and pulled out a loose-leaf binder. He flipped to the back and scanned several pages carefully, and I watched him do it with my breath on hold.

"Fuck," he said as he dropped the binder in the drawer. "We didn't send anyone to that room in June, and July's in the missing book."

That knocked the air I was holding out of me, and I worked on replacing it while Leon started punching buttons on the phone. I had a chance to complete several cycles before he put the receiver down.

"What?" I asked.

"No one answers at Miriam's."

"What's that mean?"

He didn't respond immediately, but his eyes began to narrow while we stood there until I was looking at the same slits he had shown me at the end of Friday night.

"It means somebody out there scares that fat fuck more than I do," he said finally. Then he turned and walked back into the deepening Saturday night, and I followed in his wake like ice follows a freeze.

THIRTY-THREE

The kid was a mutt, a crossbreed squared, a regular poster child for diversity. Fernando couldn't keep his eyes off him, couldn't stop trying to trace the roots of the family tree in that silent face. He could see three continents in that face, all blended together into something new, something unique to this particular kid.

The kid was a quiet one. Fernando liked that, a kid who could keep his fuckin' mouth shut, could just sit on the sofa next to mama-san or grandmama-san or whatever the fuck she was and wait for whatever was coming next.

The woman was quiet, too, her eyes closed, her right arm around the boy, waiting silently. Fernando liked that, both of them knowing how to wait. *All things come to those who wait,* he thought. *Yeah, if you're ready to move your fuckin' ass when the time for waiting is done.*

You must have been a hot one once, Fernando thought. *You must have fucked the blond right off some boy to get this crazy quilt started. Another fuckin'* puta *with a kid.*

You still look pretty good, Fernando said to himself. *You still have that face, you still have those black eyes. Maybe I should give you a try, take you for a spin, give the boy a show he'll never forget.*

No, Fernando thought, *give the kid a break. Let him die before he finds out the truth.*

THIRTY-FOUR

Leon pointed the Mercedes at Miriam's house, and neither of us said a word until well after we got there. We went up the stairs to the porch two at a time as soon as we saw the front door was ajar, and I followed as Leon shouldered his way through the opening without breaking his stride.

He disappeared in the direction of the bedroom while I gave the living room a wasted glance, so he was already checking Miriam's carotid for a pulse by the time I caught up with him.

"Get me some ice and some wet towels," he said, words which soothed the worst of my fears. I crossed the hall into a cramped but tidy kitchen and rummaged in some drawers until I came up with several dish towels. I threw the towels in the sink, turned the water on, and foraged in the freezer for the ice. After a moment or two, I was back at Leon's side with both elements ready for application.

Leon took the towel holding the ice and placed it gently across Miriam's broken nose. Her right eyelid began to flutter a little after that, but the swelling around her left eye seemed to prevent the same thing from happening on that side.

"Hold this, bro'," he said, and I dropped to my knees beside the bed and replaced his hand on the ice pack with mine. He picked up one of the wet towels and gently began to sponge away the blood splattered liberally across her face.

"Easy," he said softly, bending down to speak quietly into her ear as he worked. "It's me."

Miriam opened her good eye and began to tense until the effort caused her to cry out sharply.

"Easyeasyeasyeasy," Leon murmured in her ear. "I've got you now."

His velvet insistence seemed to work; Miriam slumped back on the bed and closed her eye again.

"That's good," Leon said. "You just relax. Let me check you out, nice and easy. That's right." And while he continued to speak, he worked his fingers gently around her face, wiping and probing simultaneously. After a few moments, he finessed a couple of ice cubes out of the pack I was pressing to Miriam's nose and wrapped them in the towel he had used on her face.

"Easy, baby," he said softly, and he placed the towel gently on her left eye. Then he stood up and turned his slitted eyes in my direction.

"Trade places with me, bro'," he said, so I slid over a foot or two and took command of the new ice pack while he stepped around to my left. He grabbed another towel and began to give her torso the same examination he had just given her face, gently sponging and probing and speaking softly while he worked.

"You're gonna be fine, baby," he said. "Leon's got you now." When he was done, he wrestled a comforter from the tangle at the foot of the bed and draped it across Miriam's naked body. Then he hit his phone three times and began to talk into it.

"This is Portland Police Lieutenant Sam Adams," he said. "I need an ambulance at Nine-twelve Northeast Prescott—I have a victim of an assault, possible concussion, badly swollen eye, broken nose, maybe a broken rib or two. Got that? That's correct— Nine-twelve Northeast Prescott."

"When did Sam get promoted to lieutenant?" I asked as I watched him cut the connection.

"You know what they say," he said. "Rank has its privileges."

"Maybe," I said. "Do you think Lieutenant Adams could get a pizza delivered to this address?"

"Probably not," he replied, working another combination on his phone, "but this is a whole 'nother thing. Some of these public-servant motherfuckers respond affirmatively to rank.

"Hey—this is Leon," he said into the phone. "Looks like Fat George is the guy who called the motel, if you're still interested in that.

"Yeah, he still lives there," he added after a short pause, "but the last I heard he was shacked up over on Ninth and Prescott.

"How would I know the address?" he asked after another pause. "That's where you do some police work, Sam. I do know it's the white house in the middle of the block on the south side of the street, if that helps you any. Look—I gotta go. Keep us posted, hear?"

I watched what was available of his eyes as he put the phone away, but I couldn't see a thing that matched the lightness of his conversation with Sam. He knelt at the side of the bed again and whispered a kiss along Miriam's cheek.

"You're gonna be fine," he said softly. "An ambulance is coming, and so are the police. They'll take care of you until I see you tonight. You just rest—I've got you now."

When she nodded slightly, Leon put one of her hands on each of the ice packs as I relinquished them. "Just hold these like this," he said. Then he got up and left the room. I did the same until we were both sitting in his car across the street from the house. He started the engine, pulled away from the curb, drove to the end of the block, and parked again with the motor idling.

Neither of us spoke while we waited, but we didn't wait long. Within a minute or two, flashing lights were visible in both directions—a fire department rig coming at us and an ambulance coming up from behind. As soon as they both were stopped and spilling uniforms toward the house, Leon eased into the street and drove west.

He fished the phone out of the jacket of his suit as we approached MLK. "Talk," he said, and then he listened while we waited for a chance to turn north. The chance came long before the listening ended, because we were all the way to the Safeway at Ainsworth before Leon said another word.

"Cut the shit, Albert," he said finally. "Just tell me where you are, and we're cool. Anything else you don't want to think about."

After another moment of silence, Leon slipped the phone back into his jacket. He turned right on Ainsworth when the light allowed us to move, and then he spun immediately to the right again and stopped in the Safeway parking lot.

"What?" I asked.

He didn't respond at first, so I sat there silently and watched the tension ripple over him as he clenched the steering wheel. When it subsided, he looked at me through those heavy lids and almost smiled.

"That motherfuckin' Albert just hung up on me," he said. "Can you fuckin' believe that?"

"What'd he say?"

"First Fat George pulls this shit, and now Albert." He paused for a moment, his head shaking almost imperceptibly. "Feels almost like the world is turning inside out—everything is backward."

"What'd he say?" I asked again.

"He said he bailed when he heard the shot, and he's sorry about that, but he doesn't know anything else and he's afraid to see me, so he hung up."

"Sounds reasonable to me," I said with a shrug. "I'd be afraid to see you myself in the same situation."

"Then you'd be thinkin' backwards, too, homeboy."

"Meaning?"

"Meaning Albert shouldn't be afraid to see me now—he should be afraid to *not* see me now."

"I see your point," I said, but he didn't appear to hear me. He slipped the car back into gear and drove us in a loop that put our noses at the edge of Ainsworth. As soon as the traffic permitted, he pulled out of the lot and headed east.

"Where are we going?" I asked.

"It's time for some Chinese food," he answered.

"I don't really feel like eating," I said.

"Believe me, bro'," he replied, "neither do I."

THIRTY-FIVE

Leon didn't speak while he pushed the Mercedes east to Thirty-third, and he repeated himself while we veered south to Knott, east again to Forty-second, and then to our right on Sandy and Broadway. I watched him closely for the first couple of blocks, but after that I leaned back in my seat and matched him word for word until he stopped in the Pagoda's parking lot.

The Pagoda is supposed to look like its namesake, and for all I know it does—the Pagoda is the only pagoda I've ever seen. It's the kind of place that captures your imagination as a kid and never really lets go, even after you know that real pagodas don't serve takeout.

Leon looked at me after he cut the engine and I looked back. "You know that fuckin' fountain they have in this place?" he asked.

"Yeah," I answered.

"I think I could hear it when I was talkin' to idiot Albert."

"Ah, so," I said, and we both climbed out of the car, crossed the lot, and strode through the nearest door. Leon hooked a right immediately, which led us up and over a cute ramp across the fish pond with the fountain and into the Pagoda's dimly lit lounge.

I could see four figures leaning up at a short bar, but Leon only had eyes for one of them. "Hey, Albert," he said as he slipped alongside a tall, skinny white kid with a brown ponytail hanging halfway down his back. "Guess we got disconnected, huh?"

Albert looked at Leon, then he swiveled to look at me coming up on his opposite side. Even in the dim light I could see the color draining from his face, and by the time he turned back toward Leon he looked like his own ghost.

"Your limo's ready, Albert," Leon said.

"What?" Albert asked.

"Get the fuck outside before I hurt you, Albert," Leon said, and all three of us trooped out of the room, across the fish pond with the fountain, and out the door into the parking lot.

Leon led us to the Mercedes, opened the front passenger door, and stood next to it until Albert dropped into the seat. I climbed in behind him while Leon walked around the car, and a moment later we were rolling west on Broadway.

"Where are we going?" Albert asked.

"Believe me, Albert," Leon said, "you aren't goin' anywhere."

Albert slumped a little after that, and no one spoke while he tried to disappear into the back of his seat. Leon whipped us onto Interstate 5 when we got to Williams Avenue, and a couple of minutes later he took us off again at Delta Park. After a turn or two, he stopped the car in the dark racetrack's deserted parking lot.

"Talk to us," Leon said.

"I told you everything I know on the phone, Leon. Come on, man, I don't know anything else."

"How long have you been driving for Lizzie?" I asked.

"Who's he?" Albert asked, nodding shortly in my direction.

"Albert," Leon replied, "answer the question."

"From the beginning," Albert said.

"Why you?" I asked.

"What?"

"Why didn't she pick someone who could actually do the fuckin' job?"

"I don't know. I guess she was trying to help me out."

"Why?"

"Why? We were friends—she needed a driver, I had already been doing it for a while. It seemed like a good idea."

"Friends how?"

"Look—what difference does all this make? I told you, Leon—I don't know anything else about what happened."

"The difference, Albert," Leon said slowly, "is that while you're talkin' you're not gettin' hurt. So you just let me know when you're through talkin'."

"Friends how?" I asked again.

"We had a class together last summer."

"What class?"

"Intro to Film Production."

"She was a film student?" I asked, looking away for a moment.

"Yeah."

"How good?"

"Probably the best in the class."

"And you?"

"I don't know—I was probably next after her."

"Congratulations," I said, bearing in on Albert again.

"What?" he asked.

"Congratulations. Now you're number one."

Albert recoiled noticeably at that, and stared out the window to his right for a moment.

"Done, Albert?" Leon asked.

"Look, I know I'm a sorry piece of shit. I don't need you guys to tell me that."

"Albert," I said, "what was Lizzie doing in the escort business?"

"It wasn't my idea, I swear to God. I took the driving gig when she asked me because it had always been easy money, but I'm not sure why she was doing it."

"You didn't ask?"

"We talked about it all the time. She was going to write a screenplay set in the business."

"So she was hookin' as a research project? Is that what you're saying?"

"What I said was I'm not sure why she was doing it. I always felt like there was more to it than that."

This time I was the one who lapsed into silence for a moment, but Albert eventually continued. "Besides," he said, "she wasn't hookin'."

"What?" I asked.

"She wasn't hookin'. That's what she thought was so hilarious about the whole scene."

"Hilarious?"

"Yeah. That these guys are so fucked up they'll pay you hundreds of dollars just to be there while they fuck themselves."

"Apparently not everyone shared her sense of humor, Albert."

"Look, I don't know what happened that night. I'm just telling you that she told them all the same thing—that she wouldn't do anything illegal, but they'd never forget the experience. And no one ever ran her out of the room before the time was up."

"If this scene was so fuckin' funny, what was the gun for?"

"She wasn't stupid," he said softly, staring out the window again while he spoke. "Not everyone out here is playing with a full deck, you know what I mean? She said it never hurts to have an ace in the hole."

"What happened Thursday night?"

"I drove her to the Evergreen, she went in One-thirty-two, a few minutes later I heard a gunshot, I panicked, I left, and that is all I know."

"Albert, you are an even worse liar than you are a driver."

"Whaddaya mean?"

"You know what I mean, Albert. What happened Thursday night?"

Albert slumped into silence for a moment before he answered, and when the words finally arrived they seemed to have traveled a great distance. "I'm as good as dead if I talk to you, man," he said.

"What do you think you're as good as if you don't?"

A blank expression crossed his face for a moment, like he

knew what he wanted to say but couldn't find the right place to start.

"Just tell me what the fuck really happened, Albert."

"There was a car parked out in front of the room when I got there," he said slowly and without emotion, as though each word had been wrung dry. "There were two guys in it. I parked a couple of spaces away from them and Lizzie went in. I heard a gunshot about ten or fifteen minutes later, and all three of us started climbing out of the cars. One of them was on me before I even cleared the door. He stuck a gun in my face, forced me back behind the wheel, and jumped in the seat behind me. He told me to get my ass out of there, and that's what I did."

"What was the other guy doing?"

"He was at the door to the room, but I guess the chain was on because he couldn't get in."

"But the door was ajar?"

"Yeah, it looked like he was talking into it."

"How'd he get it open that far? Did he have a key?"

"I don't know. I didn't see that part."

"Did you see the guy in the room?"

"No. We left before the door even opened all the way."

"Where'd you go?"

"He got out on Third and Main."

"Downtown?"

"Yeah, downtown."

"What'd he say?"

"He said if I opened my mouth about that night, he'd be back to shut it for me."

"So he gets out and you drive away, how's he going to find you again?"

"Fucker made me give him my driver's license."

"What'd he look like?"

"I don't know. I never really looked at him, you know what I mean?"

"What'd he look like, Albert?"

"I don't know—I didn't really see him!"

"Was he animal, mineral, or vegetable?"

"What the fuck are you talkin' about?"

"Was he bigger than a bread box?"

"Oh—he was about my size. You know, just average."

"Race?"

"White."

"Hair color?"

"Dark."

"How was he dressed?"

"Suit and tie, actually. Something dark with a white shirt. Seemed kind of formal for that situation."

"Distinguishing marks or characteristics?"

"I don't think so. I really didn't see him that closely. Well—except for his accent."

"What accent?"

"His voice came straight from the land of cotton, you know what I mean?"

"Old times there are not forgotten?"

"Right. You don't hear that around here very much."

I looked at the back of Albert's head without speaking for a moment, and then I closed my eyes and let our conversation roll around my mind for a while. When I opened my eyes again, nothing had changed.

"Anything else?" I asked.

"That's it," he answered. "That's all I know, I swear to God."

"When did he ask you how to find the service?"

"Oh. That was right at the end. He got a phone call after we got downtown."

"That stuff you said before about your film class," I said.

"Yeah?" he asked.

"Was that bullshit, too?"

"No," Albert said quietly. "Not at all."

"Don't worry about those guys, Albert. They kept you from seeing the guy. That's all they needed."

"Are you sure?"

"Yeah."

After that, silence descended over all of us for a while. Then Leon started the car, turned the defroster up to fight off the fog we had breathed onto the windshields, and drove us back to the Pagoda without a word. When we got there, I climbed out of the back, opened Albert's door, and watched him join me by the side of the car.

"Albert," I said, "Lizzie didn't die because of anything you did."

"Whatever," he said. "I should have done something more."

"Believe me, kid," I said. "I know exactly what you mean."

Then I claimed the seat he had relinquished, closed the door, and allowed Leon to point us back into that darkening night.

THIRTY-SIX

"What beach was she headed for?" Fernando said. "Malibu?"

"What?" the woman asked.

"She could have driven to fuckin' California by now. Why hasn't she called?"

"Perhaps she did," the woman said, looking away from him and snugging the boy a little closer. "This is not the place she was calling."

"What?"

"This is not the place she was calling."

"I heard what you said. What do you mean?"

"We were not planning to stay here. We only came to pick up a few things."

"That's fuckin' cute. How long were you going to sit here waiting for this call that was going somewhere else?"

"As long as possible."

"Well, you just got there. Call the right number and collect your message."

"No."

"No?"

"No," she said, leaning back with her eyes closed again.

"I start cutting on you, how long you think the answer'll be no?"

"I don't know. As long as possible."

"Or maybe I start with the kid. How long then?"

"You have the knife," she said. "We have no control over what you do with it. But I will do nothing to bring you closer to my daughter."

You are a ballsy cunt, aren't you? Fernando thought. *I like that in a mother—ready to step over the edge for her kid and her kid's kid, ready to make the ultimate sacrifice, ready to take this blade until she can't take it anymore.*

"She's bound to come back sometime," Fernando said. "What's the point of putting it off?"

"Who knows what the future will bring?" she said. "Perhaps lightning will strike you dead where you sit."

Yeah, Fernando thought, *perhaps lightning will strike me dead where I sit, me holding this blade in my hand. Maybe God Himself will take me out, zap me a good one, bring this whole thing to a halt. Maybe so, maybe He would, maybe—if there was a fuckin' God, maybe He just might.*

THIRTY-SEVEN

Leon was back in his jacket for his phone by the time we cleared the Pagoda's parking lot.

"Talk," he said as he drove us west on Broadway again, and someone apparently did because Leon listened until we got to Twenty-fourth.

"Don't fuck with me, Sly," he said then. "I'm not in the mood tonight.

"What's that got to do with me?" he said a moment later. "You gotta problem with Wiley, call *him*.

"You don't like what happens in my club," he said after another pause, "stay the fuck out of it."

We were approaching Ninth by this time, and Leon suddenly spun off Broadway and planted us in the credit union's empty parking lot. "Tell me what you want," he said into the phone, and then he listened with a steely silence that seeped across the space between us until I could feel it clamping down on me as well.

"Put her on the phone," he said.

"It's me," he said next. "You guys cool? Just hang loose—I'll have you out of there within the hour. Got that? Okay, girl. Put Sly back on.

"You the man," he said then, the words slipping into the phone soft and easy, but Leon's frozen face had more hard edges than a chainsaw sculpture of himself.

"I'll get you what you want," he continued, "but don't forget what you *don't* want. They get so much as a hangnail before I get there, we'll all wake up in the fiery fuckin' furnace. You hear me, motherfucker?

"Just keep your eyes on the fuckin' prize, Sylvester," he said a moment later. "He'll be there in less than an hour—I'm callin' him as soon as you hang up.

"He's out in the Grove, so you're gonna have to wait for him to get from there to here whether you fuckin' want to or not. But cheer up, sweetheart. I'll be there in fifteen minutes to hold your hand while you're waiting—and if I don't like what I see, I'll break it off at the fuckin' elbow if it's the last thing I ever do."

Leon cut the connection after that, and I concentrated on drawing a breath while I watched the wheels turn in his head. When he finally spoke, he seemed to be talking to himself more than me.

"You didn't hurt Sylvester bad enough, bro'," he said slowly. "He's got his sorry ass waaaay over the line now."

"How many are we up against?" I asked.

"I don't know," he said, still so soft and easy it almost made me shudder, "and I don't give a shit." He slipped the Mercedes into gear, guided us out of the parking lot and back to Broadway, and drove us west to the freeway and north to the Portland Boulevard exit. It only took him a minute or two from there to stop us in front of the house on Jarrett which bumped backyards with Ronetta's house on Ainsworth. Then he called 911 for the second time that night.

"We need the fire department," he said after thirty seconds or so. "The house across the street's on fire!

"It's at Five-twenty North Ainsworth," he added after a short pause. "Hurry—I can see flames coming out the kitchen window!" Then he cut the connection and pointed at the car's glove box. I fished out another phone and played a variation on the same theme.

"I'd like to report a fire," I said. "I don't know the exact address, but you'd better hurry—I can see flames shooting up. It's on North Ainsworth just west of Haight, on the south side of the street. Did you get that—North Ainsworth and Haight."

Then I cut my connection and returned the phone to the glove box while Leon dropped his back inside his jacket. Moving with what seemed to me to be excessive deliberation, he slowly reached behind his back and produced the Glock.

"Take this with you," he said. "I'll never get it in, anyway. Wait until you hear the fire engines pull up in front, then go in through the basement door."

"You taking Ronetta and the kids out the front?" I asked.

"Just as soon as the fire department gets there. But remember—you can't make a move until they leave, or Sylvester's crew will have the same counter I'm gonna use. And you don't have to take 'em all on. If you get to Sly, you can tell the rest to fuck themselves."

"And if I do get to him?"

"Tell the sorry motherfucker I'll be right back."

"Got it," I said. I pushed my door open with my right hand while I dragged the Glock out behind me with my left, but Leon spoke again before I could close the door.

"Wiley," he said, and then he said nothing more until I bent down and made eye contact with him. "If you have to shoot someone, aim a little higher this time."

"No problem," I said, and I straightened up, closed the door, and strode up the driveway and past a porch which wrapped around the front of the house. A small, stooped man with white hair fringing a bald pate opened the door and looked out at me through glasses thick enough to stop a bullet.

"May I help you?" he asked.

"I'm going through your yard to the house behind you," I said. "Just stay inside and you'll be fine."

"What's goin' on?" he asked.

I ignored the question and cut past a single-car garage that needed a little paint. I reached the laurel hedge on the property line in a heartbeat or two, and by the time I paused in the midst of the leafy branches I could see Leon's Mercedes flash by the gap between Ronetta's house and her neighbor to my left.

There were two sirens in the air by then, one more insistent than the other, and I cased the space I still had to cover while I waited for the sound to crest. I paid special attention to the kitchen windows looking over the deck and back toward me, but no one seemed to be lurking on the other side of the glass.

"That's right," I said loud enough for my ears only. "Good ol' Leon always draws a crowd."

A moment later, two fire engines rolled up in front of the house in rapid succession. As soon as the second one stopped, I sucked in enough air to last me for a while and ran across Ronetta's yard. I could have saved several steps by slashing across the mud which had been her vegetable garden during a better season of the year, but I veered around it almost automatically. I slowed to a walk when I made it to the corner of the house, and I tried to look like I belonged in the driveway while I moved to the basement door.

I could see the front end of one of the fire trucks and a couple of firemen, and I could sense the fuss at the front of the house better than I could actually hear it. I moved Leon's Glock behind my left leg as I walked, but no one looked in my direction.

Good ol' Leon, I thought again.

The door to the basement wouldn't open when I got there, but I only had to fumble through the flower pots stacked nearby for a moment to find a key that turned both locks. I slipped in, closed the door behind me, crossed to the stairs, and climbed to the door that opened into the hallway near the kitchen.

Then I waited, and then I waited some more. I tried to imagine that I was in a card game waiting for a hand I could play, and if I had been holding cards instead of Leon's Glock it might have worked. I tried to count every breath I took, but I had to stop when they started adding up too fast. But mostly, I leaned up close to the door and listened.

I could hear the murmur of voices coming from the living room, and it sounded like the door to the house was open because I could also hear the buzz of the people and machines out front. I tried to count the number of voices in the house while I listened for the departure of the fire trucks, but the second was easier than the first.

I guess firefighters get chapped by false alarms, because they made quite a show of leaving. They slammed enough doors and revved enough engines to make their departure audible a block or two away, so I didn't have much trouble estimating when the time was right to make my next move.

I opened the door and looked both ways while I filled my right hand with my own gun. I couldn't see anyone in either direction, but feet were shuffling in the living room so I got the three strides between me and it out of the way as soon as I could.

I saw Sylvester when I hit the entry. He looked as slick as usual, except he had traded one of his snakeskin boots for enough gauze and tape to wrap a mummy. He was being lifted out of Ronetta's favorite chair by two of his crew, one on each side, and the grip they were using struck me as funny considering the situation.

"Don't they call that a fireman's carry?" I asked. Everyone looked toward me and froze, but I think that had more to do with the two guns extended in Sly's direction than the dialogue. "Kind of ironic, don't you think?"

Either nobody did or nobody understood the word *ironic*, because nobody said anything. "Put him back down, fellas," I said into the edgy silence. "Sly ain't ready to leave quite yet."

The fellas did as they were told, and while they were doing it I took a quick look around. There were two more fellas in the room besides the ones fussing with Sylvester, but the bodyguard from the night before was not among them.

"No Tee?" I asked.

"Fuck you," Sylvester said.

"Oooh," I said. "If we're going to get intimate, we better send the fellas home. Tell the fellas they're off the clock, Sylvester. I'll make sure you get to where you're going."

I watched Sylvester process my remark slowly. He looked at me, he looked at his crew, and then he shook his head. "I think I like my chances better with them here," he said.

"Believe me," I said, "your chances are exactly the same either way."

"You can't shoot us all, asshole."

"True," I agreed, "but how many of the fellas here want to wait around to find out how close I can come?"

I scanned the group quickly, and it looked like every eye in the room was on me. "Sylvester's going down for sure, fellas. Is there some reason any of you should go down with him?"

I moved away from the entry to my right while all four of them filed out of the room without a word. They left the house and climbed into a maroon van parked out front. When the van pulled away from the curb and disappeared from sight, I sat down in Scooter's favorite chair.

"That wasn't a fireman's carry," Sylvester said.

"No shit?"

"What good would a fireman's carry be if it took two firemen to do it? That was a cradle, you fuckin' idiot."

"I'll be damned," I said.

"Now what?" Sylvester said as soon as he figured out that two or three minutes of silence were more than he could stand.

"Now you fuck me, I guess," I answered. "Unless you want to wait for Leon—he said to tell you he'll be right back. Then you can fuck us both."

"Shit," he said, more to himself than to me, so I just sat there and watched the bravado drain out of him like diarrhea. He didn't even look up when I heard Leon's Mercedes stop in the space recently vacated by the van, and his eyes had glazed over by the time Leon walked into the room.

Leon held out his right hand and I put the Glock in it. Then he stepped across the room and stood on Sly's bootless foot. The pimp screamed the fog right out of his eyes, and when Leon was satisfied with the level of focus he stepped away from the injured foot.

"You went too far, Sly," Leon said quietly. "You can't get back from where you are right now."

Sylvester nodded slightly, watching without a sound.

"Give me your hand," Leon said.

Sylvester slowly extended his hand, and Leon placed the Glock in it.

"Grip it," Leon said, and Sylvester gripped it.

"Now open your mouth," Leon said, and Sylvester's jaw fell open. Then Leon placed both of his hands over Sly's, turned the gun, and placed it in the pimp's slack mouth.

"Now pull the fuckin' trigger, Sly," Leon said, and that's exactly what Sylvester did.

THIRTY-EIGHT

Leon stepped away from Ronetta's favorite chair and I got up from Scooter's. The only one who didn't move was Sly, who stayed where he was with his feet stuck out in front of him and the back of his head splattered across the wall in the opposite direction.

"Shit," I said, and for a while that seemed to say it all. I watched Leon look around the room blankly for a minute or two, and then I couldn't stand the silence anymore.

"I'm sorry I started this mess, Leon," I said.

"You didn't start it, bro'," he said, looking at me for the first time since the Glock had spoken. "I should have cleaned this shit up a long time ago." Then he walked into the hall, opened the closet door, and began to fumble through the stuff on a shelf above the coats hanging in a tidy row.

"I think there might be some empty boxes in the basement," he said quietly. "Could you bring a couple up?"

There were and I did, and when I got back I found him rummaging in Ronetta's room. He took a carton from me and started filling it with selections from the top of Ronetta's vanity—the mahogany jewelry box, the framed prom photo, the collection of glass birds, the studio photo of the twins at two, the tiny porcelain doll—and her closet, which yielded several thick scrapbooks and photo albums.

I followed him upstairs to Scooter's room, where he picked up a ragged doll and a ball autographed by the '77 Blazers, and then to JJ's, where he took a photo of himself off the wall—the one of him dunking during the state tournament that ran in the *Oregonian* when we were young—and a worn white buffalo from the bed. He looked at me soberly for a moment, then brushed past me and carried the box downstairs to Ronetta's den while I trailed behind him like a memory.

He dropped his box next to the desk and nodded at the one I was carrying. "Could I get you to empty these drawers?" he asked, and I fell to it while he went through the kitchen and out the door to the deck. The drawers were filled with the official paper trail of Ronetta's life, but it wasn't really all that much paper. I had the contents moved to the boxes by the time Leon returned.

"Ronetta needs some wheels," he said, tossing me a set of keys. "Could you take the Mercedes over there?"

"Where is she?"

"They're all at your place," he said.

"What about you?"

"I'll finish up here," he said. "Hang on to the phone in the car so I can hook up with you later."

"What about Sylvester?" I asked.

"I don't think Sylvester needs anything, bro'."

"You know what I mean."

"Elmer's on his way over," Leon said, around the cold shadow of a smile. "We'll take care of him."

"How?"

"We'll take care of it," Leon said. "Go on. And take these boxes with you."

"Why?" I asked.

"Go on—they're waiting for you."

"Answer the question," I said.

"Because some things are easier to replace than others," Leon said. "Okay?"

I didn't discover exactly what he meant until the TV news revealed it to me later that night. But when I chewed on the words themselves, they left the bitter aftertaste of truth in my mouth. So I nodded, picked up the boxes, walked out the front door, loaded the boxes in the car, and drove across the line between what is and what might have been without a backward glance.

THIRTY-NINE

My house was dark when I nosed the Mercedes up to my Subaru. I tried to still the stutter in my heart as I climbed the stairs to the kitchen door, but I made no progress until I entered the room and saw Ronetta and the twins seated in the shadows at my table.

"Are you all right?" I asked.

No one responded for what seemed like an hour or two, so I moved over to the table and joined them. Ronetta had one arm around each of her kids and a cold wall of silence over all three of them, so I sat there and waited for a thaw.

"We got scared, Uncle Wiley," Scooter said finally.

"I know, sweetheart," I said. "Everything's okay now."

"Daddy came and got us," she said.

"I know," I said. "He'd never let anything happen to you guys."

"Is he okay?" JJ interjected.

"He's just fine. It's all over."

"What about those men in our house?" JJ asked.

"They left," I said. "Everything's okay now."

I could feel the anxiety in the kids drop a degree with every new assurance, but it only took one look at Ronetta to see how far from fine things still were. I tried to catch her gaze, but her eyes were turned so far inward that her first words caught me by surprise.

"Give me the keys," she said quietly. I laid them on the table in front of her, and she unwrapped JJ so she could pick them up.

"Let's go, kids," she said, scooting them off her lap as she rose. As soon as they were all on their feet, she led them across the room and out the door I had entered. I trailed down the stairs behind them and stood by the driver's door while Ronetta belted the twins securely into the backseat.

"Where are you going?" I asked when she finished with the kids and walked around the car to where I was standing.

"Away," she said flatly.

"That's all you have to say?"

"No," she said, "that's just all I'm *going* to say. Open the door, would you?"

I opened the door and stood there dumbly while she slid behind the steering wheel. "Would you hand me the phone in the glove box?" I asked after she was settled.

She reached across the empty space beside her, extracted the phone, and handed it to me without a word. "Do you know the number for this phone?" I asked.

"You don't quite get it, do you?" she asked, shaking her head slightly.

"I don't get what?"

"I don't need your number, Wiley. I won't be calling either one of you fools."

"Look, I know how you feel right now, Ronetta. But we need to know where you're going."

That drew a broken smile to her face. "Do me a favor, Wiley would you?" she asked, still looking somewhere I wasn't. "Don't talk about how I feel. I can't even imagine a subject you know less about."

"We need to know where you're going, Ronetta."

"I don't know where I'm going," she said. "But when I find out, you two will be the *last* to know."

"Look," I said, "at least stay away from the house for a while."

"Why's that, Wiley?" she asked, locking her ruthless eyes on mine at last. "Everything's just fine now, right?"

I felt skewered by her gaze, and she knew it. She kept me

twisting there for a moment, then she broke it off and cranked the car to life. "Do me one more favor, Wiley," she said.

"What?" I asked.

"Close the door," she said.

I did as she asked, and she backed the Mercedes into the street, turned it toward Alberta, and drove away. I followed as far as the end of my driveway, where I stood with Leon's second phone in my hand while the mother of his children turned left at the stop sign and slipped out of sight.

FORTY

Leon's phone vibrated in my hand as I turned back toward my house.

"Hey," I said, after fumbling clumsily with the contraption for a moment or two.

"Are they okay?" he asked.

"Yes and no," I said.

"Meaning?"

"Ronetta's not a happy camper," I said.

Leon didn't respond to that, so I walked through the silence on the line to my Subaru.

"Where are they?" he asked finally.

"She wouldn't say where she was going," I said, "except away from us."

"Can't really blame her for that, can we?" he asked softly, but it didn't sound like he was looking for an answer so I didn't try to offer one. After another long pause, he shifted gears.

"Where do you want to go from here?" he asked.

"Who are we dealing with? Who was the guy in the suit?"

"I don't know, homeboy, but I do know we're not gonna like whatever the answer turns out to be."

"I'd like to see Fat George again," I said.

"I know he needs his butt kicked, but I don't know if he needs it done right now."

"We don't know if Fernando and friends got the logbook until we're sure George doesn't have it, and maybe he saw who took it even if he doesn't have it anymore. And he needs his butt kicked."

"Something made him run, that's sure as shit. Start with Miriam. Call me if she can't help you, and I'll try to think of another way to work on that."

"You're not coming?"

"I need to stay out of sight for a while, so I'll follow up on our other lead."

"What lead is that?" I asked.

"Rebecca," he replied.

"Rebecca?"

"The girl our mystery guest asked for Thursday night. Maybe she remembers a Fernando-lookin' fuck in Room One-thirty-two at the Evergreen."

"Right—Rebecca. Didn't George say she was in Vegas?"

"I'm on my way to the airport as we speak."

"The airport? Who has flights to Vegas this late on Saturday night?"

"That's why charters were invented, bro'. I should be back by morning."

"Shit, Leon. Remind me never to get you on *my* ass."

"In for a penny, in for a pound," he said soberly. "It's just money, my friend. And it don't take too many nights like this to figure out what that's worth."

"Yeah," I said. "Keep me posted, hear?"

"Likewise. And Wiley—if you find that fuckin' George before I get back, hang onto him for me."

"Will do," I said. Then one of us broke the connection, so I pocketed the phone, slipped into the Subaru, cranked it up on the first try, backed out to the street, and pointed myself at the woman Fat George had left behind in a senseless heap when he decided to run.

FORTY-ONE

There are only two turns between the house I was living in then and Emanuel Hospital—a left at the corner of my block and a right on Vancouver. The Subaru navigated both without incident.

The night was still hooked on the cusp between wet and dry, so even in the three or four minutes of that brief ride it flipped from one side to the other a couple of times. I felt the same way, except my volatility veered from hot to cold—one minute flushed with fever, the next chilled to the core by an icy fist in my gut.

I tried to line up what we had learned so far, but either the information was unusually resistant to order or my mind didn't have the tools for the task that night. The only thing I knew for sure by the time I parked the Subaru was that a fat man with a mean streak was looming somewhere in my immediate future, and I went into the hospital to find out where.

I had to bounce around the building for a while before I caught up with Miriam, which probably sounds a little strange considering I was ambulatory and she was not. But you can forget everything you know about geometry in hospitals, because the straight lines there are never the shortest distance between any two points anyone is ever trying to connect.

I finally found her in a private room with a TV set and Sam. He was watching a news bulletin without sound, but one of her eyes was covered with gauze and the other was closed so I couldn't see what she was watching.

"How is she?" I asked.

Sam didn't reply, so my eyes drifted in the same direction as his. A newscaster was mouthing something I couldn't decipher, but Sam seemed to be hanging on every word. Then a live feed began to roll, and I saw Ronetta's house engulfed in flames. The fire boys were on the scene again, but this time they were throwing enough water at the house to float it. The fire seemed to be water-resistant, though—the flames were still ripping through the house when the TV cut away from the feed.

After a few more minutes of silent commentary, the TV returned to its regular programming—apparently something about a guy and a girl who were not living happily ever after yet. Sam got up and walked out of the room, so I followed him into the hall. He looked at me intently, but I focused on the wall behind him until he started talking.

"Where's our buddy Leon?" he asked finally.

"I don't know," I replied. "Why?"

"How 'bout Ronetta?"

"I don't know where she is, either."

"When's the last time you saw either one of them?"

"Why? What's goin' on?"

"When we have some time to kill, we'll work on your questions. Right now, we'll work on mine."

"I'm not workin' on shit until I find out what's goin' on, Sam."

Sam kept his eyes on me but started shaking his head back and forth a little. I put on my best poker face and looked back at him blankly, and after a while he spoke again.

"You recognize that house?" he asked.

"Should I?"

"Cut the crap, Wiley. You had breakfast there this morning."

"If you already know the answers to your questions, Sam, why the fuck do you ask?"

"It establishes a baseline, if you really want to know. Tells me right away if I'm talking to a liar."

"A guy can start lying anytime, Sam. It doesn't have to be right away, like I do it."

"Yeah," he said. "It does work best on fools like you. But then again, I don't need a special test for fools like you, do I? I know from the jump what you're going to do."

"I'm happy to be able to simplify your life, Sam."

"What would simplify my life is to lock you up until this is over, smart guy."

"What's stopping you?"

"Nothing, yet."

"Is that a threat?"

"Let's just say our collaboration is starting to look a lot like a crime."

"What crime?"

"How about withholding information relevant to a police investigation?"

"We aren't withholding shit."

"If you had mentioned Fat George a little earlier, maybe he wouldn't be gone right now and this lady here would be."

That didn't sound like a question, which was a good thing because I didn't have an answer for it. We both stood there and stared at each other some more, and when he finally had his fill of that he answered my original question.

"She's okay," he said, glancing at the doorway behind me. "Assuming that's what she was before this happened."

"What did happen?"

"I was hoping you could tell me that."

"If I could, I wouldn't be here."

"Well, it's going to be a while before she says much. They've got her drugged up pretty good."

I turned, walked back into the room, and stood at the side of the bed. Miriam's one good eyelid fluttered occasionally and her head moved slightly, but Sam appeared to be right—she wasn't in the vicinity of her next conversation.

"This is probably her normal condition," I said quietly.

"What—beat up?" Sam asked. He had followed me into the room and was standing at the foot of the bed.

"No," I answered. "Drugged up."

"What makes you say that?"

"How else could someone be with a guy who would do this?"

"There's other reasons."

"Such as?"

"Some people don't know anything else—they start thinkin' that shit is normal."

"Maybe," I said. "But I have a hunch Miriam here hasn't felt 'normal' for quite some time."

I pulled back the thin sheet draped over her and put my hand on her side. I could feel tape under her hospital gown, which confirmed Leon's earlier diagnosis.

"Two broken ribs," Sam said, "although it looks like you already suspected as much."

"Nothing gets by you, does it, Sam?" I said as I covered Miriam with the sheet again.

"Is this another subject you won't talk to me about?"

"I didn't say I wouldn't talk to you—I said I wanted to know what's going on first."

"And do you?"

"I know this—Leon told Fat George to stay put and to never lay another hand on this woman here, and we are oh-for-two on those instructions."

"Maybe Fat George is the one on drugs," Sam said. "I didn't think he had the balls to spit in Leon's face."

"He doesn't," I said.

"Which means what—someone out there scares ol' George even more than Leon does?"

"Apparently."

"And you're hoping Miriam here knows who."

"Like I said—nothing gets by you, Sam."

He let that slide, so I pulled a padded metal armchair up to the side of the bed and put myself in it.

"So now what?" he asked.

"So now I wait," I replied.

"When's the last time you saw Leon or Ronetta?" he asked, picking up as though the time since he initially asked that question had somehow never passed. I sat on my answer for a minute while I sifted through the events of the last hour or so in my mind. I knew Sam was watching me as I did it, but I didn't give a fuck. I was looking for things that might have been observed by Ronetta's neighbors, and when I thought I knew what they all were I answered his question.

"Right before I came over here," I said.

"Where?"

"Ronetta and the twins were at my place when I got there, and a couple of minutes after that Leon picked them up."

"Where'd they go?"

"They didn't say."

"Why were Ronetta and the twins at your place?"

"I'm not clear on that. Ronetta wasn't exactly speaking to me at the time."

"What happened at her house, Wiley?"

"Looks like it caught on fire," I said.

"You can't help me out here?" he asked. "You can't tell me what I'm going to find when I get there?"

"How would I know, Sam?" I said. "The last time I was there, not even the hotcakes were burning."

Sam sat behind his big black glasses and chewed on that for a while, and this time I did the watching. His mind was working better than mine; I could almost see it hammering what he knew into manageable rows.

"And you guys split up why?"

"He said he had some business to take care of, so he dropped me off and said he'd meet me here."

"I thought you said that Ronetta and the twins were at your house when you got there."

"I did."

"And a few minutes later, Leon picked them up."

"See what I mean? Nothing gets by you, Sam."

"Keep it going. What are you going to say next?"

"He didn't drop me at home. I needed some air, so he dropped me on MLK and I walked from there."

"That's good—I like it."

"Fuck you, Sam."

"You know it's only a matter of time before I put the real story together, so why don't you just tell me in the first place?"

"A person only has so much time on this earth," I said. "Maybe I'm counting every minute."

"Maybe so," he said. "Let's just hope you can count better than you can lie." Then he walked out the door and disappeared down the hallway, leaving me with a wounded woman and a television that didn't make a sound.

FORTY-TWO

I sat in the dark and listened to Miriam breathe hoarsely until a
nurse the color of a marshmallow roasted just right entered the
room. She was about my height and just as wide as she was tall,
and when she slapped her eyes on me it rocked me back in my
seat a little.

"What are you doin' in here?" she asked, just as the man and
the woman in the movie on the silent TV were about to usher
in the closing credits with a kiss.

"Waiting," I said.

"Waitin' for what?" she asked.

"For her," I said, nodding toward the bed.

"Well, you better do your waitin' in the waitin' room. Ain't
supposed to be no one in here right now."

I didn't have an answer to that, so I sat there like the TV and
watched her study Miriam's chart. When she was done, she put
the chart back where she had found it and turned her attention
back to me.

"Out," she said.

"I can't afford to do that," I said.

"Believe me, mister, you can't afford not to."

"To you, this woman is a patient," I said. "To me, she's a wit-
ness. I need to be here when she wakes up."

"You sayin' you're a cop?"

"No. The cops have lots of people to talk to—I just have this
one."

"What's that supposed to mean?"

"It means I'm the only guy looking for whoever did this to her right now, and I need to know which way the slimeball rolled."

"Either way," the nurse said emphatically, "she ain't gonna be talkin' before mornin'. I'm fixin' to give her another pain shot right now."

"Couldn't you wait until you finish your rounds? Maybe she'll wake up in the next few minutes, and we'll both get what we want."

"You can bet yo' brown ass I'm gonna get what I want," she said. "You the one outside the loop here."

"True," I said. "But what would you want if you were the one on the bed?"

"Ain't no man aroun' who could put me on a bed like that."

"Maybe," I said. "But it looks like Miriam can't say the same."

She turned the octane up in her eyes and tried to burn a pair of holes through me, but when I didn't go up in smoke she shifted on her feet and headed for the door.

"I'm gonna be back in fifteen minutes," she said as she paused in the hallway. "You don' wanna be here then."

I didn't move as soon as she left the room; I watched the TV news first. The show began with a live feed from Ronetta's, not because the fire was still burning but because a body had been found in the rubble. I was pretty good at reading the TV by then, so I could see that the charred corpse had not been identified and the mystery of an earlier false alarm at the site of the fire had not been solved.

Sam came on the screen, but the camera turned away as soon as he spit the words "no comment" out of his silent mouth. That's when I got up and turned my attention to the wordless woman on the bed next to me.

"Can you hear me, Miriam?" I whispered, bending low so my lips were close to her ear. She slowly rolled her head away from me, so I stayed right next to her ear and tried again.

"Are you ready to talk to me?" I asked softly.

This time there was no hint of a response, so I reached across her body and pressed my hand against her side through the sheet. I probed slightly, applying pressure here and there until she flinched in her sleep.

"This'll only hurt for a minute," I whispered in her ear, and then I increased the pressure of my fingers on her broken ribs.

First her eyelid began to flutter more quickly, then she rocked her head back in my direction and her teeth began to clench. She couldn't breathe through her broken nose so her mouth fell open again, and then she began to moan loud enough for me to hear it. I eased the pressure and waited, but every time she began to drift in the wrong direction, I increased the pressure again. After three or four cycles of this attention, her unbandaged eye blinked open.

She had to work a little to focus on me, and I stood up and dropped my hand to my side while she did it. "Do you remember me?" I asked, when it looked like the job was done.

She looked away for a moment, then back again. She seemed to be rolling her answer around in her mind, and when she had it right side up she nodded slowly.

"Do you know what happened to you?" I asked.

After another extended pause, she nodded again.

"Where's George?" I asked.

Miriam closed her eye and shook her head slowly.

"Where is he?" I insisted.

"Gone," she said finally, in a voice so faint I almost had to read her lips to hear it.

"Gone where?"

"Just gone."

"Miriam," I said, letting some steel creep into my soft insistence, "I need to find George tonight. Where is he?"

She opened her eye in response to the change in my tone, but she continued to shake her head slowly. "George is gone," she said softly. "There is no George."

"What do you mean?"

"He's running from himself," she said, "and he can't run that fast." Then her body tensed, she clutched my right arm, and her single good eye arced an electric current into my gaze that made the hair on the back of my neck stand on end.

"Can you?" she hissed. "Can you run that fast?"

I felt the temperature in the room plummet by thirty or forty degrees, but I tried to keep the frost out of my voice. "What are you talking about?" I asked.

Miriam slumped back on the bed with a groan and laid her right hand over her eye. "Don't hurt me anymore," she said softly, all of the hiss from the moment before drained out of her voice. "I'm so tired."

Her words stuck like errant fish bones an inch or two east of my heart. I swallowed hard, but the burning in my chest didn't budge. The room was suddenly hot and close—I felt my cheeks redden and a fine sweat break across my brow. After a moment, I leaned over her again and gently pressed my lips to her forehead.

"Your nurse will be here in a minute," I murmured against her flushed skin. "Try to get some rest."

Miriam turned her head away from me and didn't say a word. I thought of something more to say, but those thoughts couldn't find my voice so they came out of my mouth as air. After a silent moment like that—Miriam disappearing behind her hand on the bed and me bent over her like a bad dream—I stood up, turned toward the door, and walked out of the room.

FORTY-THREE

Fernando turned on the news at eleven. A skinny black dude started talking about a body found in a house fire somewhere in north Portland, and Fernando listened all the way to the weather report without hearing about a girl with her throat slashed on the southeast side of town. Then he turned the television off, walked to the wall phone in the kitchen, and punched in Morton's number.

"This is Morton," Morton said.

"You guys still outside?" Fernando asked.

"Where the fuck else?" Morton snapped.

"You might as well split. The bitch won't be back until tomorrow afternoon at the soonest."

"Split where? Avina'll tear us new assholes if we show up without you."

"Go somewhere she ain't gonna be. Just get back by noon."

"This shit is gettin' deep, Fernando."

"Shit washes off, believe me. I'll take care of Avina when this is done. Go get a room, get some bitches, get Jimmie his fuckin' Whopper, do whatever the fuck you want."

Fernando hung up the phone and looked from where he was standing in the kitchen to the sofa in the living room. The boy was asleep, but the woman was watching him through those slanted black eyes.

"Go to sleep," he said.

The woman made no response. He looked into her eyes some more, and her gaze did not waver.

"Then act like you're sleeping," he said. "I'm tired of seeing your fuckin' eyes."

"Look somewhere else," the woman said quietly. "My eyes will always be on you."

"I can fix that anytime I feel like it."

"I know you can," the woman said, but her slanted eyes didn't even blink.

Why doesn't everyone have a mother like this? Fernando thought. *A ballsy mother like this one. Not that it was going to make a difference in this case—this family was fucked either way. But if everyone had a mother like this one, wouldn't it make all the difference in the world?*

FORTY-FOUR

I leaned on my Subaru in the hospital parking lot for a moment before I slipped behind the wheel. The rain fell softly, cooling my face when I tipped my head toward the sky, but the fiery knot in my chest burned unabated. I stood like that, poised on the outer edge of nowhere, until Leon's phone began to throb in my coat pocket.

"Hey," I said, after I got the thing out and working.

"What's up with Miriam?" Leon asked.

"Looks like she'll be okay, so to speak."

"So to speak?"

"Assuming she was okay to start with," I said.

"Yeah," he said, his voice trailing off a little. "Assuming that."

"I'm afraid she wasn't much help," I said after a moment of silence.

"What'd she say?"

"She said George is running from himself, but he can't run that fast."

"That's it?"

"Actually, she said one other thing. She asked me how fast I could run."

"What was your answer?"

"I asked her what she was talking about."

"Next time the question comes up," Leon said, "tell her fast enough to run right up Fat George's ass."

"That fast?"

"Oh, yes. Every bit that fast."

"Where in the hell are you, anyway?" I asked.

"You don't want to know, bro'," he said with a short laugh. "Gives you plausible deniability next time Sam asks. Besides, I don't know myself. Do you realize how dark it is up here?"

"What makes you think you can find Rebecca when you get there?"

"Same thing that makes a bear think he can find a honey tree—he knows all he has to do is put his nose in the wind and sniff."

"You're not lookin' for the honey tree, Leon, you're lookin' for one of the bees."

"My nose is keener than a bear's, bro', and Vegas is smaller than the woods. If she's still there, I'll find her. You just worry about findin' George."

"I'm on my way over to Miriam's now. Maybe he left a trail of bread crumbs to mark his path."

"You're more likely to find the slime a slug leaves behind, but don't worry. It may be harder to see in the dark, but the birds'll leave it alone."

"Thanks for the tip," I said. "You take care of yourself."

"Back atcha, bro'," he replied, and then I couldn't hear him anymore. I put the phone back into my pocket, climbed into the car, cranked it up on the first try again, and drove on automatic pilot to the place where a weary bird had flown too close to the ground and a fat man had flown too high.

FORTY-FIVE

The front door of Miriam's house was no longer ajar, and it didn't open when I tugged on it. I walked back down the steps and around the house until I came to a door with a window in it, but I didn't need to put a rock through the glass because that one opened when I turned the doorknob.

I entered on a small landing with stairs descending toward a dark basement to my left and ascending to a dark hallway right in front of me. I chose to rise rather than fall, found a light switch at the top, and killed some of the darkness. The hall ran to my left past the bedroom where we had found Miriam and into the front room; the kitchen where I had found the ice for her face was directly across from me.

I turned left, paused in the bedroom doorway, found another switch, and threw some more light around. It looked the same as I remembered it except Miriam was no longer sprawled on the bed and Leon was no longer hovering over her like Florence Nightingale.

I didn't see Fat George anywhere. I got down and peered under the double bed, I flipped the mattress over, I manhandled the pillows, and I fumbled through the blankets and sheets still balled at the foot of the bed, but I didn't find the missing logbook and I didn't find George.

I kicked my way past a small table tipped on its side and began to paw through a chipped white dresser. I found out that Miriam was overdue for a stop at Victoria's Secret, but nothing else; and when I went through the tiny closet all I came out with was the tight roll of hundreds that Miriam had squirreled away from George in the pocket of a light raincoat.

I made a similar survey of every room in the house, not because I hoped to find what I was looking for but because I couldn't think of anything better to do. I uncovered a few things I was not looking for, of course, such as a small stash of grass and a few other substances I had questions about but did not recognize, but no logbook and no Fat George.

When I was finished, I flopped in the same living-room chair that George had used on our first trip to the house. I leaned back and closed my eyes for a moment, but I saw even less that way than I had seen while my eyes were open.

"Where are you, George?" I said out loud, but no one answered until the phone on an end table next to my chair began to ring. I jumped on the first sound and picked it up on the second.

"Yeah?" I said.

"Oh," someone said from the other end of the line. "I was trying to reach Denise."

"Do I sound like a Denise?" I asked.

"No—no, of course not," the someone said. "I'm sorry—I must have the wrong number." Then the phone went dead and I put the receiver back where I had found it.

It was not that someone asked for Denise instead of Miriam that surprised me about the call, because women who get calls that deep into Saturday night tend to change their names almost as often as they change their underwear. What surprised me was I didn't notice the address book on the end table until I hung up the phone.

I picked the book up and flipped through the pages. The rough scrawl inside didn't fit Miriam no matter what name you called her by, so I turned back to the front of the book and started dialing. Every time someone answered, I asked to speak to George, but that turned out to be infrequent. Most of the time, the number was no longer in service, I reached an answering machine, or the phone rang until I got tired of listening to it.

I hit the right number on the twenty-first try.

"What!" a gruff voice said.

"Put George on the phone," I said, going to my own gruff side.

"Do you know what fuckin' time it is?"

"I don't have time for your shit," I said, sticking to the same tone because you don't have to fix something when it ain't broke. "Just put George on the phone."

"Well, if you could fuckin' tell time, you'd know he wasn't here yet. The drive is three hours minimum, you fuckin' idiot."

"I know how long the drive is, asshole," I said, doing my best to think faster than I was talking. "He was supposed to be on the road by nine."

"Who said that? Who the fuck is this, anyway?"

"Thank you very much," I said to myself as I slammed down the receiver. I memorized the address that went with the phone number, went back to the bedroom closet for a small suitcase, threw in a few things Miriam would need to check out of the hospital dressed in more than gauze and tape, and walked back out the side door of the house to start a journey to somewhere I had never been before.

FORTY-SIX

The phone call had given me a Seattle address, so I put Miriam behind me and George in front as soon as I got the Subaru back to Interstate 5.

"Age before beauty, Miriam," I explained wryly. "When I finish with your boyfriend, I'll be back for you." Since no one heard it but me, I was the only one who might have smiled had I been in a smiling mood.

And I might have set the cruise control at seventy-five and the tape deck on B.B. King by the time I rolled past the fairgrounds, except my Subaru didn't have either of those devices and had to be flying downhill to break seventy. All the car offered me for this trip was a reasonable certainty of arriving at the other end, but I considered that offer more than generous. So I sang the blues in my mind and controlled the cruise with my foot while I followed my headlights north.

And the farther I drove, the deeper in my own mind I went. There is nothing quite like stacking interstate miles on top of each other for tapping into your subconscious—no matter how hard you pull in the opposite direction, you always start angling toward the abyss. So I began my ride in George's wake with my mind on "Why I Sing the Blues," but by the time I noticed Centralia slipping by in the darkness, I was wrestling with why I had never tried to scale the wall of my daughter's anger toward me.

They say a child loves its parents unconditionally, and I believe it. What other options does a child have, when you get right down to it? But children grow up—well, some of them do—and options are what they gain as the years go by. I eventually squandered every ounce of Lizzie's unconditional love for me, and she eventually responded by exercising some of those hard-won options. Such as hanging me out to dry for what turned out to be the last year of her life, which is why I didn't know she had been the best student in the film intro class I didn't know she had taken.

In some ways, Lizzie's life remained a greater mystery to me than her death. I understood that I had turned her heart to stone, but not exactly how I had done it. And illumination failed to find me on the way to Seattle that dark night.

I probed my memory for clues as the landmarks slipped by, but none emerged. I took no solace in this, however, because I don't have a lot of faith in memories. People tend to forget what they can't afford to remember, and that's what most haunted me that night:

What was it that I could not afford to recall?

Questions without answers are like scares without screams—you get the adrenaline rush but not the release. By the time I caught sight of the Kingdome, I was more than ready to focus on finding the West Seattle exit and the fat man who had found it before me.

There is a remarkable range of lifestyles on the west side of Seattle—an address there could turn out to be anything from a city housing project to a yuppie condo with a view of the Sound. The numbers I had memorized took me somewhere in the middle—up a notch or two from the High Point project but still on the wrong side of the hill.

The street was quiet when I got there, but light poured through a plate glass window at the front of the well-kept house with the right numbers on it. I cruised the neighborhood slowly and turned up three cars with Oregon plates, but only one of them had a backseat stuffed with clothes.

I had to park about two blocks beyond the house, but I didn't mind the walk back in the quiet rain. I turned a few approaches over in my mind on the way, but nothing had jelled by the time

I got back to the house so I just walked up to the door and knocked on it.

The door opened after a moment or two, but it might as well not have bothered. The woman who stood in the doorway was bigger than the door and harder-used. The only thing thin about her was the wiry hair on the top of her head; otherwise, she appeared to be descended from the same gene pool as Fat George.

"You Leon?" she asked, revealing a gap where her two front teeth should have been.

"Almost," I replied. "Where's George?"

"He ain't here."

"I didn't ask if he was here—I asked where he is."

"Ask whatever you want. He still ain't here."

I didn't see any point in repeating my line again, so I shut my mouth and looked at her. She stood there in what might have once been a blue muumuu with large white flowers all over it and looked back at me. I believed her to be unmoved and probably immovable, so I eventually stopped staring at her and reconsidered the front of the house instead.

I was standing on the right edge of a tidy porch which extended the width of the house to my left. I could see two wrought iron chairs flanking a small table and beyond that a planter box overflowing with blooms of some kind. Then I looked at the woman again, confirming my suspicion that she took better care of the house than herself.

"Nice place you've got here," I said.

"I like it," she said simply.

I didn't respond to that except by stepping over to the nearest chair, hefting it to test its weight, and hurling it against the front window. The chair didn't penetrate all the way into the house—it landed astride the windowsill after the glass shattered.

"Hey!" the woman shouted, her fat face puffing up so that it almost swallowed her beady eyes. "What the fuck are you doin'?"

"Where's George?" I asked again.

"Are you crazy?" she said.

"I don't know," I answered as I returned the chair to its previous location. "Does it matter?"

"Yeah. I'd like to know what I'm dealin' with."

"That's nice to know," I agreed, "but you never really do. Guy can be fine one moment and just go off the next."

"I don't know where George is," she said then. "He left as soon as he heard about your phone call."

"Where's the guy I talked to on the phone?"

"He went with him."

"Whose car did they take?" I asked, turning toward the driveway and the Pontiac Firebird to my right as I said it.

"George's," she said.

I stared at her again, nodded as if in agreement, and took a shot in the dark. "Tell George I'm going to burn this place down around him if he doesn't get out here," I said.

She stood and stared at me for a while more, and then she turned and walked away from the door. I stood on the porch and waited, and a moment or two later George and a guy with a gun in his hand came up a little short in an effort to take the woman's place.

"Step out here, George," I said.

"Leave me alone," George said gruffly, but he looked a little sheepish around the edges to me. I kicked him as hard as I could in the groin, and he crumpled in front of me like the air had been let out of him.

"Hey, you idiot!" the guy with the gun shouted sharply, brandishing the weapon. "Can't you see this?"

I ignored him and waited quietly for George to recover. It took a while, but I was in no particular hurry. The guy with the gun kept looking at me and then at George, back and forth, like he would understand what was happening if he could just get in the right number of repetitions.

Finally George began to moan and squirm a little, which meant he could breathe again, and when he raised his head and looked at me I kicked him as hard as I could in the face. This caused George to start spitting blood and teeth and his friend to spit more words.

"What the fuck?" he said. "Cut it out, I'm tellin' ya'!"

"Go back in the house," I said, focusing on him for the first time. "I'm tired of hearing you."

"Look!" he said. "I'm the one with the gun. You don't tell me shit!"

"Go back in the house before I stick that thing up your ass," I said, turning my attention back to George. When the guy began to sputter again, I looked up and nodded toward the house behind him, and he finally spun away and disappeared inside.

George, on the other hand, was going nowhere fast. He had flopped over on his back, but not before blood and saliva had drooled from his mouth all over the front of a gray sweatshirt which had rolled up over his bulging gut. This time I kicked him in the side, at approximately the same place he had kicked Miriam and I hoped with approximately the same result. But I had to figure that his ribs were padded by a lot more flab than Miriam's, so I kicked him again just to be sure. Then I cleared away some residue from the broken window with my foot, bent down on one knee, and leaned close to his ear so I could cut through his moans and cries for mercy.

"I feel like kicking you to death, George," I said softly, "but you can still stop me."

"Wha'?" he croaked. "Whaddaya want?"

"I want the logbook, George."

His beady eyes blinked at me, and then they blinked again. "What?" he said.

"The logbook."

"Aaaaahhhhh," he said, moaning over the top of his words. "I don't have it, man. I don't have it."

"Who does?"

"I don't know, I swear I don't."

"Who else has keys to your place?"

"No one, man," he said, shaking his head slowly with his eyes scrunched tight. "No one."

I chewed on that for a minute until it went down right, then I stood up. "Why didn't you do what you were told, George?" I asked. When he didn't respond right away, I urged him to reconsider by tapping him sternly on his side with my foot.

"I couldn't stand it," he said with a grimace and a groan. "I couldn't just sit there, man. I had to *do* something."

"You might be a *stupid* sonofabitch," I said, nodding more to myself than to him, "but I know exactly what you mean." Then I stepped off the porch, walked across the yard, and strode into the wet darkness without another word.

FORTY-SEVEN

Leon rescued me from another fruitless reverie about two-and-a-half hours into my return drive.

"Hey," I said, after I dug the phone out of my pocket and got it working.

"Hey," Leon said. "What's up?"

"You first," I said. "Did you find her?"

"Yeah, I found her," he said, but I didn't like the way his voice trailed off as he said it.

"What?" I asked.

"She's dead, bro'."

"She's what?"

"She died early last night."

My will to speak faltered after that, so I drove for a mile or two in silence. I couldn't quite swallow the news of Rebecca's demise no matter how hard I chewed on it.

"Do you believe in the random nature of the universe?" I asked finally.

"Sometimes," Leon said without hesitation, as though he had been reading my mind. "It makes a little sense when you think about it in general."

"But what?"

"But I lose it when you get down to the particulars."

"Like the coincidence of these two deaths, maybe?"

"I guess that's my problem with the thing. I understand the

concept of a coincidence, but I don't believe I've ever really seen one."

"Neither have I," I said soberly. "What happened to her?"

"They've got it down as an OD," he said.

"But what?" I asked again.

"But I'm not buyin' it yet."

"Why not? Even you don't always know which of your girls are into drugs and which aren't, or when exactly they get started."

"Maybe so," he said. "But why go to Vegas to OD? Kind of defeats the purpose of going."

"People don't always end up doing what they started out to do," I said quietly.

"I heard that," he said. "But I'm still not buyin' it yet."

"What'd she supposedly OD on?"

"Horse."

"Heroin? You're shittin' me."

"It's not the choice of drug that bothers me, it's the choice of location. That fuckin' shit has been born again, bro'."

"I thought Gene Hackman cleaned out all that shit in that flick with the killer car chase."

"The guy on that train got away, homeboy."

"But Hackman got the heroin."

"Which all disappeared from the police evidence warehouse later. Besides, you've forgotten the sequel. Hackman was a fuckin' addict in that one."

"Yeah," I said. "But he kicked it."

"Well, if the locals are right, you can't say the same about Rebecca."

"But you don't think they're right."

"Not yet."

"Neither do I, Leon. So where's that leave us?"

"I've been giving that some thought."

"And?"

"I don't know yet. What's up with my friend George?"

"He's in Seattle. I can tell you where if you still want a piece of him, but his ass has already been kicked."

"He didn't have the logbook, did he?"

"How did you know?"

"Because I think Fernando used it to find Rebecca."

"How would that work?"

"The logbook could give him her number, her number could give him her roommate, her roommate could give him her location in Vegas."

"Oh, fuck," I said.

Leon didn't say anything in response to that, but I could hear him thinking as I continued to drive into the dripping darkness between me and Portland. I was three minutes past the LaCenter exit when he finally spoke.

"I feel like the fuckin' *Titanic*," he said. "There's a lot more of this 'berg below the surface than there is on top."

"No shit," I said.

"Every question I can answer leaves me with a new question I don't have a clue about."

"Like what?" I asked.

"Let's say I'm right about Rebecca. If this guy iced her, how'd he do it?"

"If you have enough muscle, it can't be that hard to fake a heroin overdose."

"I get that part of it—what I'm wondering about is the timing. Fernando's got some serious quicks if he snatched the logbook in Portland *and* killed Rebecca in Vegas early last night."

Leon dropped back into silence after that, and I let him fall. I followed the freeway through Vancouver and was halfway across the interstate bridge when his voice came back into my ear.

"What are you doin' next?" he asked.

"I'm going to check Miriam out of the hospital," I said. "I should be there in about ten minutes."

"Where are you takin' her?"

"My place, I guess."

"I'll meet you there in about an hour."

"Gotcha," I said. Then I broke the connection and continued to drive into the soft rain. The night was drifting toward the day, although it looked like one was going to be a lot like the other. *That's the trouble with January mornings in this damned town,* I thought to myself as I eased off the freeway at the Broadway bridge exit. *You don't get a sunrise, just another shade of gray.*

FORTY-EIGHT

"I need your help," Fernando said, slipping out of his shirt.

The woman looked from his eyes to his bandaged torso and back again, but she didn't make a sound. The boy beside her had his eyes on him, too, the sleep chased out of them but the kid still wrapped in the same cocoon of silence Fernando had admired the night before.

"These dressings need to be changed," Fernando said, motioning toward the hallway with the hand holding the knife. "See if you can find something to use."

The woman rose from the sofa, and the boy rose with her. "The kid stays here," Fernando said, and the boy sat down again. The woman moved past him down the hallway and disappeared into the bathroom.

Fernando watched the kid while he waited for the woman to return. "How old are you?" he asked.

"Five," the boy said.

Five's as good a place to stop as any, Fernando thought. *They don't get any fuckin' better from there.*

FORTY-NINE

Sam was the only one awake when I arrived at Miriam's room. When I appeared in the doorway, he rose from the padded metal chair I had drawn next to the bed the night before and led me into the hall.

"I need to see Leon," he said quietly.

"I still don't know where he is, Sam."

"You haven't heard from him?"

"We've talked twice since I saw you last night, but he wouldn't tell me where he was. Said it would give me plausible deniability when you asked me."

"Cute," he said.

"He gave me something for you. The guy who did Lizzie originally asked for someone else, and that someone suddenly died in Vegas last night. Are you interested in that?"

"Died how?"

"They have it as a heroin overdose."

"No shit? What's her name?"

I told him, and he wrote it down in a small spiral notebook. When he was done, he put the notebook and the pen in his jacket pocket, removed his glasses, massaged his eyes, and spoke again.

"Why go to Vegas to OD?" he asked.

"My question exactly. Leon doesn't buy it, either."

"Fuck," Sam said, putting his eyes behind the ugly glasses again and training the whole mess directly on me. "Unfortunately, this isn't the case I need to talk about right now."

"I'm not a cop, Sam. This is the only case I'm working on."

"If only that were true," he said. "Every time you guys turn around, you get another case started."

That didn't sound like a question, so I made sure what I didn't say didn't sound like an answer. I walked back into the room and peered down at Miriam.

"How is she?" I asked while I placed the bag with the clothes I had collected at the end of her bed.

"She seems to be resting easier than she was last night."

"That's good," I said, thinking back to the rest she wasn't getting the last time I had stood over her bed.

"How well did you know Sylvester?" Sam asked.

"Sylvester the pimp?" I asked, looking over my shoulder for confirmation while I considered my answer.

"The very one," Sam said.

"I don't know him at all, really. Why?"

"Cute," Sam said for the second time.

"What's cute?" I asked.

"The way you turned the tense around. I used past, you used present."

"Signifying what, in your twisted mind?"

"Signifying you don't know Sylvester has slipped from current events to history."

"He's done what?"

"He was part of the rubble at Ronetta's last night."

"I'll be damned," I said.

"Quite probably."

"Now that's cute, Sam."

"Does anyone actually like your fuckin' repartee, Wiley? I'm sure as shit sick of it."

"What makes you think it was Sly?" I asked, giving his last comment all of the attention I thought it deserved.

"Anonymous tip," he said slowly, eyeing me unblinkingly through those black-rimmed glasses.

"Anonymous tips are always good?"

"This one was—looks like the corpse had Sly's teeth."

"I'll be damned," I said again. "That's some first-rate police work, Sam."

"Why is everything so fuckin' funny to you?"

"Believe me, Sam, I'm cryin' on the inside."

"As sorry as your ass is, you should be cryin' front to back."

"How'd he die?" I asked, turning away from him and his most recent jibe in favor of watching Miriam breathe some more.

"Kind of looks like he tried to eat his own gun and didn't chew fast enough."

"He killed himself?"

"Maybe. Hard to figure out why, though, what with the fire making it tough to leave a note."

"Might have been an act of contrition for being somewhere he wasn't supposed to be," I suggested.

"What makes you think he wasn't supposed to be there?"

"What? You think Ronetta invited him over? Maybe share some coffee and a little TV?"

"Be nice to chat with Ronetta. Maybe she could straighten me out on that."

"And it would be something to watch, too, believe me. I'd tell you where she is just to see it. If I knew where she is, of course."

"Yeah," he said. "If you knew where she is."

"But I don't, Sam. So let's talk about my case."

"So talk."

"Is it safe to assume that you've already checked all the usual places a guy with a bullet he didn't want might go?"

"I'm pretty sure he's not in the room next door," he replied, "or anyplace like it in the metro area."

"So where did he go to get it taken care of?"

"That's a good question."

"Do you get the feeling this motherfucker is not alone?"

"Yeah, I do."

"Then who's with him?"

"That's another good question."

"You don't have even a preliminary guess?"

"I find preliminary guesses get in the way more often than they help."

"Cut the shit, Sam. There aren't that fuckin' many possibilities."

"What do you mean?"

"We've got a motel room paid for a year in advance by a company that doesn't exist. For what? So some fucker named Fernando can get laid? I don't think so, Sam. Gettin' laid is not that hard."

"Fernando?"

"That's the name that came with the request for Rebecca. Don't try to change the subject—who does devious shit like this?"

"There's lots of devious people out here, Wiley."

"Really? I don't know too many of them. The kind of people I know, they want an escort, they call one and invite him or her over."

"None of the people you know are married?"

"Yeah, they might be a little more devious than the others. They might get a motel room before they make the call. They just wouldn't set up a dummy company and rent the room for a year first. See what I'm sayin'?"

"Not really," he said slowly. "Why don't you just spit it out?"

"I'm sayin' I think you know people a lot more devious than I do."

Sam didn't say anything more for a moment or two, he just slouched there in the doorway and studied me like I was a new letter in the alphabet.

"You're not as dumb as you look," he said finally.

"I've never been able to figure out what that means," I said. "How dumb does that make me?"

"It's nothin' local. I've rattled all the cages I can think of downtown, and no one is runnin' anything like this."

"Meaning what?"

"Meanin' it's nothin' local," he said.

"What, then? FBI, DEA, what?"

"I don't know. But I think we're double-fucked whatever it is."

"How so?"

"Number one," he said, his voice drooping a little around the edges, "we're probably looking for an out-of-towner."

"And number two?"

"That just about sums it up."

"What does?"

"Number two—stacked very deep."

"I don't quite follow you."

"We're in shit as deep as it gets if your Fernando is tied in with *any* of those alphabet combinations. I'd like our chances better if he was mob-connected."

I looked back down at Miriam while I processed what Sam had said. She was still breathing only through her mouth and shallowly, but she seemed to be at ease as she did it. I put my hand on her nearest shoulder and nudged it as gently as I could.

"It might matter somehow to you, Sam," I said with utter certainty as Miriam began to stir in front of me. "But it makes *no* fuckin' difference at all to me."

F I F T Y

Checking Miriam out of the hospital required the dotting of I's, the crossing of T's and the exchange of filthy lucre. I found out in the process that Leon had already done the dirty work, so all I had to do was push the paper around until they let me wheel her out to the Subaru.

Miriam didn't speak until we were heading north on Williams, but for some reason I felt at ease in the silence. I could see the battered side of her face out of the corner of my eye as I drove, and I watched it idly as she stared out the window in front of her.

"Where are we going?" she asked finally.

"My place," I said.

She turned toward me until her good eye came into view, and I noticed for the first time a hint of green in her gaze which reminded me of Ronetta. She studied me quietly through that single lens, and I sat there and let her do it until she turned her attention to the road in front of us again.

"I need something from my house," she said.

I reached inside my jacket and extracted the tight roll of hundreds I had found in her closet. She turned and looked at me again, but this time the brow above her good eye was arched slightly. After another quiet moment, she reached over and took the money from my hand.

"Thank you," she said simply.

"You're welcome," I replied.

She slipped the money into a small handbag and went back to looking out the window without another word. By that time I had already cut over to Mississippi, and a moment later I pulled into the driveway beside my house.

I got out, walked around the front of the car, and opened the passenger door. Miriam took my hand and stepped out gingerly.

"Are you all right?" I asked.

She nodded with a grimace, but followed gamely as I led her back around the car to the steps.

"I can carry you up if you think it'd be easier," I said.

"I think I'll be better off if I walk," she said, and that's what she did. She went slowly, and I followed behind her at the same pace. She was wearing the loose nightgown and light robe I had found in her house, and her legs were bare all the way to the furry slippers on her feet. I remember thinking as I reached around her to open the kitchen door that Miriam had the legs of a beautiful woman, and then I forgot about thinking for a while.

The first bullet splintered the frame of the door about two inches from my head and the second saved my life. When it slammed me high on my left shoulder, I thought I had been dropkicked rather than shot. The force of the impact sent me crashing into Miriam, and we both sprawled through the door and hit the kitchen floor in a tangled heap.

Three more bullets ripped in behind the first two, and one of those burned across my back like it was made of fire. I tried to roll away from Miriam and find the .38 on my hip, but I seemed to be swimming in wet cement. By the time I got my hand around my gun, Tee was standing in the doorway with something snub-nosed in one hand, a crutch in the other, and a twisted grin on his face.

He watched me struggle to unholster the .38, and then he watched me try to force my arm to point the gun in his direction. "Put it down," he said, when he had seen all he wanted to see.

I ignored him and continued to struggle with my arm, so he pivoted on his good foot and cracked my wrist with his crutch. My eyes followed the arc of the crutch, and I could see my gun and my last faint hope skidding across the room.

Tee knelt down beside me. "Hello, motherfucker," he said simply. "Remember me?"

"I think so," I said. "Didn't you use to have two good feet?"

"You're a real funny guy, huh?" he asked. "Funny right down to the end."

"Yeah, that's me."

"Well, laugh this off, asshole," he said, and he slowly extended his gun until the tip of the barrel was resting right between my eyes. Then he leaned on it a little, and I could feel the gun punching a third eye into my forehead.

"Typical, Tee," I said, looking up his arm all the way to his narrow, nervous eyes when nothing went boom after a minute or two. "All prick and no balls, you sorry piece of shit."

"Say bye-bye, motherfucker," he said, and I took his advice because I could see his eyes icing over as he said it. But that's when the funny stuff actually happened, because when the gun went off Tee's head exploded in my face.

FIFTY-ONE

Leon followed his blast into the room, brandishing something short, thick, and beautifully lethal as he came. He set the weapon down on the floor next to what had become a bloody threesome and tugged on Tee until there were only two.

"What's the damage?" he asked.

"Left shoulder and across the back," I replied softly. "All this shit on my face isn't me."

"How 'bout you, babe?" he said to Miriam, and she responded by shaking her head slightly. It struck me then that she had not made a sound for several minutes in a row, and I watched her watching Leon to reassure myself about her condition.

"All right," Leon continued. "Rest easy right there for a minute, okay?"

If she signaled a response to that, I didn't see it. My eyelids kept dropping over my eyes, and I thought about holding them up with my fingers until I found out it hurt to move either arm.

Leon started fussing with me, but I couldn't follow what he was doing very well at first and then I couldn't follow it at all. I did snap back a little while he was washing Tee off my face, and I noticed then that my jacket and my shirt were shredded on both sides of me. But I had nothing to hold onto that focus with so I lost it and drifted away again.

The next thing I remember was Leon ramming red-hot pokers into both of my shoulders or Leon picking me up off the floor. I was confused at the time about which one it was, and my recall of the event is similarly clouded. Maybe it was something that happened simultaneously.

I do know that sometime later I was sprawled on my side in the back of Leon's Cadillac wrapped in a white cocoon of tape and bandages. Miriam was sitting in front of me and Leon was behind the wheel. I could see out the side of the car, but my angle made it hard to recognize what we were passing. I remember trying to figure out where we were going until I drifted off in my own direction and it didn't matter anymore.

The next time I woke up Leon was helping me stumble up a short flight of stairs. We were in the foyer of a small apartment building—two units down and two up, I found out later—and Linda opened the door to one of the upper units as we got to it.

With a little more storage capacity, Linda could have doubled as a Deepfreeze. The atmosphere around her was absolutely arctic as she stepped out of the apartment to let us walk in, me leaning on Leon and Miriam trailing behind under her own steam.

"This is bullshit, Leon," Linda said as she followed us into a smartly decorated living room and closed the door behind us.

Leon led us across the gleaming hardwood floor without responding, and a moment later I was sitting on the edge of a king-sized bed that could have rolled into the room directly from a catalog shoot.

"Do you realize how long it's been since the last time you were here?" Linda asked from the doorway of what was obviously her bedroom.

"Try to get some rest," Leon said to me, ignoring Linda again. He rose and turned toward the door.

"Let me show you where you can get settled in," he said to Miriam, but she had her one good eye locked on Linda. I tried to read the expression in it but failed—I could see something there, but it was too far back to decipher. On the other hand, it only took a quick glance at Linda to figure out what she was thinking. Or you could close your eyes and just listen.

"Why me?" she asked. "Out of all your sorry bitches, how did get singled out for this distinction?"

"Because you're the one with two bedrooms," Leon said. "Look, I'll talk to you in a minute, all right?" Then he motioned to Miriam, and both of them walked past Linda, turned to the left, and walked out of my sight.

I let my eyes rest on Linda for a moment, and she returned my gaze unblinkingly. "You look like shit," she said finally.

I couldn't say the same about her, even though her type didn't really ring my bell. Linda had the brown-skinned blonde surfer chick thing down tight, and you could tell by the way she looked at you that she knew it. But she could turn on the ice machine with the flick of a switch, and suddenly you were hanging five among swimmers in shaggy white furs with huge teeth in their mouths and big claws on their feet.

"I *feel* like shit," I said.

"What happened to you?"

"It's a long story," I said.

"Aren't they all," she said, and then she shut down and waited for Leon to return. When he did, he handed her a set of keys.

"What's this?" she asked.

"I need to trade residences with you," he said. "Those are the keys to the Lake Oswego house."

"That's bullshit, Leon," she said again. "I'm not a fucking ball you can just roll around town any time you feel like it."

"I realize it's an imposition," Leon said. "I apologize for that."

"And what? That makes everything okay?"

"No. It just means that I'm sorry for the imposition."

"This imposition is the tip of the fucking iceberg, Leon."

"I'm sorry for that, too, kid."

"God, I hate men. I really do. I haven't met one yet worth a shit."

"I haven't met too many myself," Leon said.

"So how long am I supposed to sit out in Lake Oswego before you bounce me out of there?" she asked.

"The switch is permanent," Leon responded. "Stay there or don't stay there. Do whatever you want with it."

"What are you talking about?"

"I'm giving it to you. I'll have someone come by with the paperwork in a day or two."

"Are you shitting me?"

"No."

"Leon, that place is worth three-hundred-fifty grand if it's worth a penny!"

"You always did know how to count, kid."

"Now I really don't know what to say."

"You'll probably get over it," Leon said, and he wrapped his long arms around her as he said it. She stepped into the embrace and burrowed her blonde head into his chest.

"This is happening too damned fast," she murmured against him.

"I know," he said. "I feel like everything is upside down or inside out all of a sudden. Just make sure you land on your feet."

"I will," she said, reaching up with both hands to pull him down far enough to plant a kiss on the top of his nose. "I will."

"Good. The only thing I ask is that you tell anyone looking for me that you don't know where I am."

"That's not a problem," she said. "I haven't known where you were for weeks." Then she skipped out of his arms, through the doorway, and out of sight, leaving Leon standing alone by the door and me sitting like a stone on the side of the bed because I couldn't think of a way to lay down that wouldn't hurt.

FIFTY-TWO

I woke up on the early edge of orgasm, the delicious point at which you know it's going to happen but not exactly when. I savored the unmistakable sensation of lips and tongue artfully administered for a moment, riding close to the line between awake and asleep.

Then panic kicked the air out of my stomach. For a terrible instant, I could identify neither the room I was in nor the mouth at my genitals. I jerked myself upright, ripping a sharp pain through my torso that made me cry out loud.

Miriam raised her head slowly and looked at me, her hand replacing her mouth while she did it. She let her hand and her good green eye do her talking until it was clear that my cock was going to speak for me, and then she briefly broke the silence.

"Lie down," she said softly.

She waited patiently until I followed her directions, and then she put her mouth in close proximity to her hand and worked them in tandem until she finished what she had started. When I began to throb, she took her mouth away and milked me relentlessly into a warm, wet washcloth until I was spent.

She turned her good eye toward me again when she was done and regarded me without a word.

"Why did you do that?" I asked finally.

"One thing sort of led to another," she responded. "I started out just trying to clean you up."

"Why?"

"Why not?" she asked. "Believe me, it's not a big deal."

"That's where you're wrong, Miriam. I don't take this kind of thing lightly."

"Well, good for you. Now go back to sleep."

"I'm serious."

"So am I," she said. "You need some rest."

"Miriam, I want you to understand what I'm saying."

"Which is what, exactly?" she asked.

"I'm not the same as every other guy you've ever met, I guess."

"I know that," she said quietly, looking at me intently through that single insistent eye. "But you're not as different as you seem to think."

"What do you mean?"

"You'll take whatever you can get, just like everyone else."

"I'm not so sure I agree with that."

"Cut the shit, okay? I don't remember you asking me to stop anywhere along the way, or did I miss something?"

That knocked the argument out of me, and her relentless eye continued to hound me until I let my eyelids drop in my own defense.

"Don't be so hard on yourself," I heard her say. "I thought you needed something, and I felt like giving it to you. So relax, okay? It was a short story, but it had a happy ending. Just think of this as your lucky day."

"Miriam," I said faintly, already beginning to drift away again. "I was shot two times today."

"That's what I'm saying," she replied softly. "Fucked and blown in the same day. How much luckier can one guy get?"

I couldn't think of a response to that, so I just shook my head slowly.

"Now go back to sleep," she whispered, and I laid there and did as I was told.

FIFTY-THREE

"Why doesn't her fuckin' phone ever ring?" Fernando asked as he picked up the receiver in the kitchen and checked for a dial tone. The tone buzzed in his ear right on cue, so he returned the receiver to its perch on the wall.

"What do you mean?" the woman asked.

"Her line of work, seems like she'd starve to death on this level of phone activity."

"This is where she lives, not where she works."

Of course, Fernando said to himself. *She uses a fuckin' service. No, she's the* fuckin' *service: what she uses is a* phone *service. Wouldn't want all this shit in the kid's face, would she?* Unlike some mamas he could think of, one in particular he could name.

He continued to pace hallway to kitchen, hallway to kitchen, not too fast but fast enough to keep the throbbing alive in his shoulder. But the throbbing was good, the throbbing was working for him, he was riding on the edge of the throbbing.

The television flickered quietly from the corner of the front room, the kid watching a video and the woman watching Fernando, neither of them making a sound. The video was good, a young lion learning how to take over for his papa when his papa died. Fernando thought he recognized a couple of the songs.

Enjoy it while you can, Fernando thought, up on the balls of his feet a little and riding the waves of pain. *It's as close to king of the fuckin' jungle as you're ever gonna get.*

FIFTY-FOUR

The next thing I remember, Leon was fussing with me again.

"This is gonna hurt a little," he said.

"Don't worry about it," I replied. "It hurts anyway." Then he started ripping tape off my skin, and I found out no matter how much you hurt you can always hurt more.

I'm not sure how long it took Leon to replace all the tape he had torn away and the dressings that went with it, but after a while he was done and I was sitting on the edge of Linda's bed staring at him blankly.

"I feel bad about busting in on Linda like this," I said finally.

"She's feelin' great about it, believe me," he replied.

"You really giving her the house?"

"If I can sign the papers when they're ready, I'll be more than happy to."

"What's that supposed to mean?" I asked.

Leon rose from the chair he had pulled up alongside the bed and walked across the room to a window screened by a Venetian blind. He pulled some strings and gray light leaked into the room. I couldn't see the view into the grass-covered courtyard from where I was sitting, but Leon looked down on it for a while before he answered.

"I feel like I'm comin' to the end of somethin' here," he said. "I'm certain of it."

"But what?" I asked.

"But I'm not so sure I'm makin' the jump to whatever's takin' its place."

I immediately wanted to contradict his comment, but the words wouldn't roll off my tongue. I didn't have a house in Lake Oswego, but I remembered sending most of what I did have out the door with Alix Saturday afternoon.

"I know what you mean," I said reluctantly. "But when did we ever know what was coming next?"

"Maybe you're right," he said, turning away from the window and locking eyes with me for a moment. "But I sure as shit thought I knew."

"I guess we'll just have to wait and see what happens, like everybody else."

"Let's start with the shit we do know," he suggested. "We know we have a happy camper in Lake Oswego, and we have Miriam in the other bedroom here who might be headed in the right direction. Is that about the extent of the good news?"

"I don't know. Tee tried to kill me and failed—I like to think of that as good news."

"You put it like that, it is good news. But you're shot to hell, which means I'm gonna have to carry your sorry ass for the rest of this gig."

"Don't worry about me, partner," I said. "If you ever get open, I'll still get the ball to you."

"Shit," he said with a smile. "I'm always open."

"So what's the fuckin' game we're in this time?" I asked.

"Here's what I see so far," he said, gearing right down to business with me. "We've got someone from out of town who flies in now and then. He's connected here, but the connection is on the down low or he wouldn't need all the covert shit. This part smells like law enforcement to me."

"I ran that by Sam," I said. "He claims it's nothing local, which according to him is more bad news."

"FBI, DEA, what?"

"He doesn't know yet."

"Whatever. I think this guy has serious connections back home, too, and those *don't* smell like law enforcement to me."

"What do you mean?"

"If I'm right, our Fernando can make a phone call from here and Rebecca suddenly ODs on heroin in Vegas. I'm pretty cynical, but even I don't think that call went to anybody's cops."

"So we've got a bad guy probably hooked into the heroin business."

"Which means we're probably talkin' DEA on this end."

"And this guy is on a fuckin' string between the two," I said slowly. "And someone around here can tell us who the fuck he is."

"If someone around here wanted to."

"Yeah," I said. "If someone around here wanted to."

"So one thing we do," Leon said, "is we find out who the someone around here is and have a little talk. What else do we do?"

"I don't know. All I have left are questions."

"Such as?"

"This fuck flies in here now and then and stays at the Evergreen, special room reserved in advance. But he's not there now, so where is he?"

"Back home already?"

"Maybe, but it doesn't make sense. If he did Rebecca, he's gonna want to do the one he cut last summer."

"Shit," Leon said as he reached for the phone on the table by the side of the bed. I was only a heartbeat behind him, so I didn't have to ask what he was doing.

"This is Leon," he said into the phone. "Call me as soon as you get this message." Then he rattled off the number of his cell phone, replaced the receiver, and looked at me bleakly.

"Nobody picked up?" I asked.

"Put Caramelle at the top of our list of things to do," he said quietly.

"Right," I replied. "Anything else?"

"I guess we're back to where is he?"

"And with whom," I added.

"And with *whom?*"

"Yeah, and with whom. Who is this guy's Leon?"

"Ain't nobody else got a Leon, bro', no matter how you say it."

"Then the motherfucker's nowhere near as lucky as me."

"Well, I can only see one way to approach this question—shake the top of the agency around here and see what falls out. What else?"

"That's about it, except for a few on a more personal note."

"Such as?"

"Such as what am I going to wear, now that you've ripped the hell out of my shirt and coat?"

"You don't think Linda would have something around here that might work?"

"It's doubtful."

"That's what I figured. Elmer's bringing something by pretty soon."

"What'd you do about Tee?"

"Relax. I didn't burn your house down."

"Makes no difference to me."

"Same here. If I can afford to give away my biggest house, I can afford to torch the smallest."

"So what'd you do about Tee?"

"I don't know, actually. I told Elmer to make him die somewhere totally unconnected to me. It couldn't be the fire this time, though. When I finally have to talk to Sam, I'd just as soon Tee's name didn't come up at all."

"I can't help feeling responsible for this extra shit coming down on you from the thing with Sylvester," I said. "I'll never forgive myself if you don't get out from under it."

"Make a note of this, Wiley, for whatever it may be worth to you later," he said softly, but with a staccato intensity which seemed odd at that volume. "There's a lot of shit in your life that you're responsible for, but this isn't part of it. You're not responsible for this. *You're* not responsible for this. Got that?

"The tides all changed this weekend—the Earth shifted on its fuckin' axis or something. If I come out of this on my feet, I'm walkin' in a whole new direction. I'm bein' born again, bro', right before your eyes. All I have to do now is survive the fuckin' process."

I looked at him as he said this, and he looked back at me, and then neither of us said a word for a while. They say your whole life flashes by you in the split second before you drown, and I know nothing about that. But the same thing happened to me that soggy Sunday afternoon while I was looking at Leon and he was looking back at me—our entire life together spun right before my eyes, from day one all the way to that exact moment in the apartment formerly known as Linda's.

"You just get your sorry ass open," I said finally. "I'll get you the damn ball."

"Sheeit," he said, drawing it out a little and throwing a grin around it. "I'm always open."

And then I started grinning, too, and we were still sitting there grinning like fools when Elmer started leaning on the doorbell another lifetime or two later.

FIFTY-FIVE

I slipped into Miriam's room while Leon went out the door and down the stairs to let Elmer into the building. The room was dominated by a double bed decked out all the way around by a lot more than the legal limit of fancy frilly shit, and Miriam was stretched out on top of it all like she was afraid to disturb it.

"You can get in that thing if you want to," I said, when I saw that she was awake.

"I'm fine," she said simply.

"How are you feeling?"

"About the same as I look."

"It could be worse, then," I said. "I've noticed there's some angles from which you look damned good."

"I think those are some very obscure angles," she replied, "but thanks anyway."

"You're welcome," I said, turning toward the doorway behind me as I said it to observe Leon, Elmer, and the woman I had met at Elmer's Saturday morning entering the living room.

"We're going to be gone for a while," I said, turning back in Miriam's direction, "but it looks like Leon has lined up someone to keep on eye on you."

"I'll be fine," she said. "It's you I don't know about."

"What do you mean?"

"Are you going out like that?"

"Like what?" I asked, giving myself a quick once-over—bare from the floor to the bottom of my boxers, back to bare at the midriff and then the total mummy effect across my upper torso. "You got a problem with this?"

"I didn't earlier," she said with a quiet smile.

"No, you didn't."

Her smile faded then and a cloud seemed to cross her battered face. She turned her head away from me, making only the good side visible.

"What's wrong?" I asked.

"We were almost killed," she said softly into the wall across from where I was standing.

"I know," I said.

"Be careful out there, okay?"

"Okay," I said. When she closed her good eye, I turned away, walked through the doorway, and shut the door behind me.

Elmer had the solution to my wardrobe problem, but the cure was almost worse than the disease. If you've ever tried to dress yourself without using either hand, you know why I took one look at the turtleneck and slacks he was holding and felt like falling back into bed.

"I was thinking more like sweats," I said. "I don't think I can even get into that stuff."

"The clothes make the man," Leon said. "And considering the shape you're in, you better hope the fuck they're right."

"And we'll help you get 'em on, man," Elmer added with a grin.

"Gee, thanks," I said, but a couple of minutes later I actually meant it. With the assistance of just about everyone in the room, I was eventually suited for entry anywhere I was likely to wander.

Leon clipped my .38 behind my right hip and slipped a phone inside another version of the leather jacket Tee had ruined earlier that day. "Just let Elmer handle the heavy lifting," he said. "He can at least pull his own pants on."

"So I'm with Elmer?" I asked.

"That's probably best," he answered. "The first time I have to talk to Sam is going to take a while, and we don't have that kind of time right now."

"Who's doing what?"

"You take Albert, I'll take Rebecca's roommate."

"Why Albert?"

"Ask him what he can remember about the car he saw in front of the room, and see if anything else has come back to him since yesterday."

"That's pretty thin, Leon."

"I know. If you think of something better, do that instead."

"Let's go," I said, and we went.

FIFTY-SIX

Elmer headed straight for Leon's Caddy when we got outside, so I did the same. I'm sure I could have opened the passenger door myself, but Elmer didn't give me the chance. Then he stood there until I was settled into the seat, fastened the seatbelt for me, and closed the door.

"This has got to stop," I said when he dropped into the driver's seat. "You're treating me like some kind of invalid."

"That's what you are, man," he said. "You should be in bed."

I couldn't really argue with any of that, so I shut my mouth and watched Leon pull away in Elmer's Continental. We were parked on Sixteenth facing toward Sandy, and that's the direction we went when Elmer moved us away from the curb. He turned right on Sandy, and I finally stirred when he drove past Leon's porno shop and turned right again on Burnside.

"Do you know where we're going?" I asked.

"Albert's," he answered.

"And you know where that is?"

"Naw."

"So how do you expect to get there?"

"Leon knew where it is," he said simply.

I couldn't really argue with any of that, either, so I shut up again and rolled wherever Elmer pointed us. He drove across the Burnside bridge, looped around to Front, and went south all the way to Jefferson—the street, not the school. Then he proceeded west until he made a right turn on Twelfth just past the Safeway, where he swerved into a parking slot with a no-parking hood over the meter a door or two down from the porno theater.

"You'll get a ticket if you park here," I pointed out.

"This ain't my car, though, is it?" he asked, still another observation I couldn't argue with. He got out, walked in front of the car, and opened my door, but I unfastened the seatbelt myself, threw both feet out the door, and hunched my body around until I was standing on top of them.

"Not bad," Elmer said, but I would have known he was laughing at me even without the stupid grin on his face.

"Yeah, right," I said.

"That should be Albert's building across the street," he said, pointing to a narrow, five-story apartment complex between an office tower and an empty lot. We crossed the damp street without getting hit by traffic or water—the rain seemed to be on hold for a while, although the sky was heavy with possibilities and darker than appropriate for the hour—and climbed a dozen stairs to reach the landing in front of the entry.

I didn't see Albert's name by any of the buzzers on the wall next to the door, but Elmer stepped up and punched 3B like he knew what he was doing.

"He's not too likely to buzz us in," I said.

"You cain't never tell," Elmer replied. "People do some strange shit sometimes." Once again, that shut my mouth, only this time I promised myself to keep it shut. I never did figure out how the dumbest guy I knew could be the hardest guy I knew to argue with, but I finally learned that day not to get him started.

It became obvious after a while that no one in 3B intended to answer the buzzer, so Elmer stopped punching it at about the same time that I noticed Albert crossing the street with one of those plastic grocery bags hanging from each hand.

Albert didn't see me until he was almost to the curb, which turned out to be too late by at least an hour or two. I've always thought it should be against the law for someone with Elmer's muscles to have Elmer's reflexes, but Elmer didn't pay much attention to laws so it probably wouldn't have done much good anyway.

The groceries went one way and Albert another as soon as my presence registered, but Elmer was down the stairs and up Albert's ass before Albert could get back across the street. A moment later, both of them were climbing up to where I had grabbed a seat on the landing.

Elmer stopped two or three steps below me, and for some reason Albert did exactly the same. I didn't really think about it at the time, but the fact that Elmer had Albert's arm locked up behind the kid's back probably had something to do with it. Albert appeared to be suffering some discomfort, but he got no sympathy from me.

"Why were you running?" I asked.

He looked at me briefly, then collapsed on the stair in front of me when Elmer twisted something sharply. "Fuck," he said, after Elmer let up a little. "I don't really know—it was kind of an automatic reflex."

"Relax, okay?" I said, jerking my head at Elmer a little. He turned Albert loose and stepped away from him.

"Yeah, sure," Albert said, but I couldn't see that he did it.

"Have you remembered anything else from Thursday night?"

"No—nothing."

"What can you tell me about the car parked in front of the room?"

"Oh, yeah. It was a Ford Taurus, dark, not more than a year or two old."

"I don't suppose you got a look at the license plate."

"I probably did, but I didn't pay any attention to it."

"Anything else?"

"That's it," he answered. "That's all I know, I swear to God."

"The film center's not far from here, is it?"

"What?"

"I was thinking this is a great location for a film student."

"Oh, yeah. It is. The film center's the next block over, on the other side of the Safeway from here."

I stood slowly, using one of Elmer's massive arms to steady myself.

"Are you okay?" Albert asked.

"I'm just great, Albert. Now go get your groceries out of the fuckin' street."

FIFTY-SEVEN

We were cruising north on Twelfth when my first call to Leon didn't go through, so I decided to check the calls that hadn't gone through to me. I found two messages on my machine.

"This is Suzie," the second one said. "I don't know if you're still looking for Leon, but I saw his Cadillac parked by those brick apartments near Sixteenth and Glisan about an hour ago. Hope that helps. See ya!"

That one was only thirty minutes old, but the one from Julie had been waiting for several hours. "It's me," it said. "Just wanted you to know that Ronetta and the twins are here. Everybody's fine. She's going to make the arrangements for the memorial service, so you don't have to worry about that. Not that you were. But you *are* going to call when you know something, right? I deserve that, Wiley."

"Fuck," I mumbled when her voice died away, and then I punched the lying number that promised to erase the message.

"Fuck what?" Elmer asked.

"If you got what you deserved out of life," I asked, forgetting already what I thought I had learned earlier in that ride, "would you be knowing me right now?"

He turned right on Burnside and gave me a slow look before he answered. "By the time it's all said and done," he said, "we all get what we deserve."

"Do you really believe that?"

"Don't matter if I believe it, or if I don't," he said. "What you believe don't change the way things is."

Which was when I remembered not to argue with Elmer, so I changed the subject instead. "Where in the fuck are we going now?" I asked.

"East on Burnside," he said.

"*Why* are we goin' east on Burnside?"

"Is there some other direction you wanna go?"

"Not particularly."

"That's why we're goin' east on Burnside."

I shut my mouth and shook my head while I tried with more success to connect with Leon's cell phone.

"Talk to me," he said into my ear.

"What happened to your phone?" I asked. "I couldn't get through a minute ago."

"That was more than a minute ago," he said, "and I was about to return that call."

"Did you talk to Caramelle?"

"No," he said, and I didn't like the way it fell on my ear when he said it.

"What?" I asked.

"Our friend Sam is there, and so is the whole crime-scene gang."

"Oh, shit," I said.

"I know, bro'. We have got to put a lid on this sorry motherfucker."

I sat there without another word while Elmer drove us back across the Burnside bridge, and then I told Leon what I had learned from Albert. When he had that surrounded, I gave him something else.

"You know what's killin' me the most right now?"

"What?"

"One of those fuckin' suits stood outside the door while Lizzie was cut to death, Leon. I don't think I can forgive him for that."

"I don't think you have to," he said. "He'll get what he deserves before it's over."

"Elmer was just telling me that we all do."

"The thing you have to remember about Elmer is that he's always right."

"It's fuckin' irritating, too."

"Tell me about it," Leon said. "Seems like I've been with him all weekend. It's about time you took a turn."

"Hey. Ronetta and the kids are out with Julie."

"That's good," he said softly. "That's good."

"What's next?" I asked.

"You need to be the one who deals with Sam. If anything comes out of that, go for it. I'm going over to Rosey's."

"Rosey's?"

"Fernando and his federal fucks don't know quite as much as they think they do, homeboy. Rosey was just the relief operator, so she didn't handle near the number of calls George did. But—"

"But she had to log them all just like he did."

"Bingo," he said, and then he broke the connection. And if Elmer's right and we *do* all get what we deserve, I said to myself, at least one of the calls in Rosey's log came from Room 132 at the Evergreen.

I used the new space on the line to dial Sam, and a moment later his voice was pouring into my ear. "Detective Adams," he said for starters.

"This is Wiley," I said. "Just checking in."

"So I was right," he said. "That *was* Leon in that Continental."

"What are you talking about?" I asked.

"Let me guess," he said. "You're riding around in one of his cars, right?"

"If I am," I said, "who's riding around in my Subaru?"

"You're the only person I can think of who would, so that means that piece of shit is parked somewhere."

"Your job makes you too damned suspicious, Sam. How come I can't just be checking in?"

"How many times have you just checked in so far?"

"That proves my point—I'm overdue."

"Why'd you call, Wiley?" he asked.

"I've got some info for you, what else?"

"Please. Don't get me started again."

"I found out who drove Lizzie to the motel. He lives in an apartment building on Southwest Twelfth across from the Jefferson Theater."

"What's his name?"

"Albert. I don't know the last name, but it's apartment Three-B."

"What's the story?"

"You're not going to like it, Sam."

"Wiley, tell me the story."

"He said there were two suits parked in front of the room when Lizzie went in. He heard a shot ten or fifteen minutes later, but one of the suits jumped him before he got out of the car and forced him to drive downtown at gunpoint."

"What did the other one do?"

"He was talking through a gap in the doorway of the room when Albert drove away."

"Fuck me," he said.

"What's at Third and Main downtown, Sam?"

"Why?"

"That's where Albert dropped the suit."

"God, I hate this case."

"Come on, Sam, which one of those fuckin' alphabet agencies is down there? The DEA, right?"

"Why ask if you already know?"

"Hey—what a break!" I said. "You have some federal law enforcement fellas down there who witnessed your murder! Heck, your perp might be down there, too. I better get off your phone—they're probably tryin' to call you right now."

"Fuck you, Wiley."

"What are you going to do, Sam?"

"I don't know, exactly," he said soberly. "I'll try to think of something by the time I finish up here."

"Where's here?" I asked.

"The same place it was when Leon drove by in that Continental, which is why you called me, remember?"

"What's goin' on, Sam?"

"We've got another dead girl on our hands."

"Do you know who she is?"

"I know her name. What do you mean?"

"Her roommate just died in Vegas."

"Shit," Sam said, and then he didn't say anything for a while. When the while was over, he went straight for my throat.

"I want to hear it all this time," he said. "No more fuckin' around, Wiley, I mean it. All of it, end to end."

"Everyone wants something, Sam," I replied. "And the way I hear it, we all get what we deserve in the end."

"Wiley, I'm losing my patience with you."

"Don't try to threaten me, Sam. You don't have a string on me strong enough to make me jump."

"If that's really true," he said, "you're a fuckin' idiot."

"Whatever," I said. "Your situation remains the same no matter how you explain my end."

Sam lapsed into silence again, and Elmer pulled the Caddy over to the curb while I was waiting for Sam to return. I had lost track of where we were driving, so I looked out of the car for clues about our location. I saw a modest residential neighborhood in the deepening dusk, with lights shining bravely out of windows in most of the houses.

"Where are we?" I asked.

"Tenth and Failing," Elmer said. "Just north of Irving Park."

I started to ask him why we were at Tenth and Failing just north of Irving Park, but Sam interrupted me.

"Wiley," Sam said, "are you saying the guy who did Lizzie took out the other two?"

"I think the one you're with now was how he found the one in Vegas."

"How'd he find this one?"

"He broke into Fat George's place and took his logbook."

"How'd he find Fat George's place?"

"Albert."

"Shit," Sam said again. "What a bitch this is gonna be."

"Now tell *me* something, Sam," I said.

"Like what?"

"Like how did Caramelle die?"

"The same way as Lizzie, only easier."

"Sounds like ol' Fernando is feeling kind of spry, doesn't it? Do you have any idea how he got his gunshot wound fixed up?"

"Not yet."

"I'm wondering if the narc connection might give you another way to look. A bad guy wanders in off the street with an extra bullet, a flag goes up real quick. But what happens if an undercover federal agent takes a hit, and the agency wants to keep it quiet?"

"You sayin' Fernando is a federal agent?"

"No, but he could be presented to a doctor as one."

"The doctor still has to file a report."

"Yeah, but how soon, saying what, and to whom?"

"I see your point. The real question is, what doctor are they gonna call?"

"Exactly."

"Let me work on it from that angle for a while. I can think of a couple of possibilities."

"The good news is, Fernando might not be done yet. The log-book can hook him up with *everyone* George sent to Room One-thirty-two at the Evergreen."

"Why would he care? Those girls aren't going to remember who they saw in that room unless it happened in the last night or two."

"One of them might. The woman from the motel told me he cut someone else a while back."

"Funny I'm just now hearing about that, Wiley."

"Keep your eyes on the prize, Sam."

"Okay, some girl he cut might remember him," he said. "But what makes that good news?"

"It's good news because this is my hometown, and this guy might still be in it."

"You lost me somewhere," Sam said.

"This sorry motherfucker can't hide from us here, Sam. This town ain't that big. We already know where to find some people who know the guy *and* where he is. All we have to do now is figure out how to make 'em tell us."

"Yeah," he said slowly. "That's all we have to do. I'll get back to you."

The phone went dead in my ear, so I put it back inside my jacket. I looked over at Elmer, and he looked back at me. The car was still parked at the curb, the engine idling just like the two of us.

"Why are we at Tenth and Failing, just north of Irving Park?" I asked.

"Because you didn't want to be anywhere else right now," he answered, "and you need to be here sometime."

"Why's that?"

"Because that gray house across the street is where you're daughter was living."

"What the fuck do you know about where my daughter was living?"

"Nothin'," he said. "Leon told me where it was."

"Jesus Christ! Do you do everything Leon tells you to do?"

"No," he said matter-of-factly. "I just do the stuff that makes sense to me."

"Bringing me here makes sense to you?"

"Sure. Don't it make sense to you?"

"No, it doesn't."

"It will," he said, looking away from me and focusing on the gray house across the street. "We'll just sit here until it does."

FIFTY-EIGHT

It only took fifteen minutes in the Caddy with Elmer for me to change my mind about the climb to Lizzie's front door. I took the stairs one at a time—ten up a bank to the level of the house, then a right turn and six more to the top of the porch—and I took them in slow motion. There was nothing wrong with my legs, but I felt like all of my stamina had leaked through the holes in my body and every footfall had to be carefully monitored to avoid a new wave of pain.

The door opened just before I reached it and "Are you all right?" spilled out onto the porch in a rich contralto. The voice had music pouring out of it, but with a husky rasp along the edges that made me think of the blues. I didn't see the woman who went with the voice until I reached the doorway, and it didn't take a second look to see that neither of us could give an affirmative answer to her question.

She was short for a woman her size and young for a woman her age, and her face beneath the unmistakeable sheen of grief told you everything and nothing in the same glance. I despaired in that first instant of ever knowing this woman, even while something almost tangible in her presence drew me to try.

"Come in," she said, stepping nimbly aside to clear the way.

I stared at her without moving, and she stared back. Her eyes were brown and bottomless, and red seemed to be the dominant color in the parts that were supposed to be white. They peered out at me from a face unfashionably full but unquestionably beautiful, like the face of a cover girl with extra padding for protection.

She was a wide, thick woman—or a small woman in a wide, thick body—and she was dressed in black leggings and a baggy black sweater. Her white feet were bare, and the nails on her toes were trimmed and painted.

"Do you know me?" I asked when I thought I had stared at her enough.

"No," she said simply. "But I know who you are. Please come in."

I made a conscious effort to move my feet, and I rode them through the doorway and into a cluttered living room when they finally responded. She closed the door behind me, moved across the room, and seated herself in a straight-backed wooden chair, motioning me to follow her example.

"You look like you should sit down," she said softly, looking up at me from her new perch with the same unknowable eyes.

There was only one other chair in the room—a folding chair near a corner, where an overflowing bookshelf against one wall almost collided with a huge stereo system spanning the length of another. I walked gingerly across the room and sat down slowly.

"So you're Lizzie's dad," she said, in a tone that made me wonder what she meant by the observation.

"And you are?" I asked.

She turned her gaze away from me for a moment, as though an answer to my question required careful calibration. When she looked in my direction again, tears were streaming silently down her face.

"I don't know," she said softly, swiping her cheeks with one sleeve of her sweater. "I'm her former roommate, I guess."

I watched her work on her face until she stopped. "Please excuse me," she said, shaking her head emphatically. "Here I am feeling sorry for myself, when you're the one who lost his daughter."

"I lost Lizzie a long time ago," I said.

"Is that what you think?"

"Isn't it obvious?"

"No," she said. "We all lost her Thursday night. She was right here until then."

I chewed on that for a while, considering a variety of ways to correct her, but none of them seemed likely to succeed. Eventually, I pushed ahead instead.

"Were you expecting me?" I asked.

"Yes."

"Why?"

"Leon told me you'd probably stop by."

"So you know Leon," I said.

"Everyone knows Leon."

"And you knew my daughter."

"Yes," she said simply, her wet eyes fixed on me unmercifully.

"I wish I could say the same," I said, and my candor shocked me a little as soon as the words came out of my mouth. I looked at her more intensely, as if closer scrutiny of her could somehow tell me something about myself.

"I wish you could, too," she said, locking into my gaze in a way that turned my intensity inside out.

This time I looked away. My chair was across the room from a window which provided a view of the porch and the houses on the opposite side of the street, so I looked in that direction for a while. A small television connected to a VCR sat on the floor beneath the windowsill, its blue screen humming wordlessly into the room.

"I was about to play Lizzie's film," the woman said. "Would you like to see it?"

I tried to say yes, but the word couldn't work its way around the lump in my throat. She apparently read my mind, because she picked up a remote from the floor next to her chair and turned the television from blue to black-and-white.

The film started with an *a capella* gospel song by Sweet Honey in the Rock over black leader. Then the images began with a montage of some kids playing hoops in a park, followed by a close-up of someone walking to a car with a gun in his hand. After that, the film cut back and forth between the game unfolding in the park and the car knifing through the city, until the car reached the park and one of the players was shot with the gun. Then a series of jump cuts brought the viewer up to the window of the car, where the shooter turned out to be a wide range of people, including the victim himself.

"So everyone's responsible," I said, more to myself than to the woman.

"It's good, isn't it?" she asked, with a catch in her voice that made me look in her direction. Her shoulders were shaking almost imperceptibly, and her face was awash again.

"Jesus Christ," I said, again more to myself than to the woman. "What else did I miss?"

I knew as soon as I asked that the question could not be answered, and I was grateful when she made no effort to reply. What she did instead was rise from her chair and disappear into the next room. I heard water running briskly into a sink, and a moment later she returned with a glass in each hand.

"Would you like something to drink?" she asked.

"Thank you," I said, but I set it down on the floor next to me as soon as she let go of it. She settled into her chair, sipped slowly from her glass, and began to watch me relentlessly again.

"How long did you know her?" I asked.

"We met while she was with Leon, actually," she said. "I'm one of Leon's projects—he thinks I have talent."

"Do you?"

"Most of the time I think I do."

"What do you think the rest of the time?"

She paused on the edge of her answer, I think to give herself time to decide how much she wanted to reveal to me. I was suddenly aware that she owed me no revelations at all, and I was on the verge of apologizing for the questions when she decided to proceed.

"The rest of the time," she said, "I think Leon is bound to realize I'm just another fat white chick and bounce me back where he found me."

"You can forget about that," I said. "Leon's instincts are infallible. Whatever you're trying to do is going to happen."

"I know that. But I wasn't talking about something subject to reason."

I nodded, and we both lapsed into silence for a moment. She began to work with her hair. It was dark and thick, and it streamed down to the small of her back when she removed the clasp that had been holding it up behind her head. She ran her fingers through it, then coiled it somehow and fastened the clasp again.

"How long have you lived here?" I asked.

"Almost a year. The house belongs to Leon—it's part of his investment in me, I guess. I don't pay anything for it."

"I live in one of his houses, too."

"Does that make you one of Leon's projects?"

"No," I said. "I'm more like one of his lost causes."

"Really? You just told me his instincts are infallible."

"They are. Me, he charges rent."

"What do you do to get it?"

"To get what?"

"The rent."

"Nothing much," I said. "I play poker, mostly."

"You can pay the rent playing poker?"

"I don't live in a high-rent neighborhood."

"Still, I didn't know that was possible. What happens when you lose?"

Now it was my turn to decide about disclosure, but something about the woman continued to draw answers out of me like the moon draws the tides.

"When I lose, I go to Seattle and find a drug dealer to rip off."

"Isn't that dangerous?"

"I like the symmetry of it. Either I get the money, or it blows up in my face and I don't need any money."

"It sounds like you don't really care which one it is."

"I don't," I said. "That's the key to the whole thing."

"No wonder Lizzie was furious with you."

"What do you mean?"

"If you don't care whether you live or die," she asked, "what kind of a message are you sending your daughter?"

"I stopped sending messages when she stopped wanting to receive them."

"You stopped talking, that's all. Words say one thing, silence says something else—but messages get sent either way."

I felt heat rise in my face, and I started to ask her how she had become such a fountain of wisdom. But I peeled my voice off the question before she could hear it when I decided the how of the phenomenon was less important than the what.

"How long did Lizzie live with you?" I asked instead.

"She moved in when she broke up with Leon," she answered, looking away from me when the tears welled in her eyes again. "We were already friends by then."

"Did she know how you felt about her?" I asked.

She nodded silently.

"Did she feel the same way about you?"

"I don't think that was possible, really," she said, but she thought it over for a while before she said it.

"What do you mean?" I asked.

"We loved each other, but I don't think it could have meant the same thing to her as it did to me."

"Why not?"

"Just take a look at me," she said. "People who look like me don't expect to end up with people like Lizzie. It's like we're from separate universes or something. So her loving me back was a miracle of unfathomable proportions, while anyone could see why I would love her. Do you see what I mean?"

"I guess you never heard the one about judging a book by its cover," I said.

"Sure," she said. "I heard that one. I think it's the most ridiculous thing I've ever heard."

"You're the first person I've ever heard say that."

"Think about it. Are you saying that the way I look tells you nothing about me?"

"It might," I conceded. "But I'd have to get to know you to find out if what I thought it was telling me was true."

"I don't have a problem with that. But the saying should be that a book may not be the *same* as its cover, or that you shouldn't judge a book by its cover *alone*. Do you see what I mean?"

"Why are we talking about this?" I asked suddenly.

"Probably because it's easier than most of the alternatives," she said, flashing a hint of a smile for the first time. "That's a bad habit of mine, and I think you may have it, too."

"My habit is even worse," I said. "I tend to make a joke out of everything."

"That probably *is* worse," she agreed. "Not everything is actually funny, is it?"

"No, it isn't."

"Does my relationship with Lizzie offend you?" she asked, the shadow of a smile gone without a trace.

"I don't know," I said. "It never occurred to me as a possibility before. But I don't think it offends me, really—at least no more than any other relationship would."

"What do you mean?"

"I'm jealous of you, in a way."

"Jealous how?"

"Jealous in the sense that you were a part of her life and I wasn't."

"Believe me," she said, rising from her chair and motioning for me to do the same. "You were part of her life."

"How can you say that?" I asked, slowly putting myself on top of my feet. "We didn't see or speak to each other for more than a year before she died."

"And I did," she said. "So who's got the more current information? Besides, the dad is always part of the daughter's life—for better or for worse, in sickness or in health."

"Isn't that about the groom?"

"It goes double for dads, because you can't divorce 'em. We're all stuck with you guys forever."

"Or until death do you part," I said. "Whichever comes first."

"I'm not sure death has anything to do with it, but I guess we'll have to wait and see about that."

I nodded my agreement, and then I stood there dumbly for a moment. "I guess we're done for now," I said finally.

"I have a rehearsal," she said. "I kind of owe it to the others to show up, and I find it helps to keep working anyway. Will you come back again?"

"I will if I can," I said. "I'd like to very much."

"I'd like it, too." She moved to the door, opened it, and waited while I navigated the room again.

"What's your name?" I asked as I stepped past her to the porch.

"*Is it Mary or Sue?*" she sang, her rich voice caressing the words from a song straight out of my childhood.

"How'd you know about that song?" I asked.

"How do you think?" she answered as she extended her hand. "I've been living with your daughter. I'm Genevieve, going back to your initial question."

I shook her hand, and she shook mine back. Her grip was firm, and so was her gaze as I stood there and stared into her eyes.

"Thanks," I said.

"For what?" she asked.

"For being here—for her then and me now. I'll try to make it back." Then I shuffled back into the growing dusk and left her standing in the doorway behind me.

FIFTY-NINE

Elmer had the Caddy waiting at the curb on the near side of the street, still idling as before but pointed in the opposite direction. He was standing next to the passenger door by the time I got to it, and this time I suffered his assistance without a thought of complaint.

"How was it?" he asked, after I was settled in and he was back behind the wheel.

"I don't know, really," I said. "But thanks."

"You're welcome."

"What's next?" I asked.

"Beats me," he said.

"No more hidden instructions, no mystery destinations?"

"Naw. I'm fresh out of those."

I removed Leon's phone from the pocket inside my jacket, and it began to throb in my hand while I was sitting there trying to decide where to send my call. Leon's voice spilled out of it just as soon as I got it working.

"Where are you?" he asked.

"Outside Genevieve's," I answered.

"You're quite a bit closer than I am," he said. "Get over to Alix's as soon as you can."

"Elmer," I said, the familiar cold fist suddenly clenching in my gut again. "Do you know where Alix lives?"

"Yeah," he said.

"Get us there soon," I said, and the Caddy surged away from the curb before I even finished the sentence.

"What's up?" I asked into the phone.

"According to Rosey's log, Alix took a call to One-thirty-two at the Evergreen on July twenty-second."

"Fuck," I said, shivering involuntarily. "But is that a problem, Leon? The motherfucker doesn't have that log."

"It's not a problem if he doesn't know her name. If he does, he can get her number just by looking her up in the logbook he does have."

"If she's the one he wants, aren't we running a little late?"

"Extremely," Leon said. "I left her a message to get the fuck out of there or to stay away if that's not where she is, but we're gonna have to look to see if it did any good."

"Got it. Where will you be?"

"I'll be right behind you, homeboy," he said, and then he cut the connection.

Meanwhile, Elmer was making large chunks of the city between us and southeast Portland get out of our way. He started by going west instead of east on Fremont, but he only did it long enough to catch MLK south to I-84. As soon as he was on the freeway, the distance virtually disappeared. I closed my eyes for the briefest instant as we flew east, and when I opened them again we had already made the switch to southbound on I-205 and were slicing away from the freeway at the Division Street exit. A moment later, we were waiting on Eighty-second across from the Chinese restaurant to make a left turn onto Alix's street.

"Pull into the driveway of the house next door," I said when Elmer finally got the light. That house was dark and the driveway empty, so we parked and unloaded ourselves like we belonged there.

"Whaddaya think?" Elmer said as he helped me out of the car.

I surveyed the front of Alix's house over his shoulder. A nondescript sedan I had never seen before was parked in the driveway, and light leaked out of the front-room window even though the curtain was drawn.

"I don't know," I said. "Alix's car isn't here, so she probably isn't here, either. On the other hand, someone is."

"Then there's that new Ford Taurus down at the end of the block," Elmer said, directing me with a jerk of his head to look over his other shoulder. The car was on the opposite side of the street but pointed in our direction.

"What about it?" I asked.

"There's at least two people in it," he said.

"So that's two questions—who's inside, who's outside. Can you think of anything else?"

"Not right offhand."

"All right. Let's take 'em one at a time." I started to walk around the car as though I was headed for the door of the house that went with the driveway we were using. When Elmer stepped in beside me, I disappeared from the view of anyone lurking in the dark Taurus. I got my hands on the phone in my jacket and hooked up with Leon.

"How far away are you?" I asked when he came on the line.

"About ten minutes or so," he answered.

"It looks like Alix isn't here, but somebody is. And the house is staked out. There's a new Taurus across the street at the west end of the block."

"How do you want to handle it?"

"We'll take the house, you take the car."

"I'll be there," he said, and we cut the connection. By this time, Elmer and I were at the neighbor's door. We were shielded from the Taurus by the garage, which protruded toward the driveway at our right.

"The only way in besides the front is a sliding glass door on the far side of the house from here," I said. "If you'd be kind enough to take that one, I'll take the front."

He disappeared to our left. I leaned against the screen door and tried to breathe away the fist in my gut while I gave him time to circumnavigate both houses, but the fist was still there when I finally pushed off and strode back around the edge of the garage, across the driveway, and into Alix's yard. I veered diagonally across the patchy grass and pressed emphatically on the doorbell as soon as I got close enough to reach it.

No one responded directly to the bell, but I could hear the murmur of voices on the other side of the door. I rang the bell again, and when the door still didn't open I began to pound on it. When the muffled sounds from within grew sharper, I pounded even harder, and as I did it my mind started whirring through scenarios that might explain my behavior if an explanation should ever be required.

"Open this damned door," I said as soon as I had something in mind.

"Who is it?" someone asked from the other side of the door. I didn't recognize the voice specifically, but I pegged the general type as middle-aged Asian female. I cataloged that information as quickly as I could and pushed hard for more.

"Who do you think it is?" I said. "Open this goddamned door!" Simultaneously, I was praying without a sound for a little help— for a relative from one of the smarter branches of Alix's twisted family tree, perhaps, someone who might have contributed significantly to the native intelligence Alix had withdrawn from her well-stocked gene pool.

Whoever you are, I said to myself, *please keep up with me.*

"What do you want?" the voice from inside asked after another round of muffled discussion which I strained unsuccessfully to decipher.

"Don't start this shit again," I said sharply, making up the story as I went along. "If you don't open this door, I swear to God I'll kick it down."

"If you don't go away," she said, "I'm going to call the police."

"If you don't open this door," I said, "I'm going to call them myself."

"What do you want?" she asked again.

"You know what I want. Why do we have to go through this shit every time Quincy spends the weekend? The weekend is over—he goes back with me now. Period."

This intensified the murmurs a notch or two, but I still couldn't make out any of the words.

"Quincy isn't ready," the woman said. "Come back in an hour."

"I'm not goin' anywhere. Just open the door—I'll get him ready myself."

"Hey, podnah," a voice from behind me said. "Is theah problem heah?"

The sound of that drawl almost froze me, but I instinctively pivoted on my right foot so that my body was between my gun and the voice. Two men in dark business suits were moving up the walkway behind me, and the sight of them switched my internal plumbing from cold to hot.

"Nothing that concerns you," I said.

"Now why don' y'all jus' step back and let us decide that, podnah," the one on the right said. "Okeydokey?"

"Okeydokey?" I asked.

"Yeah, okeydokey. You know, as in shut the fuck up 'cause weah askin' all the questions heah."

"Are you lost?" I asked.

"Was that a question, assho'?"

"Not really. It's pretty obvious you're on the wrong side of the line."

"What line is that?"

"The Mason-Dixon line. The guard must have been takin' a shit when you crossed over."

"Cut it out," the second suit said, and he had enough edge in his voice to stop the one with the drawl almost in mid-strike. Then he turned his focus to me. "You're messing up a federal investigation here, so I'm going to have to ask you to leave the area."

I met his change of focus more than halfway. He was taller, darker, thicker, and probably smarter than his partner, with cold black eyes that peered out at me from beneath bushy black eyebrows. I tried to picture him talking through a crack in a motel doorway while a girl was being cut to death on the other side of the door, but I failed.

"An investigation of what?" I asked.

"I'm not at liberty to discuss that, sir," he said. "May I ask what your business here is?"

"I don't have any 'business' here," I said. "I'm just trying to pick up my son."

"Your son?"

"Every Sunday I have to go through this shit when it's time to pick him up."

The suit looked at me, and I looked back at him with my best imitation of a father who was not going anywhere without his son. Then he looked at his partner, shook his head, stepped around me, and tapped on the door.

"Let's go," he said.

"What the fuck are you talkin' about?" someone, not a middle-aged Asian female, said from inside the house.

"Don't give me any shit," the suit said. "The alternative is not acceptable, understand? Let's go."

"Wait a minute," I said. "Who's in there with my kid?"

"Cool it," the suit said to me. "Everything's fine."

"Fine, my ass. What the fuck is going on?"

"Believe me, you don't want to know. Fernando—let's go, I mean it!"

"I know what I want to know, motherfucker," I said, "and I want to know what the fuck is going on." I whipped my .38 away from my hip and lodged it hard in the handy little notch at the base of the second suit's skull. My upper torso screamed in objection to this, of course, but I used the pain as fuel and forged ahead until he was flattened face-first against the door.

"Are you crazy?" the suit asked.

"I just might be," I said. "You might tell your 'podnah' there to keep that in mind. Now talk to me."

"There's really nothing I can say," he said.

"Wrong answer," I said. I moved the .38 a couple of inches to the right and raked it across his ear. He flinched involuntarily as a small trickle of blood emerged.

"Now try again," I said. "Who are you guys?"

"We're DEA," he said. "Jimmie, show him your ID."

"Easy," I said as Jimmie began to move his hand inside his suit coat. He stopped the motion and flashed both hands at me, front and back.

"Nuthin' up eithah sleeve, son," he said, "just as easy as can be." Then he reached into the inside pocket and gently pulled something out using only his thumb and forefinger. It was encased in leather, and when he flipped it open I could see a seal of some kind and some writing I didn't really bother to read.

"Who's the guy inside with my kid?" I asked.

"He's with us," Jimmie said. "Like we said, we've got a federal investigation goin' on heah."

"Bullshit," I said. "My ex is no drug dealer."

"We ain't sayin' she is," Jimmie said. "It's kind of a complicated situation, podnah."

"I'll bet," I said. "Get the other guy out here where I can see him."

"Fernando," said the one with his nose mashed against the door, "get out here, now." Then he pounded on the door a couple of times for added emphasis.

The door opened inward, which lessened the pressure on the suit's face significantly. An older, darker, more Vietnamese version of Alix stood in the doorway, her dark eyes sweeping over us without expression.

"He left," she said quietly.

"What?" the suit said.

"He went out the other door," she said.

"Where's Quincy?" I asked, rolling over the top of assorted cries of incredulity from the suits. She stepped away from the door, and Alix's five-year-old son by way of a father heretofore unknown stood in front of us with one arm around his grandmother's leg.

"Are you guys okay?" I asked him.

"We're fine, Daddy," he said, proving to me that his gene pool was just as deep as his mama's. "Can we go home now?"

"I think you better go home with Grandma, Quincy. I'll catch up with you there when I'm finished with these guys. Is that okay, Grandma?"

"Yes," she said. "That's fine." Then she took Quincy by the hand, picked up a purse she had stashed beside the door, and walked past all three of us to the car in the driveway. She walked

around to the far side to get Quincy belted in, and I called out
to her when she came back to the driver's side.

"Hey, Grandma!"

"Yes?" she said, looking over her shoulder in our direction.

"One moment, please. Jimmie, I need your gun—nice and
easy, now." Jimmie obliged as requested, and after some clumsy
fumbling to reverse which gun was ready to fire, I put his piece
where mine had been and extended mine in Grandma's direction.

"Take this with you," I said. She came back to me and took
the gun from my hand. "I'll pick it up when I see you again. It
won't fire right now, but just push this thing right here and
you're good to go. If you ever see that guy again, point this at
him and pull the trigger until it won't fire anymore."

She stared at me soberly, and then nodded.

"One more thing," I said. "These guys probably have your
license number, so if you don't want to see them again right
away, don't go home."

"Yes, I see," she said. "Thank you." Then she walked to the
rear of the car, put the gun in the trunk, got behind the wheel,
and backed into the street. I stood with Jimmie's gun jammed
against the second suit's head until she reached the light at
Eighty-second, turned right, and drove out of sight. Then I made
Jimmie's gun a little less lethal and handed it back to him.

"Well, now," I said, "that wasn't so hard, now was it, podnah?" Then Jimmie jammed the barrel of his gun into my gut
with considerable vigor, fracturing the frozen fist clenched inside
my skin and shutting my weary mouth for a while.

SIXTY

Everybody froze when the doorbell rang, but Fernando didn't freeze for long. He went straight to the sofa and wrapped the kid up close enough to nestle the knife just under the bump in his five-year-old throat.

"Who the fuck is that?" Fernando said.

"How would I know?" the woman answered calmly, but she flinched in spite of herself when the bell rang again. Then someone started pounding on the door, and the woman flinched again.

"Don't do anything stupid," Fernando said.

"I won't," the woman said.

"This boy needs you to get rid of whoever's out there," Fernando said. "Do you understand me?"

"Yes," the woman said. The pounding on the door intensified as she rose and began to move in that direction, and then the voice of a man filtered inside.

"Open this damned door!" the voice said.

"Who is it?" the woman asked.

"Who do you think it is?" the voice said. "Open this goddamned door!"

"What do you want?" the woman said.

"Don't start this shit again," the voice said. "If you don't open this door, I swear to God I'll kick it down."

"If you don't go away," the woman said, "I'm going to call the police."

"If you don't open this door," the voice said, "I'm going to call them myself."

"What do you want?" the woman asked again.

"You know what I want," the voice said. "Why do we have to go through this shit every time Quincy spends the weekend? The weekend is over—he goes back with me now. Period."

"That's the fuckin' father?" Fernando asked.

"Yes," the woman said flatly. "It will be hard to make him leave."

"Are you through trying?" Fernando asked, putting a little wiggle into the blade at the boy's throat.

"Quincy isn't ready," the woman said to the voice outside the door. "Come back in an hour."

"I'm not goin' anywhere," the voice responded. "Just open the door—I'll get him ready myself."

"Hey, podnah," a second voice said, and this was a voice Fernando knew, "is theah problem heah?" The voices continued back and forth, but the volume dropped so that Fernando couldn't follow the conversation. Before long, he heard a third voice, and he recognized that one, too.

Fuckin' idiots, Fernando thought. *How long do they plan on shootin' the shit out there?* Then he heard a sharp tap on the door and learned the answer to his silent question.

"Let's go," Morton said through the door.

"What the fuck are you talkin' about?" Fernando asked.

"Don't give me any shit," Morton said. "The alternative is not acceptable, understand? Let's go."

"Wait a minute," said the voice Fernando didn't know. "Who's in there with my kid?"

"Cool it," Morton said. "Everything's fine."

"Fine, my ass," the voice said. "What the fuck is going on?"

"Believe me," Morton said, "you don't want to know. Fernando! Let's go, I mean it!"

"I know what I want to know, motherfucker," the voice said, Fernando having no trouble hearing this at all, "and I want to know what the fuck is going on."

Sure you do, Fernando thought. *But believe me,* amigo, *you won't find out from those clowns at the door.*

"The boy and I are leaving," Fernando said to the woman. "What happens to him while we're doing it depends on you. Do you understand me?"

"Yes," the woman said. "I understand you."

Fernando could hear a scuffle at the door, but he ignored the sounds and rose from the sofa. The boy got up, too, and Fernando removed the knife from the boy's throat and pointed across the room.

"We're goin' out the side door," Fernando said. The boy led the way across the living room and the small dining area. When he got to the drape which shielded the sliding glass door, he pulled it aside and let the damp evening air blow over them.

I thought I closed that fuckin' door, Fernando thought, and then a massive black shadow slammed all the thoughts right out of his head.

SIXTY-ONE

I'm not sure how long you can balance on the line between life and death. Maybe you can balance just as long as you want, but the problem is finding the fucking line in the first place. I felt like I was flopping from one side to the other while I bounced along in the back of the Taurus—now you see the damned thing, now you don't.

The pain finally convinced me that I was still sprawled in the land of the living—the dull, aching pain in my upper torso and the sharp, blinding pain in my gut. I don't pretend to know what death is like, but I think my logic was unassailable: If death hurts just as much as life, why call it by another name?

I slammed against the front seats when the car suddenly screeched to a stop. The wrenching fanned the pain in my shoulder for a moment, but I must not have screamed out loud because no one in the front of the car seemed to notice me. By the time I bounced back to my starting point and the car was moving again, my mental deliberations had shed several levels of abstraction.

"Jeesus!" Jimmie's partner said sharply. "Watch it!"

"Would you relax?" Jimmie said. "You sound like y'alls about to bust into teahs."

"Fuck you, all right?" Jimmie's partner said. "If I hadn't listened to you in the first place, I wouldn't have my ass in a sling right now."

"Listen to yo'self," Jimmie said. "Everythang's fine."

"Ever'thing's fine? Are you retarded, or just stupid?"

"Nothin's changed, Mo'ton."

"Nothing's changed? Unless that fuckin' spic is in the backseat, *something* changed."

"Keep yo' eye on the big pictuah, Mo'ton. Only the details are different."

"That fuckin' Fernando ran on us," Morton said. "I'd say that was a helluva detail."

"He didn't run, Mo'ton."

"What?"

"Who's he runnin' from, huh? Us? Weah on his side, remembah?"

"Then what?" Morton said.

"What's left?"

"Someone snatched him?"

"God, y'alls quick."

"Who?"

"Who else?"

"Him? That fucker can't snatch his own ass."

"He not only can, he did. He had some hep, but he did it."

"Shit," Morton said. "I forgot about the guy with the muscles."

"Him and at least one moah."

"One more?"

"Weah talkin' about another cah, don'chall think?"

"Fuck," Morton said slowly. "I still don't see what's so fine about it."

"If Fernando really were runnin', we wouldn't know wheah to find him."

"We still don't know where to find him."

"True," Jimmie said. "But Daddy-o does. Like I said, nothin's changed. As long as we have Daddy-o heah, we can still put ever'thang back togethah again."

"I don't know if I *want* it all back together again. When we started this, we weren't talkin' about him killin' half the whores in this fuckin' town."

"True, but y'alls missin' the big pictuah again."

"What?"

"Fernando is about to go deepah into his pocket than he evah imagined when this stahted. If we were wuth what he was paying befoah, how much moah are we wuth now?"

"I see your point, I do. I just don't know if that fuckin' bitch is gonna see it."

"She don' have to see shit. We get Fernando back, she don' need to know any moah than she knew befoah."

"Yeah," Morton said, "but we ain't got Fernando."

"True. But it won' be long befoah we do."

"If this idiot really snatched him, why'd he do it?"

"Now that's a good question, Mo'ton. That's the question of the day. If I hadn't knocked all the air out of him, we'd probably know the ansa by now."

Then the conversation and the car stopped simultaneously. I heard the front doors open and the rustle of my traveling companions leaving their seats behind. Then the door next to my head opened and Jimmie leaned over me. He jammed an arm under each of mine and pulled until he had my sprawl thoroughly redirected.

As soon as he was standing up straight with my back pinned against his chest, he began to walk backwards. My feet were dragging on the ground, but they didn't seem to impede our progress much. After a moment or two, I heard a door open behind us and a light came on. Jimmie and I combined with the light to throw a shadow like nothing I had ever seen before, but the shadow vanished when we cleared the door and Jimmie bounced me off the cement floor where a car would have been if the cars had been at home.

I can't describe the pain associated with this transfer. At some point, your system overloads and you can't really feel it all, anyway. I *can* say that it left me dizzy on the floor when it abated, and that the pain remaining in its wake actually felt good.

"Take it easy," Morton said as I settled into a new sprawl. "We don't want him fading out again."

"Fuck it," Jimmie said, and then he squatted down beside me like those tenant farmers studying the dirt in *The Grapes of Wrath*—except Steinbeck's guys didn't wear dark suits and wingtip shoes. I tried to picture Jimmie scuffing that Oklahoma dust with his bare feet, and somehow it wasn't really much of a stretch. I almost had it when he started talking to me.

"Can you heah me, assho'?"

"I'm hanging on every word," I said.

"Don'chall jus' love this guy?" Jimmie asked. "He's jus' so *funny!*"

"Yeah," Morton said. "I love him."

"Y'all heah that?" Jimmie asked. "We jus' love y'all, Daddy-o."

"It makes me feel kind of tingly all over," I said.

"That's jus' great!" Jimmie said. "So if ah stick mah cock up youah ass y'all prob'ly bust a nut, huh?"

"Prob'ly," I said. "If you could get it up, of course."

"Now see," Jimmie said, "that's funny. Ah admire y'alls sense of humah, ah do. Ah cain't remembah when ah've enjoyed anyone this much."

"See if we can do it the easy way first," Morton said.

"Daddy-o don't want it the easy way," Jimmie said. "Y'all know that no pain means no gain, don'chall?"

"Actually," I said, "easy does it is my motto."

"Now ah am disappointed," Jimmie said. "Ah nevah had y'all figuahed foah a pussy."

"Must be kind of a jolt," I said. "Pussy prob'ly isn't really your thing, is it?"

Jimmie moved a lot quicker than he talked, so I didn't see it coming when he cracked me on the side of my face. The blow had more snap to it than you would expect from someone sitting on his haunches—it turned my head around until the opposite side of my face slapped against the concrete floor. My mouth filled with blood, and I didn't want to give him the satisfaction of seeing it so I swallowed it all.

"What's wrong, Daddy-o?" Jimmie asked. "Cat got y'alls tongue? No snappy comebacks? Sheeit—y'alls about to disappoint me again!"

"I thought we were going to try it the easy way first," I said finally.

"Believe me, Daddy-o, that's what this is."

"What do you want?" I said.

"We want Fernando," Jimmie said.

"I don't have him," I said, and he cracked me again, this time a little closer to my eye than my mouth. I could feel my eye swelling almost immediately, and I had to rotate my head around before I could see Jimmie looking down on me.

"We can see that, assho'," Jimmie said. "But y'all know wheah to find him, don'chall?"

"Not at this moment, no," I said.

"But y'all know who to call."

"Yeah," I said. "I know who to call."

"Give Daddy-o his phone," Jimmie said. "He knows who to fuckin' call."

Jimmie's partner reached inside his suit coat and produced Leon's second phone. "Tell me the number," he said. "I'll do the calling."

I did as he asked, and watched him try to make the number work. Then the door to the garage swung open and Leon stepped in behind a cut-down shotgun.

"You probably don't need the phone," he said. "I'm not all that far away."

"What the fuck?" Jimmie said, but one look at the scattergun in Leon's hands drained away whatever else he had in mind to say.

"So you're the other guy," Morton said while he cut the connection on the phone in his hand and spread his arms away from his body in acquiescence to the shotgun.

Leon walked around him until he was within a stride of Jimmie, who looked up at him from his perch on his haunches.

"I'm never the other guy," Leon said, just before he kicked Jimmie in the face. Jimmie sprawled backwards on the floor with both hands clutching his nose.

"You broke it!" he said, as though he couldn't believe the blood pouring through his fingers belonged to him. Leon stood next to me so I could use his leg for leverage, and after a moment of concentrated effort I was somewhat unsteadily back on my feet.

"The other guy is always someone else," Leon said, turning his slitted gaze on Morton.

"You broke mah fuckin' nose!" Jimmie said again.

"Shut him up," Leon said to Morton.

"Jimmie," Morton said, "shut the fuck up."

"He broke mah gawdamn nose!" Jimmie said, but after looking at Leon and his partner he settled back on the floor and bled into his hands without further comment.

"Do you know who we are?" Morton asked.

"More or less," Leon said, extending his empty hand. Morton passed him the phone. Leon relayed it to me, extended his hand again, and received a .38 police special for his trouble.

"Can you get *his* piece?" Leon asked, motioning toward Jimmie on the floor. I nodded and did as he asked, and Jimmie laid there like he was in the house next door while I did it.

"If you know who we are," Morton said, "you know we have to get Fernando back."

"Fernando's dead," Leon said. "Forget Fernando."

"What do you mean, he's dead?" Morton said.

"What part don't you understand?" Leon said.

"I don't understand the why."

"That's the easiest part to understand. You didn't think anyone would care about the girls he iced?"

"I guess I didn't, really. You get locked in on trying to plug all the holes, and you lose sight of the peripheral issues."

"Peripheral issues?" Leon asked.

"So to speak," Morton said.

"The thing is," Leon said, "you guys are the peripheral issues now, and we're the ones trying to plug all the holes."

"I see that."

"Then you can see what comes next."

"You don't want to kill us."

"We don't?" Leon said.

"If you did, we'd be dead already."

"Maybe I'm not the one who wants to do it."

When that registered, Morton rotated his focus from Leon to me. I released the safety on Jimmie's gun and raised it with both hands. "I can't stand like this very long," I said. "Get down on your knees."

Morton did as he was told, and I walked up and propped Jimmie's gun on the bridge of his nose. He looked up at me quietly and waited.

"What were you talking about when you were standing at the door of Room One-thirty-two at the Evergreen Thursday night?" I asked.

"I was trying to get the asshole to open the door."

"Asking him to do it was the only way you could think of?"

"You have to understand my point of view. My job was to protect *him*, not her, and when I got to the door he was all right. Then it wasn't really an issue anymore."

"You couldn't hear what was going on inside?"

"I could hear it, but I didn't know what it was."

"What'd you think it was?" ·

"I thought someone was getting hurt. I didn't know someone was dying."

"What'd you think was happening to the other two he killed?"

"We didn't know about those until after. That's why we were outside the place you found him—we didn't want it to happen again."

"You're pretty good," I said. "Not many people can stare up a gun and lie as well as you can."

"What makes you think I'm lying?"

"You were there to give him a ride when he was done. Otherwise, you'd have been inside with him."

"Nevertheless, you don't want to kill us."

"Why not?"

"It's not the kind of killing you can get away from."

"I'm not trying to get away from it."

"I take it the girl at the Evergreen was someone to you."

I didn't respond to that, but he continued as though I had.

"Is this really the best you can do for her?" he asked. "Just roll your life up and flush it down the toilet?"

"I did that a long time ago," I said. "There's nothing to be lost by it now."

"Maybe so, but there's sure as shit nothing to be gained by it now. If she really meant something to you, why don't you do something constructive instead?"

"Such as what?" I asked.

"Shit, I don't know! Get that damned gun out of my face, and maybe we can sit down here and think of something."

I looked over his head at Leon, and he looked back at me. "It's up to you," he said with a shrug. "I'm with you either way."

I looked back into Morton's quiet eyes, and then I lowered Jimmie's gun. Morton rose, walked over to Jimmie, gathered him in both arms, lifted him to his feet, and then turned them both toward the door.

"I've had about enough of this fucking garage," he said. "Let's go in the house and think."

SIXTY-TWO

The first thing Fernando noticed was the pain in his head, the second was the new level of throbbing in his shoulder, and the third was the short, muscular black man seated next to the bed.

It was the *puta*'s bed, and Fernando was sprawled across it on his back. The black man was toying with Fernando's knife, releasing the blade and then retracting it, first one and then the other, like he couldn't get enough of it. That was the fourth thing Fernando noticed—the quiet, comforting click of the knife's release, over and over again.

"Is this the knife you used on Lizzie?" the black man asked, still flicking it open and closed as he looked at Fernando sprawled on the bed.

I don't think so, Fernando said to himself. *On her, I think I used the one strapped to my leg right now. The same one I'm going to use on you.*

Fernando closed his eyes without a word to the black man and used the darkness behind his eyelids to grow a plan. *This is a very strong man,* he thought, remembering the blow to the side of his head. *Severing the artery in his neck will require a strong base and good balance—a wild swipe on the move can't be counted on to do it.*

That means the first cut must be somewhere else, Fernando thought, *somewhere immobilizing enough to give me time to set my feet for the kill. But where, on a guy this strong? The wrong cut, he'll bleed, but he'll still have those muscles.*

No problem, Fernando thought. *The problem is getting to the knife in time.*

"Who are you?" Fernando asked, his eyes still closed, his mind still working.

"The hand of God," the black man said. "I'm God's fuckin' fist."

There is *no God*, Fernando said to himself. *What's that make you?*

"I don't believe in God," Fernando said.

"What you believe don't change what is," the black man said.

"What are you doing here?" Fernando asked.

"What?" the black man said. "You thought no one would notice what happened to that girl? No one would give a fuck?"

No, Fernando said to himself as he opened his eyes and focused on the black man. *I didn't think that. I didn't think at all.*

"I need to use the john," Fernando said. The black man looked at him calmly, still releasing and retracting the blade of Fernando's knife, and finally rose with the blade glistening and motioned toward the door of the room.

Fernando rose with him, moving stiffly, and slowly walked around him to the doorway. He stumbled slightly as he entered the hall and fell hard, landing squarely on his left shoulder so he wouldn't have to fake the cry of pain that he wanted.

Let's see how smart you are, Fernando thought, but the black man just stood in the doorway and watched him writhe on the floor.

"What's wrong?" the black man asked.

"I lost some blood," Fernando said. "I guess I'm a little dizzy."

"How'd you do that?"

"The girl shot me in the shoulder. Hurts like hell."

"Good for her," the black man said.

"Not really," Fernando responded. "That's why the fuckin bitch's dead now."

The black man was quicker than Fernando expected, so the kick caught him a little fuller on the side of his face than he wanted. He rolled with the kick until he was flat on his back, and when blood started to leak out of his mouth he reached up with his left hand and tried to wipe it away.

"Get the fuck up," the black man said, standing clear again.

"I don't know if I can," Fernando said.

"How 'bout I kick the shit out of you 'til you do? Whattaya know then?"

Fernando rolled over slowly and struggled to his hands and knees. He was facing away from the black man, so he closed his eyes and measured the distance in the dark as he wobbled to his feet. He stood unsteadily for a moment, then dropped to one knee. His left knee, of course, which allowed him to lean unsteadily over the opposite leg and brought his right hand where it could reach the knife in the pull-away sheath nestled above his ankle.

Now just take a step this way, Fernando said to himself. But the black man stayed in the doorway to the bedroom, the clicking of the knife in the black man's hand as it opened and closed the only sound for a long moment or two.

Just one step, Fernando said silently. *That's all I need.*

"The fuckin' *puta* deserved what she got," Fernando said.

"Maybe," the black man said. "But maybe she got what *you* deserve."

This time Fernando was exactly in synch with the black man's move. He turned inside the kick with the knife in his right hand, drawing the blade hard across the black man's genitals as the kick rocked the side of his head.

The blow drove him into the wall, but he brought his right hand with him as he rolled with the kick so the blade was clear by the time he bounced back on both feet.

The black man, on the other hand, was slowing to a stop. He didn't make a sound, which took Fernando by surprise, but he dropped Fernando's knife and brought both hands to his crotch just as Fernando had envisioned in the darkness behind his closed eyelids.

Fernando set his feet and threw his hips and shoulders into the next cut, the knife doing its job like it always did, and Fernando leaned back against the hallway wall and watched the black man in front of him slowly turn red.

SIXTY-THREE

Morton led the way, with Jimmie under his arm and Leon on his butt. They all started and moved more quickly than I did, so I was already several steps behind them when they passed through the garage door and turned to the right.

By the time I reached that door, Morton was fumbling with the front door of the house. The rain had intensified since the last time I had taken note of it, and I stood under the eave of the garage and watched it pelt the walkway between the others and myself.

The house had some heft to it. I could see a second story rising above the cluster of people at the door and an impressive spread to their left. I was idly admiring a twin set of picture windows which overlooked the street when a light came on behind the curtains, and I switched my focus to the door in time to see my companions disappear inside.

I stepped out onto the walkway and lifted my face to the rain. It washed some things away; some things it did not. I was drenched by the time I started moving in the watery footsteps of the others, and I was ready for a respite when I entered the house.

My mother used to say there is no rest for the wicked. I could hear the echo of her words in the back of my head when I crossed the threshold between outside and in and discovered that no respite was forthcoming.

I was moving slowly and thinking at a similar speed, but I still

ad a point guard's peripheral vision. Leon was four or five
trides ahead of me and slightly to my right, and he was raising
is shotgun in that direction as I cleared the door. Morton was
ut beyond Leon's cut-down barrel, and I could see or feel or
ense him bringing cold steel rather than ice out of a small re-
rigerator on the counter of a wet bar along the wall on that side
f the room.

Jimmie was two or three strides to Leon's left. He seemed to
e arranging a dried floral display in a ceramic vase, until he
traightened up with the vase in his hand like a club.

I could only focus on one of those scenarios—the one to my
ft or the one to my right—but the decision required no delib-
ration. I immediately turned away from what Leon could see
nd toward what he could not, a move which turned out to be
etter for us than it was for Jimmie.

I was still carrying Jimmie's primary piece in my right hand,
I raised it as soon as I saw his arm begin to arc in Leon's
irection. I remember that I squeezed the trigger twice, because
felt like I was watching myself do it from a neutral vantage
oint somewhere near the ceiling.

The bullets didn't cluster the way they're supposed to—Jim-
ie died almost by random chance. The first one hit the arm
olding the vase right below his shoulder, and the second en-
red his right cheek and came out just below and behind his
ft ear. I remember seeing the vase fly one way and the blood
latter another.

"Hold it!" Morton shouted as I turned my attention in his
rection. "Just hold it!" He had a pistol in both hands, as I did,
ut he was looking down Leon's short barrel into Leon's slitted
es.

"You so much as twitch," he said, apparently to me, "and
omeboy here is dead!"

I looked at Leon, but he was deep within himself and the
ecarious moment which had enveloped him. Then I looked at
orton, who was pouring every drop of his life's energy into
olding Leon at bay. He didn't seem to have enough attention
ft over to see whether or not I twitched, so I pulled the trigger

of Jimmie's gun again and shot his left eye out the back of hi
head.

The impact threw Morton back against the wet bar, wher
he seemed to hang for a moment before he slipped slowly to th
floor. Leon lowered his shotgun, drew a handkerchief from th
pocket of his immaculate slacks, and turned in my direction
He looked at me and began to shake his head.

"What?" I said.

"What a fuckin' weekend."

"Yeah," I said.

"Hand me that gun," he said. I did as I was told, and he wipe
it clean with the cloth in his hand and dropped it on the floo:
Then he refolded the handkerchief, returned it to his pocket, an
turned to check on Jimmie. When he was satisfied that Jimmi
needed no more of our attention, he walked past me and ou
the door.

I followed in his wake, leaving the light in the front room o
and the front door open. A moment later, I was seated next t
him in Elmer's Continental.

"How bad is that going to be?" I asked.

"It's hard to say," he answered. "It depends on who aroun
here saw what." Then he cranked up the car, pulled away fro:
the curb, and drove without headlights into the rain.

After a cautious couple of blocks, he hit the headlights an
the accelerator. Laurelhurst Park slipped past Leon's side of th
car, and when I looked out the front windshield Thirty-nint
Avenue began to creep up on us. Leon turned south when w
got to the stop sign, then east when we got to Division.

"How did you happen to show up?" I asked finally.

"You guys took the house, I took the car."

"That's it?"

"That's it."

"So what happened to Fernando?" I asked.

"I have no idea," Leon answered. "But I think it's about tin
we found out."

SIXTY-FOUR

learned that you don't have to be standing for your knees to
nock just as Leon rolled up on the left-turn lane at Eighty-
econd. I was sitting there staring at the light when it began to
lur right before my eyes, and the next thing I knew I was shak-
1g from my shoulders to my knees.

When I couldn't stand the wrenching anymore, I leaned for-
ard and wrapped my arms around my quivering legs. That sur-
ounded the shudder without diminishing it, but I continued to
old on as hard as I could because I didn't know what else to
o.

I felt the Continental veer to the left and then Leon's right
and gently massaging the back of my neck. "What you did isn't
apposed to be easy," he said softly. "Otherwise, people'd be
oin' it all the time."

"How'd you get so used to it?" I asked, but the words spilled
ato the crack between my knees and I wasn't sure he could hear
1em until he answered.

"I'm not like you, bro'," he said slowly, the earlier softness in
is voice laced with a melancholy I could almost taste. "I've al-
ays been used to it."

The car slowed to another stop as I straightened up to reply,
at whatever I was going to say died on the back of my tongue.
'e were opposite the Chinese restaurant waiting to make a left
rn onto Alix's street, and Leon was looking at me so quietly
1at I somehow didn't want to intrude.

"Are you okay?" he asked finally.

I launched a silent inventory before I answered, and I was still in the midst of it when Leon caught the light and put Eighty-second behind us. The tally turned out to require some complicated mathematics: My head was throbbing, my face was flushed, my right eye was swollen almost shut, my torso had holes in it which had not been in the original design, and my gut ached every time I breathed—but the shakes seemed to have subsided. By the time Leon pulled into Alix's driveway, my answer was mired in the obscure mechanics of adding positive and negative numbers.

Leon cut off the Continental, leaned back in his seat, and watched me wrestle with my calculations without a word. When he thought he had done that long enough, he asked the question again.

"Are you okay?" he said.

"Yeah," I said simply. "I'm fine."

"Do you know where we are?"

"Sure," I said. "We're sitting in front of Alix's place."

"No," Leon said. "Do you know where we are in this fucked-up scenario."

"Not really," I said, looking past him to the empty driveway next door. "The Caddy's not here, so I'm not too sure why we are."

"We're here to find out what happened to Elmer," he said softly. "Are you ready for that?"

"Whaddaya mean, what happened to Elmer?" I asked.

"He hasn't called in, bro', and I don't think we're gonna like the reason why."

Leon's words fell on me like slabs of granite. I slumped back in my seat, and for a moment I felt like breathing might require more energy than I could muster. But that moment passed, so I drew in a deep breath and slowly let it out just to demonstrate to myself that I could do it. Then I opened the passenger door and began to unload myself from the car.

Leon followed my example but not my technique, so it seemed like he'd been lounging along his side of the car for a hour or two by the time I got there. He fell in behind me as I shuffled by, and we walked up to Alix's door at my pace rather than his.

The door was shut, but all I had to do to change that was turn the knob and push. When we spilled from the porch to the entryway, the first thing I noticed was the absence of the rain—even though the rain had failed to penetrate my consciousness during the walk to the door or the drive which had preceded it. This struck me as odd when it happened, but it shouldn't have—it was not the first time I had noticed something only after it was gone.

I noticed two more things when we got to the hallway in front of Alix's bedroom: that it takes more than muscle to stem the flow of blood from a severed artery, and that Elmer had been wrong after all—we don't all get what we deserve. He was sprawled on his back with most of his blood on the wrong side of his skin, his red hands still clutching his neck.

I sagged against the hallway wall, and when Leon edged round me I turned my back to the scene and staggered to the kitchen. A wave of nausea bent me over the sink for a moment, but nothing came out of my mouth when I heaved.

I was splashing water on my face when Leon joined me. He looked at the sliding glass door for a moment, then slouched next to me while I gingerly dried myself.

"What do you think happened here?" I asked when I was done. "The last thing I heard, Fernando had gone out the side door there. How'd we get from that to this?"

"Where'd you hear that?" Leon asked.

"Quincy's grandma said it when the narcs asked her where he was."

"It sounds to me like Elmer had Fernando under wraps at that point, and Grandma was helping him get rid of the heat."

"You think they were in the house the whole time?"

"Kinda looks like it."

"Then how'd that happen?" I asked, shrugging toward the hallway.

"Elmer was like a lot of really strong guys," Leon said quietly.

"Their strength ends up being their biggest weakness."

"You lost me," I said.

"They eventually start thinking their strength means more than it does. Like this situation here didn't turn out to be about strength—it turned out to be about quickness."

"Elmer was quick," I said.

"Keep that in mind when we catch up with this fuck," Leon said. "Elmer was damned quick, but it looks to me like he wasn't quick enough."

I stood there without a word for a moment, my head bowed, and then I fished the phone out of my jacket and punched in Sam's number. He answered almost immediately, like he'd been waiting for the phone to ring.

"Detective Adams," he said.

"You know Elmer, don't you?" I asked.

"Fuck Elmer," he said. "Where are you guys?"

"That's no way to speak about the dearly departed, Sam," I said.

"What?"

"Elmer is over at Alix's place with his neck sliced open," I said. "I'm calling you 'cause I'm pretty sure it's a homicide."

"There's lots of that going around tonight," Sam said. "Matter of fact, I want to talk to both of you about that very subject."

"Why's that, Sam?"

"Because two people matching your general descriptions were seen leaving the scene of a double homicide less than an hour ago."

"You can't be serious about us."

"I can be, and I am."

"Who died?" I asked.

"Two narcs in town on a special, sensitive, top-priority assignment which has now been put in extreme jeopardy—or so I've been told."

"Or so you've been told by whom?" I asked.

"By the agent in charge of this special, sensitive, top-priority assignment."

"Is this agent in charge a woman?"

"Why?"

"Answer the question, Sam."

"I give you the answer, what do I get?"

"You give me the right answer, Sam, you get whatever the fuck you want."

"Then the answer is yes," Sam said.

"You just won the lottery, Sam. Whaddaya want?"

"I want to see you guys now," he said.

"I don't know where Leon is, Sam, but I'm at your disposal. Where are you?"

"I'm where you were recently seen, wise guy."

"Where someone who matches my general description was seen, Sam. Look, I've got a better scene for you. I'll meet you at Room One-thirty-two at the Evergreen. Tell your new friend to join us—maybe we can swap crime-scene stories."

"You're at the end of your spin on this fuckin' merry-go-round, Wiley. You're in no position to set the parameters here."

"Take a deep breath and look again, Sam," I said. "I'll be there in fifteen minutes—and if I can get in touch with Leon, he'll be here, too."

Then I cut the connection, put the phone back in my jacket pocket, and locked eyes with Leon. He looked back at me peacefully, as though he had no concerns more profound than selecting the next color of the day.

"Did you follow that?" I asked.

"I think so," he said. "Let's go."

SIXTY-FIVE

My eyelids dropped as soon as I hit the seat of Elmer's Continental, and I didn't force them open again until I felt us cruise under the freeway on Division. I stared blankly past Leon as the on-ramp sailed by, and then I stared the same way at him.

"Wasn't that our turn?" I asked.

"That depends on the plan," he said.

"There is no plan, Leon. I'm making this shit up as we go."

"Then no," he said. "That wasn't our turn."

I waited a moment for further elucidation, but I slumped back into blindness as soon as that moment drifted away. After another moment or two, Leon eased the car to a stop in front of his topless club, abandoned the driver's seat, strode around the front of the car, and opened my door.

"Everybody out," he said.

"I'm not sure I'm in the mood, Leon," I said.

"I've got some real mood-changers in there," he said with a smile. "Let's go."

I went—in waves, just like the Marines. First I sent both feet out to establish a beachhead, then Leon led the rest of me into an upright position on top of them.

"Can you make it to that silver Camry over there?" he asked, pointing to a car parked three spaces away.

"Yeah," I said.

"I need to swap keys with Henry. I'll meet you over there in a minute." Then he disappeared inside the club and I began to slowly demonstrate my ability to navigate a small slice of the parking lot.

We arrived at the Camry's passenger door simultaneously. Leon unlocked it and I pulled a reverse Marine landing to fold myself into the seat.

"I don't know about this trade," I said. "What're we gettin' to make up for the loss of legroom?"

"Anonymity," Leon said, after he rolled around to his side of the car and joined me inside.

"Anonymity?"

"I don't think we can slip the Continental by Sam at this point."

"Why would we want to?"

Leon let my question linger until he got the Camry rolling toward the freeway, and then he let it linger some more until we were knifing north through a light rain.

"Why'd you set up this meeting?" he asked finally.

"It was the shortest line between the only two points I give a fuck about."

"Him and us?"

"Bingo."

"You thought we'd just ask her where he is?"

"She seemed the logical person to ask—she knows the fuckin' answer."

"I like your thinking, as far as it went."

"Meaning?"

"She's the person to ask, but this might not be the place to ask her."

"I thought it might encourage her to tell us if she could see why we're asking."

"It might," he said. "But even if it did, it wouldn't solve the problem with this scenario."

"Which is what?"

"Which is how we'd get away with the answer."

He let me chew on that until the Camry made the transition from the interstate to Airport Way, and then he let me chew on some more until he pulled into the Arco station across the street from the Evergreen. He stopped with our nose pointed back at the freeway at a pump with a good view of the motel parking lot from his side of the car.

By the time the skinny kid in the blue Arco shirt headed from the office toward our car, I was finally up to speed. I was on the office side of the car, so I rolled my window down and fished a hundred out of my pocket as the kid approached.

"Who's in charge here tonight?" I asked when he got close enough to see what I was holding in my hand.

"I am," he said.

"We need to sit here for a while," I said, extending the bill in his direction. "Is that a problem?"

"No sir," he replied, plucking the bill from my fingers. "Not at all. Is there anything you need while you're waiting?"

Leon hit the hood release, and that's all the kid needed to hear. "Right," he said. He walked to the front of the car, raised the hood, and then headed back toward the office.

"Just give me a signal when you're ready to go," he said over his shoulder, "and I'll be right over."

"Thanks," I said, and then I settled down to wait. I was just getting started when we saw Sam's Dart approaching the Evergreen's parking lot. The right turn signal came on near the motel entrance, as did the signal of the Taurus behind Sam's Dart. We watched them turn off Airport Way and backtrack through the lot until their headlights bounced off the yellow crime-scene tape on the door of Room 132.

"What is it with these fuckin' Fords?" Leon asked.

"Now that you mention it," I said, "there are a couple more in the parking lot."

"Looks like everyone's there but the guests of honor."

"Now we find out how long they're willing to wait for us."

"I don't think so," Leon said, pulling his phone out of his coat and putting it to work. "I don't have that kind of time tonight.

"Sam," he said into the phone. "We're not coming. We'd like to meet your new friend, but we can't call it a night just yet."

"Cut the shit, Sam," he said after a pause. "Even if we were the guys, your new friend's little buddy makes us look like fuckin' beginners. If you still feel like a little police work tonight, find *his* sorry ass."

Leon looked at me soberly while he cut the connection and made the phone disappear, and I looked back at him until he was done. Then we both turned our attention to the parking lot across the street, where we saw Sam climb out of his car and bend down to the window of the car next to him. Then he stood up, the Taurus backed away from the building, and the lights of two more cars came on. A moment later, Sam was standing alone in the parking lot watching a Taurus parade pull away.

Leon brought the Camry to life, which activated the skinny kid in the office. He was already coming out the door by the time I turned to motion to him.

"Thanks," I said, when we were locked down and ready to roll.

"No," the kid said with a grin. "Thank *you*."

Leon eased up to the edge of the street and watched the traffic carefully. The first Taurus was poised on the opposite side of the street, but its driver had to negotiate both lanes of traffic. When Leon saw the opening the Taurus was going to use, he moved us out in front of it and headed for the interstate. A moment later, the Taurus was right behind us.

"Cute," I said. "Following from in front."

"Yeah," he said. "It's cute if she's headed downtown. If she's headed for the airport, how cute is it?"

I didn't know how cute that would be, so I made no attempt to reply. But when Leon pushed us onto the southbound ramp of the freeway, the first Taurus followed us and the other two kept their noses pointed at the airport.

"Good girl," I said softly. "You're doin' just fine."

"So that's how those guys got there before we did," Leon said. "They probably came from the airport."

"That's not good," I said.

"No," Leon agreed. "That's not good. Boss lady might not now where her little buddy is just yet."

"Still, she's likely to be the first to know."

"Yeah, there's still that."

Leon was holding up his end of the conversation, but most of his energy was flowing into the mechanics of keeping the Camry in front of the Taurus. It was still in position when we switched from I-205 to I-84 westbound, and he made his move as soon as we cleared the ramp between the two.

"Hang on," he said quietly. "We're about to be rear-ended a little." Then he popped his brakes just long enough to close the cushion the Taurus was riding. I heard the squeal of brakes behind us and the crunch of metal, but we were already firing forward when the contact was made so the impact was not what I expected.

"Fuck, Leon!" I said. "You could have killed us!"

"I suppose," he said, his eyes glued to the rearview mirror while he pulled the Camry onto the shoulder and glided to a stop. "But there's a lot of ways we could be dead right now, homeboy. What the fuck difference does one more make?"

When the Taurus stopped behind us, he handed me a .38, opened his door, and climbed out of the car. "Let's go," he said. "You've got the boss lady, I've got the driver."

Adrenaline makes liars of us all—I was out of the car and on my feet before I had time to think about it. I slipped the .38 into my pocket and followed Leon's lead. He stopped to look at the damage to the back of the Camry, so I did the same. I didn't see anything that would stop us from rolling, so I turned my attention to the Taurus.

The driver was out and bearing down on us, but I didn't have to think about him. I started to wonder how I was going to get to my assignment when the passenger door opened and my assignment climbed out of the car.

"What the fuck were you doing?" the driver said.

"Was anybody hurt?" Leon asked.

"No thanks to you, you fuckin' idiot!" the driver said, and then his legs buckled and he fell in a heap on top of his feet. didn't see the punch that toppled him, and neither did the boss lady. She was examining the damage to her car when she heard the driver fall, but by the time she turned toward the action had the .38 in her face.

"Easy," I said, stepping between her and the traffic to shield the .38 from the eyes streaming by. "Don't make a mess out of this."

"You're doing that all by yourselves," she said, but she stood without moving while Leon disarmed them both.

"Cuff his hands behind his back," Leon said.

"I don't carry cuffs," the boss lady said, and Leon slapped her sharply enough to bloody her lip.

"Pay attention and do what you're told," he said quietly. "I didn't ask if you carry cuffs—I told you to cuff his hands behind his back. Do you understand me this time?"

She leaned over the driver without another word, and used the cuffs on his belt to do as instructed. The driver was starting to get his breath back by then, so Leon helped him to his feet and stacked him in the back of the Camry.

"Get in beside him," Leon said, and the boss lady did as she was told once more. Then we climbed in the front and Leon started the car.

"Do you know what it means if you drive away from here?" the boss lady asked.

"Yes," Leon said, as he put the car in gear and edged us back into the flow of westbound traffic. "In the context of this fucked-up weekend, it doesn't mean shit."

SIXTY-SIX

"What's your name?" Leon asked as soon as he got back from securing the driver in the bedroom.

"Agent Avina," the boss lady said.

"What's your given name?"

"Agnes."

"Triple-A," I said with a smile.

"Triple-A?" she asked, without a smile.

"Agent Agnes Avina. That's kind of cute."

"I'm so relieved that you think so," she said. She was sitting in the same boxy armchair Fat George had used during our first visit to Miriam's place, but she didn't have the same demeanor Fat George had broiled in that seat, but Agent Agnes Avina was sitting there like an air conditioner was blowing in her face.

I regarded her silently from my perch on the edge of the recliner across the room, but my search for a trace of humor or kindness in her countenance was fruitless. She had a thin face dominated by piercing brown eyes and framed by tousled brown hair streaked occasionally with gray. Her charcoal suit and the white blouse beneath it were smart, but they hung on her wiry body like an afterthought. She was calm but not calming—thought she was coiled as casually as a cobra while she waited for the next development in her very busy day.

"Now what?" she asked finally.

"Now we wait for your phone to ring," I said.

"I haven't seen him since Thursday. You expect him to suddenly call me?"

"You might not have seen him since Thursday, but he was with your people until today."

"How do you happen to know that?"

"I don't know if it was nurture or nature," I said, "but I know a lot of things."

"You don't know the first thing about what you're doing."

"Possibly, but that still leaves a lot of things I might know."

"You don't know shit."

"On the contrary," I said. "That's one of the things I know the most about. For example, I know that you've never been in it any deeper than you are right now."

"Please," she said. "You'd have to be stark raving mad to even contemplate killing us."

"That's a strange thought, considering."

"Considering what?"

"Considering we're already suspected of killing two of you."

That shut her up for a moment, while she looked from me to Leon and back.

"Besides," I said after the moment was over, "what makes you think we're not?"

"You're not what?"

"Stark raving mad. Underneath this angelic appearance, I have lots of unresolved issues."

"It doesn't really matter," she said with an almost imperceptible sigh. "I'd rather die than give him to you, so do whatever you want."

"Why do you care what happens to him?" Leon interjected. "He's killed four people since Thursday night, and he'd like to kill at least one more."

"Don't talk about numbers," she snapped. "You guys can't count worth a damn."

"Almost everyone can count to four," I said, "but we'd be here even if we could only count to one."

"That's my point exactly."

"No," I said. "That's *my* point exactly—it's your point *inexactly.* Your numbers are a rationalization, so you can run 'em all the way to infinity to try to make your point. You're the one who can't count worth a damn."

"This is not a debate," she said slowly, looking at me with her head tilted slightly to one side and drawing it out a little. "I don't have to make a point, and you don't have to like the way I count. In spite of your belief to the contrary, this is not about you."

"So what is it about?" Leon asked, and he drew it out a little, too.

She shifted her gaze to his position on the sofa and studied him before she spoke. "It's about flushing a lot of really bad shit down the toilet," she said finally. "That's what it has always been about, and nothing that has happened this week has changed that."

"Nothing?" I asked. "Not even the tragic loss of two trusted agents?"

She glanced at me briefly before turning her attention back to Leon. "Not even the tragic loss of two trusted agents," she said.

"So it doesn't bother you that the little engine that could has jumped the tracks?" Leon asked.

"Yes," she said, still low and slow. "It bothers me, okay? It's just that the shit he's going to help me flush bothers me a lot more."

"Sure it does," Leon said, his voice still matching hers for tempo and tone. "Plus you personally have a lot to gain from this flushing operation, correct?"

That made her tilt her head again, and she skipped a beat or two before she continued. "Do you expect me to apologize for that?" she asked.

"Correct?" Leon asked again.

"Correct," she replied.

"Good," Leon said softly. "Then we should all be able to get what we want."

She made no reply to that, and she made no reply to that for quite a while. I listened to the silence that enveloped us and rotated my attention between the two of them. She was zapping some heavy wattage in his direction, but he was leaning back against the sofa with his eyes almost closed.

"How?" she asked at last.

"We let you get what you want now," he said, "and you let us get what we want later."

"At what price?"

"First, you get Sam off our butts."

"How do I do that?"

"You tell him your two trusted agents were dirty, and whoever killed them did it in self-defense."

"Would I be telling him the truth?"

"It doesn't really matter, does it?"

"No," she said, after the slightest of pauses. "Not really."

"Then the answer is yes."

"And second?"

"You get your little buddy off our butts."

"And how do I do that?"

"I don't know. He's your little buddy, you figure it out."

"What's the problem?"

"He thinks he has another loose end around here. You have to convince him that it's tied."

"Is there a third?" she asked.

"Yes."

"What is it?" she asked, when it started to look like she wasn't going to find out otherwise.

Leon leaned forward and turned on some heavy wattage of his own. I could feel the intensity of his gaze from my side of the room, and he was looking in the opposite direction. Agent Agnes Avina looked back at him without flinching and waited.

"How long until this toilet flushes?" he asked.

"Another week or so, give or take a day or two."

"And then the justice system grinds on forever, give or take a day or two?"

"Probably. But I don't need my little buddy for that part of it."

"So in a week or so, what? He gets a new life somewhere?"

"Yes. A new life and a lot of money."

"Third, you tell us where."

"I see. In other words, I use him and then sell him out to you."

"Exactly," Leon said softly, but the energy coursing between them almost crackled.

Agent Avina finally broke the connection and turned her gaze toward me, which is when I found out that I am not the judge of character I sometimes think I am.

"God," she said, "I fucking *love* it!" And she was grinning from ear to ear when she said it.

SIXTY-SEVEN

"Do you realize how long I've been waiting for this call?" Avina asked.

"Yeah," Fernando said. "As long as I fuckin' wanted you to."

"Nice," Avina said. "And now what do you want?"

"I want your two fuckin' stooges. Where are they?"

"In the morgue."

"What?"

"You heard me."

Fuckin' idiots, Fernando said to himself.

"Who put 'em there?" he asked.

"I don't know that yet, but I do know it doesn't have to concern you."

"How do you know that?"

"They don't know you or where you are, and we can keep it that way."

"I guess it's just you and me, then," he said into the phone.

"It was always just you and me," Avina replied.

"Look, I still have a problem."

"No," Avina said, "you don't. Just come back in."

"What the fuck do you know about it?"

"Everything."

"Then you know I still have a problem."

"No, you don't. And if you had come to me in the first place, I would have solved the others, too."

"What—you'd have kissed 'em and made 'em all better, just like a good little mama?"

"Yes, actually. Something a lot like that."

"How'd you neutralize the *puta*?"

"She's facing a possession beef that was more than enough to make her disappear."

"Come on. Possession isn't gonna scare anyone."

"The difference between possession and intent to distribute is sometimes in the eye of the beholder. I convinced her this was one of those times. Believe me, you don't have a problem there."

"So we're still in business?" Fernando asked.

"We're still in business," Avina said. "Just come back in."

I'm already back, Fernando said to himself. Then he hung up the phone, walked across the lobby, punched the button for the elevator, and rode it without a sound to where the fuckin' bitch was waiting.

SIXTY-EIGHT

I had no intention of attending Lizzie's memorial service, so it was almost over by the time I arrived at the church.

I'm still not certain why I changed my mind—or if, indeed, I actually did. One moment I was sprawled on the couch at the apartment formerly known as Linda's, talking to Sam on the phone, and the next moment Miriam was helping me dress.

I don't think the conversation with Sam had anything to do with it. Neither of us had much to say until just before I hung up the phone, and then we said it all.

"Do I want to know what you guys worked out with Avina?" he asked.

"No," I said.

"Does the fuckin' perp walk at the end?"

"No," I said again.

"I guess I can live with that."

"I guess we all can, Sam. If we can live at all."

"Just be careful, you hear me?"

"I hear you, Sam," I said, and then I cut the connection. Or maybe the connection continued, and all I did was hang up the phone.

I looked at the driver Leon had left behind, and he stared back at me without blinking. He had been doing that for sixty minutes straight—maybe that's what drove me to the service. Maybe it was the manifestation of some innate sensibilities I hadn't known I possessed, or maybe it was the fucking phase of the moon. All I know for sure is I eventually walked into the one place on earth everyone I did not want to encounter could be found.

Alix was standing on the sidewalk in front of the church when I arrived. We walked straight into each other's arms without a word, and we stayed there like that until she stepped back and looked into my eyes.

Even then she didn't speak, and when I started to she pressed a finger to my lips and shook her head a little. So I let the words roll back down my throat and tried to pry a message out of her silent black eyes.

That didn't take much work, and when she saw that I was getting it she slipped her finger along the line of my lips until her hand was softly pressed against my cheek. Then she turned and walked away, leaving me alone in the space we had shared.

I didn't know the first person I encountered inside the church, but she apparently knew me. "Come right this way, sir," she said. "Your place is ready for you."

I declined that offer, although not because I doubted its veracity. But there was a place ready for me in Hell, too, and one was just as appealing as the other that morning.

The crowd was bigger than I had expected, but the church was bigger still. I slipped into a rear pew that provided some distance from the other mourners and let the remainder of the service wash over me.

The speaker when I entered the room seemed vaguely familiar, and so did the words he was saying. I suppose nothing original is offered at a young peson's memorial—no one can ever quite understand God's design behind the death of a young person, and that's usually what they end up talking about at the service. The words drifted past me without sticking, although I drew an odd comfort from them in the process.

I found myself more engrossed in the congregation than the message, and it ultimately touched me more profoundly. I started with the cluster at front-row center to which I ostensibly belonged—Julie, weeping unabashedly, flanked by Leon on one side and Ronetta on the other; and the twins next to Ronetta, their small heads bowed and silent, as though they knew exactly where they were and what they were doing.

I recognized a lot of people in the crowd, as I had expected, but I was staggered by the number of unfamiliar faces. I might have asked how a father could observe a memorial for his daughter in the company of so many total strangers, but I knew the answer to that question.

I found out that day that memorial services are not like weddings—the separate worlds in attendance do not have separate sides of the aisle. People had mostly been seated in their order of arrival, which made for some interesting juxtapositions—Lizzie's old classmates from the Grove next to topless dancers, card room professionals next to film students, kids from the reading group she had tutored next to cocktail waitresses, policemen next to porno workers, her mother next to one of her lovers, and her father next to no one in the back of the room.

I think this somber survey would have eventually brought me to tears, but I didn't have a chance to find out. I hadn't really been listening to the speaker, so I hadn't really noticed when he stopped. But there was no doubt about when Genevieve began.

She sang a song that everyone knows but no one had ever heard before, which is the best short description of her genius I can offer. "Amazing grace," she sang,

> "how sweet the sound,
> that saved a wretch like me.
> I once was lost,
> but now am found;
> was blind, but now I see."

The words were familiar, but more comfortable than comforting. I remember thinking it was a safe choice of song, and vicariously appreciating her tone and delivery. Then she sang some more:

> " 'Twas grace that taught my heart to fear,
> and grace my fears relieved.

> *How precious did that grace appear,*
> *the hour I first believed."*

Maybe I'm not like other people—maybe other people know
the songs they know from front to back. I know the beginning
of hundreds of songs and the ends of almost none, so Genevieve
quickly had me lurching down an untraveled lane.

And then she sang some more again, and turned my remote
vantage point on the morning's proceedings inside out:

> *"Through many dangers, toils and snares,*
> *I have already come,"* she sang directly to me.
> *" 'Tis grace hath brought me safe thus far*
> *and grace will lead me home."*

I was standing when she finished, and when the announce-
ment was made about the viewing of the casket I knew I was
standing in the wrong place. But I was frozen to that position
with neither the will nor the ability to move.

Guilt is a great immobilizer, and it fixed me to my place at the
back of the room like a staple gun. Grace *is* the antidote, as Genevieve had whispered in my ear, but Genevieve did not have
the position in my life required to dispense it. So I stood in my
adopted spot with every intention of breaking out the door as
soon as my feet would move.

Then Leon rose and began to help my wife to her feet. I guess
hope does spring eternal, because Julie turned—against all prob-
ability based on many terrible years of contrary evidence—to
look one more time for me. And when she saw me standing
there, she stretched her right arm in my direction and waited for
grace to lead me home.

My feet started moving then, and I followed them all the way
down to my place at Julie's side.

SIXTY-NINE

Summer on the Sound is an experience unto itself—nothing compares to it, so it's hard to describe—but it was still January, which is something else altogether. The icy wind slapped me in the face, but I focused my attention on adding a silencer to the 22 in my right hand. The only other person on the ferry deck was Leon, standing to my right with his eyes locked on the lights of Seattle slowly receding in front of him.

"He's gonna come at your gun hand first," Leon said, his eyes still focused on the horizon.

"I'm going to have two of those," I said, drawing my .38 from my left pocket.

"That oughta help," Leon replied, but the noticeable lack of enthusiasm in his voice made me think he didn't believe it. I looked at him quietly for a moment, and he looked back the same way.

"He has to have a chance to walk," I said. "That's the only way I can do it."

"Yeah," Leon said, turning his gaze back to the horizon. "I know." Then neither of us said anything for a while.

"How much longer do we wait for him to wander up here?" I asked finally.

"The car deck will be lot harder. Let's give him another minute two."

And in another minute or two, the man we were waiting for

came out on the deck. He stood with his back to us by the doors
until he was able to light a cigarette, and then he wandered over
to the rail to our right.

He was about my height and complexion, but his dark hair
was longer than mine and his body looked leaner and more sup-
ple. He was dressed several degrees beyond my simple taste but
a step or two below Leon's, and he was blowing smoke into the
breeze like he was the keeper of somebody's eternal flame.

I knew better than that, of course, because Leon and I were
the true keepers of the flame that night. That's why we were
there.

"Can I bum one of those?" I asked.

He looked me over curtly for a moment and then responded
the same way. "Buy your own fuckin' cigarettes," he said.

"Actually," I said, "I don't smoke. That was just an icebreaker."

"Fuck off, asshole," he said.

"When you stop to think about it," I said, "it doesn't really
make sense. Why would someone come out in all this fresh air
and light up a fuckin' cigarette?"

"Jeezus fuckin' Christ," he said to himself as he turned away
from the rail and pointed himself at the doors. Once again, I
didn't see the punch that toppled him into Leon's arms, but I
saw him take a step and crumble. I moved over and caught one
arm while Leon kept hold of the other, and we walked him back
to the rail like his two best friends while we waited for him to
start breathing again.

It didn't take him long, but Leon used the time to lift the car
keys from his coat pocket and the snub-nosed .38 from the
shoulder rig under his left arm.

"If this is a hit," he said as soon as he could, "it's the sorriest
piece of work I've ever seen."

"Why would anyone hit you?" I asked. "Born-again fellow
like you, why would anyone want you dead?"

"Who the fuck are you guys?" he said, looking at me and then
Leon and then me again. "How do you know me?"

"They sent you to God's country, that's for sure," I said. "Just
look at this scene—even at night, you've got the lights of the

ity out there. Nothin' like it in L.A., is there? I know Bremerton
doesn't sound like much when you first hear about it, but you
get one of those places lookin' out on the bay, you'll think you
died and went to heaven. So to speak."

"What the fuck is this?" he said again, in a tone marked more
by curiosity than panic. "Is this about money?"

"Why?" Leon said. "Are you thinkin' about offerin' us the
cash in the trunk of the Jag downstairs?"

"How the fuck do you know all this?" he asked.

"Is there more than one possibility?" I responded.

"That fuckin' bitch sold me!" he said when he finally saw it,
but he sounded more incredulous than angry.

"That's a little harsh," I said. "It's more like she gave you
away."

"This is about that shit in Portland, then?"

"Yeah," I said. "This is about that shit in Portland."

"So what do you want? What are you here for?"

"That depends."

"On what?"

"On you," I said. "Here's what we're gonna do. Leon here will
bring the car out when we dock, and when he's clear we'll call
the whole thing even. How does that sound to you?"

"I don't like it worth a damn."

"Well, I guess you wouldn't. It is a nice car, and five hundred
grand is a lot of money. Still, everything is relative, right? Do
you like it better than the next alternative?"

"Probably," he said quietly.

"Okay, then. That's it."

I nodded to Leon and we both let go of Fernando and walked
away in opposite directions. I stopped after three or four strides,
but Leon kept going until he disappeared through the doors. The
ferry was nosing in on the Bremerton docks, and I watched my
new companion contemplate its progress.

"You're almost home free," I said. "Don't do anything to spoil
." Then I stuffed both hands into the pockets of my overcoat,
gripping the .38 with my left and the .22 with my right. I pointed
the .38 at him through the coat, then lowered my arm again.

"Don't get too frisky," I said. "I won't hesitate to use it."

"Who the fuck are you?" he asked.

"I'm the ghost of the girl you killed at the Evergreen, Fernando."

"I don't believe in ghosts," he said, turning toward me and taking a step in one combined motion that might have cloaked how much ground he covered if I hadn't been looking for the move.

"A mutual acquaintance of ours once told me that what you believe don't change what is, you sorry motherfucker."

I won't deny he was good—he had an expression of honest curiosity on his face as though he didn't understand my statement, but he was moving into my left arm so swiftly that I never could have hit him with the gun in that hand.

I hadn't intended to, of course—that was my shield arm. I got it up with my hand still in the pocket just enough to block the thrust of his knife, and he was satisfied with that because he sliced through the fabric and cut deep into my arm. He drew the blade back without haste, proving once more that a little knowledge is a dangerous thing.

I wasn't sure if the next thrust would be at my abdomen or my throat, but I didn't wait to find out. I pivoted with the retreating motion of his knife hand and shot him through the other pocket of my coat.

The bullet hit him in the chest and seemed to stun him. His facial expression turned from satisfaction to disbelief, and then I shot him again. He fell that time, so I stepped over him and put the third bullet in the middle of his face.

I chucked the .22 over the railing and returned the .38 to my pocket. Blood was running down my left arm, so I jammed that hand deeper in my coat and started the long walk through the ferry to the dock. I was almost the last in line, and I resisted the impulse to run with all the energy I could muster. I was almost to the terminal by the time I heard a hubbub behind me, and I was all the way to the street before I heard a siren. I kept striding, one step after another, until I got to the corner where the Jazz was waiting at a bus stop.

I opened the door, dropped into the passenger seat, buckled my seat belt, and went to work on my bleeding arm. Leon looked at me quietly, put the car in gear, and then made me an offer I couldn't refuse.

"Let's go home," he said, easing the car away from the curb.

"If you know where the fuck that is," I said, locking eyes with him for a moment, "go ahead and take me there."

"We both know where that is, Wiley," he said softly, and he pointed the Jag in that direction and drove.